Praise for THE HIGHWAYMAN'S FOOTSTEPS

"Morgan follows in the highwayman's footsteps by
stepping confidently into his leather riding boots and
galloping off with a teen novel whose strong characters,
vivid language and runaway plot not only stand,
but deliver too."
Scotland on Sunday

"Morgan is a skilled storyteller who exposes the seamiest
sides of history and explores feelings with real feeling…
A terrific tale from start to finish."
Amanda Craig, *The Times*

"The novel gallops along at a cracking pace,
packed full of plot twists."
The Glasgow Herald

"A challenging and deeply satisfying read."
The Scotsman

"A wonderfully well-written book, with well-chosen
vocabulary and serious moral dilemmas. It's meticulously
researched and a real epic of an adventure story too."
The Bookbag

"There is no let-up either in pace or atmosphere."
The Telegraph

Books by the same author

Chicken Friend
Fleshmarket
The Highwayman's Footsteps
Mondays Are Red
The Passionflower Massacre
Sleepwalking

Blame My Brain
Know Your Brain
The Leaving Home Survival Guide

The Highwayman's Curse

NICOLA MORGAN

WALKER
BOOKS

First published 2007 by Walker Books Ltd
87 Vauxhall Walk, London SE11 5HJ

2 4 6 8 10 9 7 5 3 1

Text © 2007 Nicola Morgan
Cover illustration © 2007 Christian Birmingham

The right of Nicola Morgan to be identified as author of this
work has been asserted by her in accordance with
the Copyright, Designs and Patents Act 1988

This book has been typeset in Cochin

Printed and bound in Great Britain by
Creative Print and Design (Wales), Ebbw Vale

British Library Cataloguing in Publication Data:
a catalogue record for this book is available from the British Library

ISBN 978-1-4063-0312-4

www.walkerbooks.co.uk

Dedicated ...

... to seven amazing teenagers: Brogan Donnelly, George Reader, Samantha Pearson, Peter Stalley, Ryan Liddy, Emma Quinn and Emil Franchi, all from the remarkable St John's Catholic School & Sixth Form Centre in County Durham. Their dynamism, energy and creativity were an inspiration and it was a privilege to work with them. They are stars and deserve a bright future.

My thanks as well to the wonderful Linzi Heads, the librarian at St John's, and all the staff, who entered into the spirit of an unusual project in an extraordinary way.

With thanks ...

... to Graham and Buffy Carson for showing me inside a real Galloway tower; to my husband for accompanying me on research trips and only asking for high-quality food, accommodation and golf courses in return; and to my great friend and fellow-author, Franzeska Ewart, for describing a real cave so vividly that I didn't have to go inside one.

With apologies ...

... to those who think that most of the characters in this book should speak in a more Scottish voice. The language they would have spoken is wonderful and rich but I had to accept that too many readers would have stumbled. The Scots among you must give your own voice to the characters as you read.

Chapter One

The man was dead. Of this there could be no doubt. No one could survive such a terrible injury.

Bess gripped my arm. Her hand flew to her mouth. Bleary-eyed and still not quite awake, I tried to gather my thoughts. I bent down and pulled the man's cloak so that it hid his staring eyes and the grotesque gash beneath his chin.

This man had not died by accident. Only a sharp knife in a murderer's hand could have done such damage. Old he was, with thin white wisps of hair like a ghost's breath over his head. His weathered hands were clawed in pain, or gnarled old age, clutching the soil beneath him.

"It was his hut!" exclaimed Bess. "We slept in his hut!"

We had wondered why the hut was empty when we came upon it the evening before, exhausted, hungry, and somewhat afraid, in this unfamiliar countryside of

Scotland. We had guessed it to be a shepherd's hut, nestled below trees, sheltering in the elbow of a steep hillside. Lighting a lamp with our own flint, we had looked around. A cold fire lay in one corner. Near by, two blankets were folded neatly on a thin, uneven pallet on the floor – whoever slept on such a poor bed would find little comfort. And a few small possessions – a battered tin pot, two pottery cups, a horn spoon, a wooden platter, a sharp knife – sat on a large box. Creamy threads of sheep's wool were snagged on the splinters of rough wood, or lay on the floor, drifting like puffs of smoke on the draught from the door. Two shepherd's crooks hung from a warped rafter.

Although desperate to sleep, we had tried to remain awake, to listen for an occupant's return – two four-teen-year-olds travelling alone in this strange place must surely face unpredictable threats and we were accustomed to remaining alert. But in the darkest hours, Bess on the pallet and I on the floor, each wrapped in a cloak and one blanket, it had seemed to us that no one would come here now. And at last we had slept, though fitfully, the horses standing near us, breathing softly in the small space.

My sleep had been full of scattered dreams, famil-iar to me now, of redcoats chasing us, the shattering crashes of muskets in the darkness, of my horse, Blackfoot, falling under me and my pistol failing to save me, and of spectral horsemen cursing me with words of powerful magic. In one dream I was fighting my brother again, with swords as before, but this time my brother had overcome me and I had woken, sweating, as his pale eyes and ginger moustache loomed over me and he prepared to plunge the sword into my throat. Truth mixed with terrors, until when I awoke I could not tell which was which. Which was from the past, which the product of my exhaustion, and which a premonition of future danger?

When we had arrived at the hut, in the dark, we had not stumbled across the old man's body, lying as it was by the stream some fifty paces away. Only in the weak grey light of morning did we find it, as we came to wash our faces and drink our fill of fresh water.

Now, the sight of that gruesome body brought us fully to our senses. Although it was hard to believe that the murderer could still be near by, yet I feared it, and the skin on the back of my neck crawled as though touched. Cautiously, I retrieved my pistols from where they lay on a rock. Bess took hers from the belt of her breeches. Bess, I should say, was dressed in man's garb, as she most often was, and could fight as well as any I had met. When I had first encountered her, only a few weeks before, she was holding a pistol to my head, and only good fortune had saved me from death at her hands. Since then, she had shown her unwomanly strength on many occasions and I had learnt that the word "unwomanly" had a different meaning from the one I had been brought up to know.

Now, on the run from both the redcoats and my father's militia, we both had need of courage. And trust. But we had proven ourselves each to the other. I knew I could trust her and I think she knew the same of me. I knew many things about her and her childhood; I knew what kindled the fire in her heart, the fury, the spirit. And she knew of my childhood too, my struggle against my birthright. We had no friends here, not now that we were two days' ride over the Scottish border. But we had each other.

As long as we had each other, we had some kind of hope.

We looked and listened, straining eyes and ears for signs of danger. A low mist draped nearby hillsides but to the east there gleamed the promise of a brighter day. There the sky was a buttermilk yellow, pale and watery. Dark patches of forest splashed the distant hillsides. Closer to us, large boulders and gorse bushes could be hiding any manner of perils.

As for sounds, at first we could hear only the trickling of the stream as it ran over pebbles; the slight rustling of grasses in the breeze; and then, further away, the mournful crying of seagulls. Nothing to fear.

Averting our gaze from the body, we washed

quickly, and filled our water bottles. We began to move from that place, still wary. We walked quickly, making our way back up the slope to the hut. Bess's forehead was creased; twists of hair hung down bedraggled; dirt smudged her cheeks. Her man's shirt was splashed with water from the stream, and open at the neck – where I could see, hanging on a chain, her grandmother's locket which contained her father's ring. She looked tired, and I could sense perhaps a dulling of the fire in her eyes, as though she were weighed down by something. I think I had noticed it several times over recent days, but I had thought little of it – there was too much of greater importance to occupy my thoughts.

Many terrible things had we witnessed, many dangers had we met, and we must not let our guard drop now. We were in strange lands, with different customs and people. We must be careful indeed.

"Will!" Bess whispered suddenly. "Listen!"

I stopped. I could hear nothing. Only the birds and the faintly splashing stream below us. She was pointing to a large rock set back from our path. Now she placed her finger on her lips. Our pistols were already drawn. Slowly, carefully, I used my thumb to release the catch. I was ready to fire.

And then I heard it too.

There was something behind the rock. Or someone.

Chapter Two

I could not say what might be there, only that we had heard a small noise, a whimper, the sound an injured animal might make. Slowly crouching, I picked up a stone and threw it past the boulder. A quick rustling came from there but still we saw nothing. I signalled to Bess to move round from the right, while I crept towards the left. At another signal, we both leapt forward, pistols before us.

We need not have been afraid. It was a child, nothing more. A snivelling, red-eyed, thin-faced, dirty child. A boy, of perhaps eight or nine years old, with a nest of dark hair hanging over his eyes, beneath a soft hat. He lay curled up on the ground, shivering, cowering from us as though he feared we would kill him.

When Bess bent down to him, he flinched.

"Have no fear," she said, gently. He looked confused. This man spoke with a soft voice! Bess smiled, removed her hat and nodded at him. When I had first met her, her young girl's hair had been hidden beneath a hat – now we had cut it somewhat shorter and by day she wore it in a pigtail, like a man, though now it fell loose onto her shoulders. Without her hat shadowing her face, without her garments fastened tightly to hide her female shape, it was clear what she was. Now the boy's crying ceased.

"What is your name?" asked Bess, but he answered not. She continued, "There is the body of a man down there, by the stream. Do you know him?"

The boy's eyes filled again and his lips trembled. It was clear that he did indeed know him.

"Are you hurt?" I asked. The boy was huddled, clutching his arms across his chest. There was a little blood on his leg, I saw, where his trousers were torn at the knee, but he held his whole body stiffly, awkwardly, as though injured. And his face was too pale, his eyes wide and oddly distant. He must be near frozen, dressed as he was in nothing warmer than a coat of some thin cloth. I think if he had not worn thick boots and a hat, he would have died of cold during the night.

Still he spoke not a word. His lips moved, but no sound came from them. I think perhaps he could not speak, that he was turned mute by fear and cold and pain. Or perhaps he was a simpleton, without power of speech.

Bess and I knelt beside him. To show him that we meant no harm, I removed my cloak and placed it over him. Still his eyes looked frightened, but I think he understood a little now. Together, we tried to sit him up, but he cried out, clutching one arm more tightly.

It was clear that he was badly hurt. As we raised him to a sitting position, he seemed to slip into a swoon. His eyes rolled up until we could only see the white parts, and he became limp. I have some knowledge of injured animals and I knew I must discover the nature of his injury.

It did not take me long. His right arm was broken. Between his elbow and his hand was a crooked, swollen place which made me wince merely to see it. The bones were badly misaligned, the fingers grey and lifeless. He started to moan again and his eyes opened wide. He looked down and saw me holding his arm in my two large hands.

"No!" He groaned in fear. Did he think I would hurt him more? Did he think we had killed the old man and now would torture him before we killed him too?

"Do not move! We'll not hurt you." I know not if he believed me but at least he did not move. I turned to Bess. "We need a stick, something straight and strong, and something to tie it with." While she went

14

to find such items, I supported the boy's arm and tried to show him that I meant no harm.

A smile is a smile in any language and even an animal understands a kindly voice. But behind my smile was something more, something I tried to hide: I knew enough about the broken limbs of animals to fear for this boy – a limb could atrophy and die if the bones were not set properly. And then what might happen? I did not care to think. I had heard tell of the screaming of a man while his rotted limb was amputated...

Bess soon returned. She held a stick against the boy's crooked arm and together we bound it tightly with the cloth ripped from a kerchief. He cried out – only the bravest man would not. He cried again when I lifted him and when I held him close to me as we walked towards the hut. He weighed little, his thin bones barely more than twigs wrapped in cloth, settling loosely in my arms. The smell that came from him was not to my liking, but I have known worse since leaving my home.

My earlier childhood – a life of sweet-smelling lavender, of servants bringing hot pans to warm my bed, of tables laden with succulent meats and sweet fruits, of silks and felts and Egyptian cotton and embroidered waistcoats – though in truth so very recent, seemed little more than a distant memory. A memory I preferred to forget. It would do me no good now.

At the hut, I laid the boy on the pallet. His breathing was thin and his face paler than ever, if that were possible. Bess finished dressing, and when she was done you would not have known from her shape or her hair that she was not a young man. The locket with her father's ring was hidden under her clothes.

Outside, the horses were grazing on tiny shoots of new grass that grew between stones and gorse. We gathered our few belongings into our saddlebags and slung them across their withers. Back inside the hut, I stooped towards the boy, meaning to pick him up, to lift him onto one of the horses. But Bess stopped me, placing her hand on my arm, turning me away from the child.

"What do you intend?" she said quietly, her face set in a frown.

"Why, to take him with us. To take him to his home, to his mother and father. He will show us where. This hut is not his home – you can see that."

"No, we must leave him," said Bess.

He was but a small child! If we left him, he would surely die.

Bess looked at me, her dark eyes cold. I did not much like what I saw.

Chapter Three

Seeing my surprise, Bess continued. "We cannot return him to his home." She placed her hat over her man's pigtail. "It is too dangerous by far. What if his family choose not to believe our story? There is a murdered man down there. The boy acts as though he thinks we are the murderers and—"

"The boy is merely terrified. He must understand we were not to blame."

"We know nothing of these parts. We know not whom to fear, who would be our friend. He will hinder us. What if we are pursued? How will we flee? How fight?" She placed her pistols in the belt of her breeches.

"He is a child. How can you consider leaving him to die? And die he surely will."

"This is foolish! Why should we risk our lives for a child who is nothing to us? If the men who slit the old man's throat pursue us, then we will all die. If we leave the boy here, he may be found by those who love him. And we'll be far away."

"Where is your heart?" I retorted, angry now. How could she be so cold? This was not the Bess I knew. She who had been cared for by a woman who had no need to do so, who owed her nothing, when her father and mother died at the hands of the cruel redcoats, and Bess only seven years old? I knew Bess had a hard place in her heart, a steely determination, but I had not thought her cruel.

"My head rules my heart," she answered, calmly, though I saw something like anger flash across her dark eyes. "It's too dangerous to take him with us. It's for the best, whatever your heart tells you."

"He's ill, Bess! Did I leave you when I found you injured, even though you had threatened to kill me? I knew nothing about you, and staying with you carried risks. If I had left you then, you would have died for certain. And when you killed the redcoat – I could have run away then and saved myself. But I stayed and helped you. Should I perhaps have listened to what my head told me then?"

A sneer crossed her face now, though it was fused with anger. "And where would you be if you had gone away on your own? A rich boy far from home, on the run from soldiers? Would you have your own horse now? Would you have your freedom? Or would you have returned to your father? Your father, the man of justice." That last was too close to truth, too raw with pain. But I liked not the bitter quality to her voice. Were we not friends?

She was right, I knew, but I too was right. We had need of each other. We had been thrown together by chance. If only Bess would be easier, softer ... but then, if she had been softer, she would not have been leading the adventurous life of a highway robber. And I would not have met her, strange though that encounter had been. I would be on my own, wandering, or imprisoned, or hanging at the end of a noose for thievery. She was right: I needed her.

I wished, though, that she did not recall to me my father. Sir Charles de Lacey, High Sheriff of Hexham, corrupt Member for Parliament. The man who was already hated throughout the north of England for his callous hanging of an innocent old man only a few weeks earlier and for ordering the deaths of angry rioters. Was he any better than the men who had cut the throat of that shepherd?

I regretted nothing of what we had done at that time. I did not regret fighting, and defeating, my hated brother, and showing my despised father that I was no longer his son. That I would make my own way and find my own life.

But, for now, we had to decide what to do with the

injured boy. And I knew that on this matter I was right.

"He will be of use to us," I argued. "His people will thank us for bringing him back safely. We have need of friends in this place." I still felt anger at Bess's words, but I would keep my feelings inside. We were tired, too tired, and we had been through much together. It would not do to quarrel now. "We cannot leave him, Bess. I will not stand for that. It's not right. My heart says so and what are we if we have no heart?"

She shook her head but answered thus, "Then on your head be the consequences!" And she shrugged, but I understood that she would do as we agreed. Her anger had been quick to start, but its strength had burnt out as fast. Her face once more looked tired, drained of vigour and expression.

I had thought to place the boy on my horse but Bess stopped me. "Merlin is calmer, less inclined to shy. The boy should go with me." She was right and so I agreed. Together we gently lifted the child onto Merlin and she climbed up behind him into the ample saddle. When she was ready and the boy was as secure as we could make him, I mounted Blackfoot, and we made our way slowly down the path towards the road.

There was a silence between us and then Bess

spoke. Her voice was somewhat strained. "I am sorry. I regret my words. I'm glad you stayed with me and I'm sorry I did not thank you properly."

Hiding my surprise, I smiled at her, then turned away and smiled to myself.

She had not finished voicing the thoughts in her head. "But I still believe you to be wrong. That it is foolish to take the boy. I warrant you I'm right."

I ignored her words. I preferred to remember her apology.

A soft and watery sun warmed our faces as we rode down the slope, and my spirits lifted. Here in Scotland, the land of Bess's ancestors, the country of her beloved father, the notorious highwayman, we might find a home and, perchance, a peaceful way to live.

I would put behind me the terrors of the last few weeks and the cruel deaths we had witnessed. We would forget our pain – the shame that I had felt when I had discovered my father's corruption, and Bess's despair and anger when the redcoats burnt down the cottage where she held the memories of her murdered father.

And as for the ringing words of the curse that had been hurled at me as punishment for my father's crimes, they were mere words. "The devil take the sheriff's son!" Who was any man to say so? What strength did the devil's words have when God was on my side?

No power at all. If we always acted with justice and right on our side, nothing could hurt us. Nothing at all.

Chapter Four

We were on the same path as we had ridden the day before, making our way back to the road which went from east to west. From the morning sun to our left, we were travelling almost due south. The sea glinted ahead of us.

How full of colour everything seemed, how rich and wet and fertile, compared with the stone-strewn moors around Carlisle, where we had escaped the redcoats, and the wild and windy land near Hexham where I had lived with my parents. The blue-grey of a pine forest in the distance, the bright yellows of young gorse bushes, splashes of sunlight on brown grasses, pinks and brightest greens all daubed the rolling layers of hills. Rivers and streams wrinkled the slopes, and sometimes they trickled across our path. The ground was often clogged with marsh grasses, and water birds flew up as we passed. Everywhere was the smell of wetness.

Hunger grumbled in my stomach and I thought of the few provisions we had remaining – we would need to find food before long.

Not a sound did I hear the boy make. Once I looked at his face. His head lolled weakly and his skin looked grey as hogs' lard.

I remained alert for anything to fear.

As we came near the good road – newly laid by King George's men, we had been told by a garrulous old woman from whom we had bought hot pies in a village the previous day – we would need to know which way to go. As if reading my thoughts, Bess spoke to the boy now. "We will take you home, but you must tell us which way."

The boy seemed not to hear her. His eyes were closed. My heart lurched. I had had a tutor once who had died as silently as this, lolling in front of me as I dully recited some lines of Shakespeare and wished I could be somewhere else. Was this boy dying now? He must not! We needed him alive. If he died, what would we do with him? How would people not think we had caused him harm? And the old shepherd, too, when they found him.

"Bess! Waken him! He mustn't sleep!"

Bess pushed the boy's shoulder. And again. He stirred, opening his eyes. The fear in his face was pitiful and I turned away.

"Which way is your home?" she asked. By now we had come to the crossroad, where our path met the new road. One way went south-west before veering quickly to the west, the other east.

In a valley to the north-west, some distance away, I saw a tall tower, square, with parapets, and slits for windows. Perhaps you would call it a castle, though it consisted of nothing more than that tower and a low wall surrounding some small, separate buildings to one side. The tower itself stretched towards the sky. Near by was grazing pasture, enclosed by stone walls which I think were newly built from the look of them. Many sheep, their winter coats long and straggly, grazed there.

And that was when I was struck by a thought which I should have had as soon as we found the shepherd's body. If he had been a shepherd, where were his sheep?

I noticed the boy looking towards the tower, alert now, his eyes like metal, a crease on his forehead. He shrank towards Bess. What was in his mind?

"Which way must we go?" repeated Bess, with annoyance in her voice. And perhaps fear. I cannot speak for her but I know that I did not find it easy to put from my mind the memory of that old man's throat ripped open by a murderer's knife.

The boy, after some hesitation, pointed. South-west. In that direction we set off, knowing not what we should meet. Or whom.

"On your head be the consequences," Bess had said. I could not forget that.

And so it was that a rush of fear went through my body as I saw them first. Riders, five of them, approaching us fast.

Chapter Five

Bess and I pulled our horses to a standstill and they stood, tossing their heads and breathing hard. We glanced at each other. I pointed to my hat and she pulled hers down a little so that the corner covered her face the better.

We each kept a hand resting near a pistol. We would not draw our swords now – but would do so if it became necessary. Bess, I knew, would use the boy to her advantage – she would drop him or use him as a shield. As would I have done. Our loyalty to each other was greater by far than any care for the child. Though we may have disagreed on some things, we would act as one on this.

We must do what had to be done, and think afterwards. This was something I had learned by now.

Kicking our horses to a trot, we moved towards the riders. My heart beat faster. But I have known worse fear, much worse.

They were a ragged group. The leader rode a sturdy chestnut pony, bred for the terrain, thick-coated and shaggy-maned. The man wore loose trousers and a mud-brown jacket, a black scarf tied round his tree-trunk neck, a soft brown hat on his head, with thin dark hair hanging below it, and a beard flecked already with silver. He was perhaps thirty, or less, and I did not like his eyes: deep slits beneath hooded eyebrows. But then I did not much like the look of any of them. With mostly unshaven faces, hair loose about their shoulders, they looked as though they neither knew nor wished for soft comfort. One of them was much younger, of my age perhaps, his face smooth, though he looked as fierce and angry as the others.

Another man I noticed. Red-haired and wild-eyed he was, his beard licking his face like flames.

The hands on the reins were thick and gnarled and their horses were bedecked with weaponry: nasty-looking clubs and two long guns were visible. They rode well, one-handed, with long stirrups and longer reins, wheeling their ponies around roughly.

If they decided that they did not like us, we would stand not a chance.

We could rely only on the fact that we had a sick boy with us. Though, indeed, they might care nothing for such delicacies.

From their faces, and the way they pointed at the boy, they cared very much. And it was clear the boy knew them. He began to whimper, struggling against Bess's left arm which remained tight across his chest. One man said something but I could not tell what his words were. His accent was strange to me. Two men levelled their guns at us.

Bess put her hand on her pistol. "No, Bess!" I warned. No good could come of such an action, not with their numbers. I was glad above all that these were not redcoats – I could not have answered for Bess's behaviour towards them if they had been. Her hatred of the King's army had no limits.

"English?" asked the leader. The idea did not seem to please him over much. Nor did it please the others.

"Do you know this boy?" I asked, ignoring the question.

"Give him here!" snarled the flame-haired man. He was built like a boulder, his huge arms bulging under his rolled-up shirtsleeves, his waistcoat barely containing his muscled frame. In his mouth, I saw a hole where some teeth should be.

"What have ye done wi' him?" demanded the one with the dark beard, who seemed to be the leader, though I could not be sure – the red-haired man too had the demeanour of a leader. "We heard tell o'

29

trouble and we have broken the Sabbath to come looking…"

"We found him injured. We rescued him."

But the boy did not aid our situation. He gibbered and held out his one good arm towards the men and anyone would have thought that he was terrified of us.

"He has a broken arm – we tried to help him," Bess insisted.

"Aye, and where's my grandfather? What have ye done wi' him?" demanded the red-haired man, his accent thick but his meaning clear enough.

Bess and I glanced at each other. The man with the dark beard snapped at us. "Tell us! Is he dead?"

I nodded. His face twisted and there was a groan from one of the men.

"We found his body…" I tried to explain, but the boy wailed and pointed at me and a muttering rose among the men, gruff words growled, so that I caught no more than part meanings here and there.

Bess and I moved our horses closer to each other.

One part I understood, some words spoken firmly by a pale-eyed fleshy man with no full beard, only a few curly whiskers protruding from his hat. "No' on the Sabbath." And though I did not like his soft, round face, with its nasty thick lips and smooth skin, I gave silent thanks to God that it was indeed His day and that we might be safe from whatever these men planned for us.

Very soon we were surrounded, the men moving closer until we could smell them, see their angry eyes. Still we did not touch our weapons. The two guns were pointed towards us, and I know another man was behind us. Two men leapt to the ground. They lifted the boy from Bess's saddle and he cried out.

Within moments Bess and I had been relieved of our weapons. I would like to say we put up a fight but we did not. In previous circumstances, we have fought for our lives but this was not such an occasion. We were outnumbered and we both knew that our only hope lay in doing merely what we were told.

Two men kicked their ponies to a gallop and rode in the direction from which we had come. They went, I supposed, to find the old man's body.

Meanwhile, we were taken along the road, powerless, with two men riding behind us and one in front. Few words were spoken, and those that were had the thick accent of the area.

The strange ways of fate had brought us here, to a place far from what we knew. Fate, or the consequences of our own act of revenge. For we had indeed been taking revenge, settling a score, when we came near Carlisle. But settling that score had taken all our money and so we must, of course, turn to the only means of survival we knew – highway robbery. Then we had been careless – or too desperate – and the redcoats had pursued us. In a masterly act of deception of which I was proud, we had made them believe we were going south again to Carlisle and meanwhile we went where they would least expect us to – north, across the border into Scotland.

Would we live to regret this? We were strangers to these people. Were we also enemies? From the way the man had spat the word "English?" I think perhaps they had no liking for us. I did not know of such things. Would it help us at all that Bess's father had been Scottish? He had been dead for seven years or so, and had left Scotland some years before that. And we knew nothing about his family – for had he not disowned them, leaving them at a young age, preferring the life of a highwayman over his destiny as a churchman? I think it would not have helped to tell the men this – Bess's father, like mine, was high-born, and something in the roughness of these men told me that they would feel no warmth towards such as us.

The sun rose higher, and the air hummed with new life. The beauty of the day, the salty freshness of the sea, the mossy grass and heather pillowing the rolling slopes, all this formed a strange backdrop to my fears. It was as though the earth was melting into spring, leaving me behind in a dark, cold winter.

We rode for some time, which I guessed to be less than an hour. We made slow progress, for trotting caused too much pain for the child. No one spoke. Only the boy, riding with the man in front of us, occasionally made some noise, but never a word, merely a groan or a cry at some sudden movement. We passed no one. Since it was the Sabbath, I suppose everyone was at church or indoors at some honest pursuit.

Now we turned off the road, taking a track across some flat ground, with marsh grasses on one side and grazing land on the other. In front of us, the sea shimmered like freshly caught herring, the sunlight catching the flickering water.

A pair of curlews flew noisily into the air from their nest in some reeds a distance away and one of the ponies behind us was startled. An angry curse came from the rider and I turned to see one of the men pull a gun to his shoulder and fire into the air. The curlew fell to the ground, dead, and the men's cheering had a strange intensity to it, which I did not at that time understand.

Before us lay a small farm, a few low buildings sprawling, and as we came into the yard the smell of livestock was sharp and eye-watering. Two dogs – thin lurchers, scraggy and long-legged – came from behind one of the dwellings and began to run from one pony to another in agitation.

A girl of around my age, or a little younger, came from a byre, wiping her hands on her apron, turning to chase a cat from the doorway. Thick red hair fell from the twisted cloth that tried to hold it back and it cascaded around her shoulders. I glimpsed a cow within the byre, a milking stool beneath it, and a bucket to one side.

A woman ran from the largest building, a long, low cottage, calling something to the men. Her bare arms were red and strong, her face weathered, her waist thickened. A man walked towards us, quite slowly, a man of about fifty or more, muscular, though dragging one leg slightly. His beard was trim, and grey, and he had an air of dignity. The girl went to him, standing a little behind him. The woman ran straight to where the injured boy sat limply on a pony, supported by the rider.

With a cry she held out her arms. "My Tam!" The boy was passed down to her and she gathered him up in her strong arms, lowering herself onto her knees and murmuring into his ear. He seemed now quiet, too quiet. A dog began to lick the child's face and she did not stop it.

She glared up at us over the boy's sweat-flattened hair. Seeing us as prisoners, guns pointing towards us, she guessed we had had some hand in the child's injury.

"We found—" I tried to speak, to reassure her, to assert myself.

"Hold your tongue!" shouted one of the men.

"Thomas?" said the older man, simply. The man with the black beard began to answer, pointing to us.

"'Tis bad news, father. The worst. Old John – he is killed. Mouldy and Hamish have gone to find his body. These two…" But before he could say more, there was distant shouting from behind us and everyone turned as one towards the track along which we had come. Two riders, we saw.

I caught Bess's eye – I believe she was thinking the same as I: was this our opportunity to escape? But no – we both knew that we would stand no chance. We could do nothing more than hope and pray that we could persuade these people of our innocence.

Had Bess been right? Should we have ridden away and left the boy?

Two men kept their guns pointed towards us. The man with red hair – redder by far than my hated brother's weak orange hair – had removed his hat and now I saw a thin scar down one side of his face, from his forehead to the cheek, skirting his eyelid. He held his gun absolutely steady, his large finger wrapped round the trigger.

The other man, a round-shouldered giant of a creature, had a worried look, his eyes strangely gentle-seeming, very close together and shaped like thin almonds. Soft and sparse was the pale hair on his face, as though he had not begun to shave, though I thought him around thirty years old. His gun was not steady in his hands.

"Off!" shouted the red-haired one. Obediently, having no choice, we slid from our saddles. Standing there, with the horses towering over us, we were more powerless than ever.

With every effort to appear unconcerned, I watched the approaching riders. It was the two men who had left us at the beginning of our ride. They galloped towards us and very soon I could see that one had a burden slung over his saddle – the body of the old man, hanging limply, bent double over the horse's withers.

The legs hung at an angle only a corpse could achieve. A roar came from the man with the black beard – Thomas, the older man had called him – and he kicked his pony to a fast trot. The riders met him not far from the place where we all stood.

Wheeling round, he came with them into the yard, his feelings etched deep into his face. He leapt off his pony and rushed to the dead man. He grasped the body under its arms and hefted it onto the ground, lying it on its back. Kneeling beside the old man, he wept, brushing wisps of hair from the grim face.

Dead blood matted the old man's hair. The hands were white, though speckled with the brown spots of age, the skin too loose, the nails yellowed. One of the dogs cowered, whimpering, beside the body.

The young girl, too, had rushed to his side. She took the dead man's hands and rubbed them together. If she wanted to bring some life to him, this was a vain action, and she must have known it. The older woman, cradling the child, still knelt on the ground. The older man, standing near her, had not approached the body.

And now it was his expression that caught my eye. Nothing moved on that face – his jaw, his mouth, the flesh beneath his eyes, none of it moved. Not a word, a sound, was uttered. And yet in his eyes was a sadness deeper than words. The open grief of Thomas, the desperate actions of the woman, the tears I now saw on the reddening face of the girl, these were nothing compared with the sorrow of this one man.

And at that moment I knew – the dead man was this man's father. And seeing his silent grief, I was truly sorry about the old man's death.

But how could we persuade them that we had not been responsible? And if we could not…?

Chapter Six

The woman now rose awkwardly to her feet and turned to carry the boy inside.

"Hold!" said the silent man now, putting out his hand to touch her shoulder. And he spoke to the child, his finger gently stroking the frightened boy's cheek. "What did ye see? These men, these lads…" And at this he gestured towards Bess and me. "What did ye see? Did they do this, eh?"

All the boy did was point at us, both of us, his face creasing once more with terror before he buried his head in the woman's shoulder. Anyone would have thought he was blaming us. Perhaps he was. Perhaps in his confusion he truly believed that we had had some hand in the murder. Who knows? Perhaps he did not see who carried out the killing. Perhaps fear mixed truth and fancy in his thoughts.

"Kill them!" urged one man, I know not which. Angry murmurs of agreement rose from the others.

I moved closer to Bess. The young one, the boy of around my age with thick dark hair flopping over his forehead, took the reins of our horses and led them towards the byre. He must not take them! I leapt to follow but rough hands pulled me from behind. I felt a man's arm round my neck, dragging me back-wards, and a knee pressed into my lower back until I crumpled to the ground, where I lay face upwards.

The man pressed his foot onto my stomach and stared down at me, his mouth open so that I could see his grim teeth, with their gaps and crookedness. A large stick was in his hand, held above his red head, ready to fall on me. All my anger had been held back for too long now and I would not be treated like this. I should have lain there passively, but I could not. What I did next was foolish – I know that very well – but … I twisted suddenly round, pushing myself onto my hands and knees before springing upright and turning to face him.

He swung his massive arm back, evil gleaming in his eyes, a grin spreading over his face. I leapt for-ward, believing I could move faster than he with his greater bulk. I know not why I acted so foolishly. I know only that my horse meant more to me than that man could understand, and that I had not rescued Blackfoot from my bullying brother only for him to be taken away by some stranger.

I was angry with the child for accusing us and with the boy who took Blackfoot and Merlin. I was angry with these people for setting themselves against us for no reason, and with myself for trusting them, and for letting Bess be dragged into such danger. I was angry with myself for being wrong.

And so I leapt forward.

As I did, black stars rained through a red storm and the world disappeared into darkness.

Chapter Seven

I know not how long it was before I awoke. Thoughts tumbled in confusion. The world was spinning. Pain shot through my head, my neck, my arm. My hands were tied behind me, one arm squashed beneath my body where I lay on my side. Sickness, dizzy sickness. I groaned. Before my eyes all was red, black and red, swimming, with stars swirling past. Sickness rose in my throat. I closed them again.

I was cold. Yet my head was hot.

A voice. Bess. But I had drifted away again and could not bring myself to speak a word. I think I mumbled something and then my thoughts tumbled into chaos. I know not for how long, only that my delirium took me on a journey into a dream which had become familiar to me in recent nights.

I found myself, in my confusion, fighting my brother once more, in that duel where at last I had beaten him and taught him to fear and respect me.

But now, I did not beat him: now, I was lying, writhing in the mud, while he loomed over me with his sword-tip tracing its way around my throat, his nasty ginger moustache dripping rain, his little eyes gleaming. I could not move and his foot on my chest squeezed the breath from me. Behind him I could see Blackfoot, the wounds on his sides raw from where my brother had used the spurs so cruelly. Somehow my sisters were there, with their silly frills and squeals, their soft satin shoes sodden in the mud. And then I was in thick fog, alone, in a stinking marsh with my feet sinking into the mud. Was that a ghostly horseman through the swirling fog? Was that a light? Did I hear the galloping hoofbeats of pursuing redcoats?

"Will!" It was Bess. I opened my eyes. At first her face was blurred and strange, the surroundings half dark, but quickly my sight adjusted. Everything rushed back to me: the murdered old man, the boy and his broken arm, the men who had taken us. I had been hit from behind. But where was I? No longer outside. In some kind of barn or byre, I guessed. Thin lines of white outlined the shuttered door and a few rays of sunlight pierced the holes in the thatch. Twisting my head painfully, I saw that some light also came through a high window, with partly open shutters. Over there was the shape of something that looked like a plough, and I thought I could smell the vinegar tang of apples that had been stored over winter.

Where were the horses? Blackfoot and Merlin? I struggled to sit up but something tugged at my throat. I was tied by my neck to something I could not see.

Bess was not far away, sitting on the floor with her hands bound behind her. She too was tethered like a horse by the neck to a metal ring above her. I tried to twist my hands but my bonds were too tight. Our saddlebags were gone, along with our few possessions.

"How long have I been here?" My words were thick, my lips stiff as leather.

"I know not. Perhaps three or four hours. Or more. It has seemed a long time. I thought…" She did not need to say what she had thought. She did not ask as to my suffering. I think she was angry with me. "On your head be the consequences," she had said, yet now she too would bear the results of my decision to help the child.

"What do they plan?" I asked.

"Evil, I fear. The child will not speak. Or cannot. They think we murdered the old shepherd."

She had been right. But it would not help to dwell on that now. I struggled to think clearly.

"Tell me all you've learned. Anything may help us

and for certain we need help now."

Closing my eyes, I tried to slow my spinning head, quell my churning stomach. I let my muscles soften, my neck loosen, wishing for the drumming in my skull to cease. Her words came slowly at first, then more quickly as she remembered more.

The injured boy was called Tam and the old shepherd had been his great-grandfather, Old John. Thomas, the man with the dark beard, was Tam's father and there seemed to be no mother – the other woman was Tam's grandmother. Bess said her name was Jeannie. The older man, the quiet man with the trim grey beard, must be Jeannie's husband, though Bess was not sure. Bess did not know who the other men or the girl were, though she guessed the red-haired girl was Tam's sister. He had a brother too, older, but Bess didn't know his name. There was the boy who had seemed about my age, I remembered – that must be he. And there were two or three other men but Bess did not know their names. Some of the family had gone to church while the others guarded us.

This much she had gathered from their words as they tied our limbs and bundled us into the place where we now found ourselves. She had also heard snatches of conversation from the yard as she waited for me to wake.

But she had some more to tell me: the sheep had disappeared and the men talked of reivers – raiders and sheep thieves. Tam had been helping his great-grandfather that evening; they had planned to stay in the shepherd's hut that night – much against Jeannie's wishes. But the men were not sure if we were reivers: some said that, since we were English, we must be stealing sheep. Or we could be from one of the landowners to the east, sent to raid and steal during the night. Others talked of someone called Douglas Murdoch, a name which they seemed to hate. And they said if we were from Douglas Murdoch, we would die a horrible death.

Whatever the reason for our being there, the old man was murdered, the sheep were gone and the only witness, an injured boy, was struck speechless with fear of us. We were enemies.

And we could expect their rough justice.

"And the boy? Tam?" I asked. "Why does he not speak?"

"I know not. Each time one of them tries to ask him, he cries and gibbers and seems as if he will fall into a swoon."

"Have they set his arm?"

"I know not. Nor do I care!" snapped Bess. "He has brought us nothing but trouble. We should have left him, as I said. You should care nothing for him."

"There is good reason to care," I replied, my voice level, my eyes still closed against the dizziness. "If they do not set his bones properly, his arm may rot and he may die. If he dies, what will they do to us then? But if I can set his bones and save his arm, perhaps his life, then it will stand us in good stead with his family. He could be our passage to safety. If I even seem to try, it could help us."

"How can you think you can save his life? What do you know of such things as setting bones?"

Little enough, I must admit, and what I did know came from half-remembered things my father's stablemen had taught me when a dog had broken its leg. She was perchance right: that I could not save him.

"So we should give up?" I asked. "We should let them kill us?"

"What choice do we have?" When Bess said this, I stared at her through the gloom. Her face hung, sad. I could not see her eyes, but she caught her bottom lip with her teeth, as if forcing tears away.

This was not the Bess I knew. The Bess I had met only a few weeks ago would never give up. The Bess I knew would act with impulse and bravery, with spirit. She had killed a redcoat in cold blood, through the heat of her hatred, for she had sworn death to redcoats after they had killed her father and mother. She had spat in a soldier's face when he insulted her,

46

without thought of her own danger. She had acted with passion and fury after the death of the young soldier boy, Henry Parish, whom the redcoats chased and killed for the theft of some flour. When we had ridden across the countryside afterwards to bring money to Henry's starving mother and sister, she had urged me on when I was tired – she would, I think, have ridden to the ends of the earth to fulfil our promise to Henry Parish. And when we had robbed my father's coach and then again another corrupt gentleman's carriage near Carlisle, the fire in her eyes, her contempt for danger, her strength, would have put the strongest man to shame.

Where was that fire now?

"Bess?"

After a moment, she lifted her head and looked at me. Then I saw her eyes.

"Bess, where is your spirit? Your father's spirit?" She simply shook her head, then turned aside, to look at nothing. Her lips tightened as she fought to control herself and twisted the tears away.

This was not Bess. Surely not!

"We can overcome this. We will find a way," I urged.

She shook her head. "It is pointless to try."

"Think of Henry Parish! Think of your father and mother! Think of the redcoats!"

"The redcoats have won." Her voice was flat, with neither fire nor ice.

"No!"

"They burnt everything. Everything is gone."

And then I understood what had destroyed her spirit. I was silent. The redcoats had burnt her cottage down, the cottage where she had lived alone among her father's things. They had done it, we knew, because they believed – rightly – that we had tried to protect Henry Parish. No doubt they had hoped to find us there; no doubt they would have killed us. So, in their fury at our absence, they had destroyed her home and almost everything she owned.

A little over two weeks ago this had happened, yet only now, because hope seemed impossible to hold onto, had she finally succumbed.

It was my fault. If we had not gone to rob my father, and if my father had been a better man… But no, I knew she had wanted him to pay as much as I had wished it. It was Bess's spirit, too, that had brought such things to pass. And now that spirit was broken.

Before I could think of what to say, a noise came from outside. We turned towards the door. Footsteps, and voices. The door was hefted open and daylight streamed in. Two men were silhouetted in the opening. They strode towards us. Without words, they untied our bonds and lifted us roughly to our feet.

Bess did not resist. As for me, dizziness swarmed over me like wasps and I retched and stumbled. Pain shot up my leg as one man kicked me below my knee. I wished to fight but I could not, not with my hands still bound behind me and my head throbbing. But I vowed to keep my wits about me and do what could be done to save us. There must be a way, and I would find it.

The two scraggy lurchers, brindled in colour, sniffed around our feet.

As we were pushed together across the yard, I whispered to Bess, "Do not give up hope. God is on our side." She looked at me and smiled, the small smile I had come to know so well. It seemed to say, "Little you know." This time it seemed entirely devoid of hope.

Well, I would show her. There had been a time when Bess knew more than I, but we were equals now, and I could lead as well as she.

Chapter Eight

We were pushed roughly through a low doorway into a place of heat and stench and activity. My eyes darted here and there, taking in now one small detail and then another. Speech seemed impossible, the words sticking to the roof of my mouth. I was like the young boy, Tam, in my helplessness. And perhaps more afraid. For I knew more than he of what men can do. Or mayhap I did not – for young Tam had likely seen the old man's throat cut.

And there was the child, lying on a thin pallet, with his eyes closed. The woman held his hand and stroked his hair. Little good would that do him. He whimpered every now and then in weakness and pain. Had he a fever? If he had and if I should return a few days later, I think I would not see him alive. But then, perchance he might say the same of me.

The two dogs went to the fire, where they curled up together.

A single room made up this large dwelling. A fire blazed at one end of the cottage, a chimney hood above it with a large pot hanging from the crook. The red-haired girl stirred the contents of the pot. She looked not at me, though I could see her eyes swollen from crying. She stirred and stirred, as though stirring was all she could or wished to do.

A large box-bed filled one corner, the heavy curtains almost closed. On the other side of the fire sat an old woman, in a chair shaped like an up-ended coracle, the back and sides of woven basketwork, enclosing her. Her arms were wrapped round herself. She did not shift her gaze towards us as we entered, seeming in some faraway place of her own.

Wooden shutters blocked the light from the two small windows and, apart from some tallow candles leaning drunkenly and spluttering as their wax spilled, the dwelling was lit only by the fire and the sunshine flooding through the door. The room glowed a burnished copper, though the corners were thick with darkness.

A haze of smoke filled the dwelling.

Three men sat on stools round a scrubbed table in the middle of the space. One of them, the fiery-haired man with the scar, clasped a pottery cup in his thick hands. Thomas and the older man sat with cups before them, but they seemed not to drink. The older man watched us closely, and silently, as we were pushed towards him.

I looked carefully at his face, the cheeks creased like dry leather. I could not tell if he was kind and good, or not. But this was the man who would decide our fate, I knew. There was a distant pain in his eyes, a weariness perhaps. I thought then that he was worn down by sorrow at the death of his father.

My head still hurt. Saliva pooled in my mouth and I thought I might collapse.

He spoke, and his voice was pleasant enough, smooth and musical and slow, the words plain through his strange accent. His voice reminded me of a teacher I had had once, who spoke quietly but whose voice commanded attention.

"We have need o' your help. Such an argument have we had." His eyes remained cold and steady. I thought he was a man I need not fear if I told the truth.

"Get on wi' ye," snarled the man with the fiery hair. "I'll no' see my father turn soft on some o' Douglas Murdoch's men." He took a mouthful of the drink in his cup and a biting reek of strong spirit came over me.

Thomas turned on him. "Dinna speak to our father so! Have some respect! And ye're drinking o'er much – 'tis no' right on the Sabbath!"

"Hold your tongues, the both o' ye!" said their father, exasperation snapping in his voice. Thomas flashed a look of anger towards his brother, who returned the look.

As the older man began to speak again, I could see behind him the ancient woman hunched in her chair. Near her was a spinning-wheel, and the unbidden image of a huge spider came to my mind. Her eyes were black, and her clothes dark brown, but her hair was white as seafoam and wound round her head many times. Turned as she was a little to one side, only her right cheek was visible to me: its skin was, I think, the most wrinkled I had ever seen, as though if you stretched it out it would have wrapped around her body like a fine cloak. But it was as she moved her head the other way that I saw something to turn my stomach.

Her left cheek was horrible to behold, smooth and white in the sunken pit of a broad scar, the skin stretching too tightly between nose and cheekbone and ear, pulling her nose over, tugging her lip upwards, drawing her lower eyelid downwards. It was a terrible injury, deforming.

I dragged my eyes away. The older man was speaking again. I saw him press his fingers to his temples and shake his grey head from side to side, as if to throw off some pain.

"Ye see, we're thinking, what should we do wi' such gentlemen as yourselves? My father is murdered – God rest his spirit – my grandson is sore hurt, and the sheep are taken. And so ye should be wondering why we have no' killt ye already. Ye ken, for all that they dinna often agree, my older sons say ye should be drowned in the sea, and my own mother is fair distraught," and at this he pointed to the old woman, who began to rock herself gently, though little sign crossed her face to show that she was mourning the old shepherd, her dead husband.

He then pointed to another man, one who had brought us in, and who was leaning silently against the wall, scratching at his hands. He was an older man, of Jock's age or thereabouts. He had the look of Thomas about him, with dark hair and close-set eyes under a heavy brow, though he was thinner, shorter, more wiry, his skin nut-brown and dry. "Mouldy will do as I say, being my brother and no' of a decisive inclination. There are three folks only who ye should thank that ye are alive – Hamish, my youngest son, who hates all thieves and murderers but, being a particular God-fearing man and more devout than many, would say we must wait till the Sabbath has past. He will no' have your blood spilt on the Lord's Day but will flay the flesh off your bones on the morrow."

A man nodded from where he stood by the door, a pale-eyed man with curly, sand-coloured whiskers and a bald pate. He stood taller, straighter, than the others, though he carried some extra weight, being somewhat soft and rounded.

Jock continued. "And then, o' course, there's Billy, my other son, who says ye should live, but what would poor Billy ken o' such matters? Calum, my grandson, is too young to ken. And Jeannie, good Jeannie, my wife, is no' sure ye are to blame. Soft she is, as women often are, and she would have the truth from Tam afore we kill ye, but Tam canna speak, and she fears for him, for his mind and his body. And I tell ye now," and his eyes blazed of a sudden with a fearsome anger, like a fire that takes new strength from a gust of wind, "if he slips from this world, ye will pay the full price, Sabbath or no Sabbath."

The one called Mouldy spoke now. "Aye, and we'll have no reivers here, no friends o' gipsies. Nor no King's men. Nor excisemen, nor English, nor lairds, nor Catholics, nor bishops nor any popery at all..."

"Thank ye, Mouldy," said the man, quietly.

"Sorry, Jock," said Mouldy, blushing and meek. He scratched and scratched at the back of his hands, rubbing and twisting them together. I saw dry red skin there, and another patch on his neck.

Jock nodded. "My oldest son, Thomas, he says ye

are English so ye must be after stealing our sheep. Why else would ye be there? Ye must be reivers, and reivers we canna abide." Now he gestured towards the red-haired man, speaking to us again. "And my other son, he would have that ye are from Douglas Murdoch. And since that man is hated here more than reivers, that will go ill wi' ye. Though whoever ye are, if ye killt my father, ye will surely die a terrible death at God's hands." He looked at us, trying to see into our hearts.

"We know no man of that name," I insisted.

"Aye, well, ye would say such a thing, would ye no'?" A hawking sound came from the red-haired man who said this, and he spat onto the floor.

Jock spoke again. "But I am thinking ye are too English and too educated in your voice, and Douglas Murdoch is no' kent for such affectations. It is the only thing I can say well o' him. He is the son o' a Highland laird and has all the evils o' those people. But he hates the English wi' such a burning power that he wouldna have ye in his pay. Though 'tis no' just the English we should waste our venom on, but any man who will no' put God above all else. If an Englishman worships God aright – though many dinna, preferring to worship the bishops – he may go to Heaven wi' us." Jock stared towards the roof, as though he would find God there.

I knew not of what he spoke, except that it seemed perhaps my Englishness would not cause my death. As long as I did not worship bishops, which I had not thought on before. I knew there were bishops in my church but I would keep that to myself.

The red-haired man could no longer keep silent. "Dinna argue and blether! Take them to the cave and have done wi' it!"

"No' on the Sabbath," said Jock firmly. "Have a mind to a place in Heaven." He pointed with a weathered finger at his son, before turning back to us and continuing his speech.

Now, of a sudden, pain crossed his eyes and he swallowed hard. He shook his head as though a cloud had fallen over his senses. But, just as quickly, his face cleared and he spoke again, to the young girl this time. "Give our guests a drink o' whisky, Iona. They will have need o' it afore this night is out. But no' o'ermuch for 'tis no good to be drunk o' the Sabbath."

The girl continued to stir the pot a moment longer, and then stopped, a shrug of her thin shoulders as though she wished nothing to do with giving us a drink. And I must say I could not see why anyone should give us a drink before they killed us, though I was sore in need of both food and drink.

Iona came towards us with an earthenware flagon, which she set on the table without grace or gentleness. Tossing her tumbling red hair behind one shoulder, she then fetched some pottery cups, which she proceeded to fill with an amber liquid that glinted gold in the firelight as it fell. Still she looked not at us. I did not like the set of her lips – though of a perfect shape, like a bow, they looked not to smile very much at all. Freckles spread across her nose and cheeks like sand. My sisters would have thrown up their hands in horror if they had found freckles on their skin – freckles were the mark of a person who has spent too much time outside, unprotected by a bonnet as ladies should be. No longer did I think as my sisters did, but still I found Iona's looks strange, like something from the fairy world. Such green eyes, deep like a forest, could not be honest, I thought.

Never had I seen such flame-red hair. It gleamed in the firelight, brighter by far than anything in the room. There was a beauty in her, if only she would smile.

Thomas looked towards her with a father's fondness. She hung her head a little, and he reached to touch her softly on the arm. I think she knew her prettiness very well, and would use it, and I did not much like such cunning.

It had not escaped my attention that these people thought Bess to be a man. I could not at that time decide whether this was for good or ill. I thought it might help us were she to reveal herself, but perhaps it might make things worse. Who knew how these men might treat a young girl? I would bide my time and not act until it seemed right. Or necessary.

The old woman with the terrible face had stopped her rocking movement now. Her eyes were closed.

"Drink," said Jock. "Ye may need it and I wouldna have it said that we care no' for our guests."

"Afore we kill 'em," muttered the man with the fiery hair. The rims of his eyes were bloody, inflamed by drink and the smoke and whatever anger he carried within him.

Obediently we brought the cups to our lips. My own eyes began to water at the smell before ever my mouth had touched the liquid. I took a tiny sip and gasped at the power of that fire water. It burned my throat and I thought I could not breathe.

"English!" said Jeannie, with a sniff, before turning back to stroking the forehead of Tam, who had now set up a constant soft moaning.

Bess was affected by the drink as I was, and had difficulty not to choke and cough. I could not tell whether they meant us to enjoy their hospitality before they killed us or whether they wished us to become drunk as lords so that we might be easier to kill. Though I believed the latter to be the truth, we had little choice but to drink. When the liquid

59

reached my stomach, as it quickly did, burning a path down my gullet like fire along a tar-soaked rope, I experienced a short moment of pleasure before my head began to spin further. Yet, within a few moments more, I felt warm within and without. The taste on my tongue and through my nose was of peaty smoke and burning oil and of heat itself, if heat can have a taste, which I had never before thought.

I looked around. Along one wall were wooden chests, and shelves with objects ranged in some semblance of order – pots on one, cups and plates on another. A few books lay on one – I know not why I noticed this; perhaps because I had not seen books since I left home and I was surprised to see them now. Bess could read and write, but I had seen no books in her cottage. Did these people read?

At the other end of the room, away from the fire, a curtain was suspended from a rafter, which could make a private space if one were needed. I glimpsed another box-bed here. There was a small fireplace at that end of the cottage, though it was not lit now.

On a trestle at that end of the dwelling lay what I suddenly knew was the corpse of the old shepherd, now wrapped decorously in a sheet, the face hidden.

Near by, a large cupboard hung open, bundles of cloth or clothing on its shelves. Different sorts of dried plants hung from beams.

The smoke, drifting upwards slowly, hung among the rafters, seeping into the heather-lined thatch.

But I must try to think on a plan. I must keep my senses in check, not let the whisky take over my mind. I watched my captors, tried to measure them all, to judge their characters. The man called Jock took small sips from his cup, screwing his face up after each one, as though he drank without pleasure.

Apart from the red-haired man, the men drank little, looking to Jock for guidance, yet their noise swelled until the place swarmed with splenetic oaths and blazing eyes, and a strange excitement which I did not at that time understand.

Was it for our death? I thought so then.

Chapter Nine

At that time, warmed from within by the whisky and from without by the fire and the fug of bodies and breath, and yet with a chill fear crawling down the skin of my back, I began to think on tales I had heard of the wild Scottish people. Of brutal murder, the theft of girls, the slitting of an enemy's throat, and the most terrible thing of all – trepanning, the gruesome punishment we heard of in cautionary tales, the terrible cruelty of drilling a hole in an enemy's skull while he still lived. I had not thought much on it before. But now my mind dwelled on such things. If the Scottish people were as fearsome and cruel as the stories told, surely there would be no mercy for us.

Gradually, more whisky was downed by the men and the noise swelled further. Thoughts of the Sabbath seemed to be disappearing fast. Jeannie scowled at them, looking at Jock, but Jock seemed not to notice any more. "Hush! Let the bairn sleep!"

she chided them, to little effect.

Iona had, I saw, been crying again for the loss of her great-grandfather, and Jeannie put her arm round the girl's shoulders, giving her a small hug and murmuring a few words. Jeannie had a kindness to her face, a softness in the eyes, a roundness to her pinked cheeks. Though there was tiredness too, and sadness, of course.

Every now and then I glanced at Bess. Her face showed no emotion. I know not if she was afraid or if she tried to think on a plan, but she simply stared in front of her, her eyes distant and glassy.

One thing I did not understand – why had they brought us into this dwelling, if they meant to kill us? Would they do so here, in front of the women and Tam, once midnight passed and the Sabbath was over? How long might it be till midnight? Some hours, I knew, as I thought it was only late afternoon.

I suppose even a condemned man receives a last meal and prisoners are fed and given water even if they are doomed to die. These men seemed intent on playing the part of hosts before they did what-ever they planned to us. Meanwhile, it gave me the only chance we had. We could not escape, but we could persuade them to change their minds, could we not?

"We did not kill him," I said, as boldly as I could.

63

"We found him dead, and the boy injured. And we saw no sheep." I looked Jock in the eye. He stared back at me, no emotion showing. A growl came from one of the other men and I whipped round to see a hand fly towards my face. I ducked, but too slowly. His rough fingernails stung my cheek as they passed. It was the man with the red hair.

"Red!" said Jeannie. "Let the laddie speak! We should find the truth or we are no better than them." Red was the man's name, then. Red by name and by nature.

"If you kill us," I continued, with more desperation than reason, "then the men who did this will yet be at large. They may return. My friend and I are handy with pistol and sword. We are two more men to join you." I had no wish to fight their wars for them, but I could think of nothing else to say.

"Pah! Bitty lads ye are! No stronger than my own son," said Thomas. I thought at first he meant Tam but a movement in a dark corner away from the fire caused me to peer in that direction, and I saw the boy a little older than I. Nothing showed on his face. Thick hair flopped down, fringing his eyes, and he did not push it back. I thought he looked sullen and I sensed no fellow feeling, nothing that I could like.

"Drown 'em, I say. Down the cave wi' 'em," said Red, his face split into a grin as he swallowed another mouthful of the whisky. He gestured with an arm towards one side of the dwelling, but I knew not why he did so. Jock raised his hand for silence.

"We will find the truth. Let it no' be said we are afeard o' that. We are good men, no' like some I might talk of. And God is our guide. What o' the other lad? What d'ye say for yourself?"

Bess had not spoken since we came into the dwelling. She did so now, her voice low, disguised in the way she knew well, so that they would not know that she was a girl. The gloomy glow in the room was not sufficient for them to guess that the smoothness of her cheeks was a mark of her sex, not her age. "My friend speaks the truth. We are guests in this country and you should not treat us in this way. Are we to meet our deaths after saving the life of your child? Is this the hospitality of Scottish people? My father was Scottish and he did not tell me this."

Her quiet voice held the room, and no one spoke. Even Red said nothing. The fire hissed and crackled and a dog yelped gently in its sleep. Only I knew that her voice lacked its usual bite. Had her spirit been doused by the whisky and by exhaustion? Or had she in truth given up? Her words were couched in reason, but the fire in them had gone out.

But whether or not her words would have helped

us, I know not. For at that moment, we heard hoofbeats outside. Mouldy scurried to the still-open doorway.

"'Tis Mad Jamie!" he called over his shoulder.

Within a few moments, in the doorway, leaning against the frame, bending over to catch his breath, stood a gasping, skinny, raggedy boy who spat over and over again to rid his mouth of excess fluid.

Some of the men stood. Jeannie did so too. "Jamie, where's the bonesetter? Where is he?"

Mad Jamie simply shook his head, spittle flying everywhere. He wiped his huge hand across his wet mouth and stared in all directions. Thomas hurried towards him and dragged him to the table, where the smell of him came to me even over everything else. Its foul sweetness made my stomach rise.

Jeannie took him by the shoulders. "Where is he, Jamie? Why will he no' come?"

"The wifie say no," said Mad Jamie, his eyes wide, his head flopping back and forth as Jeannie shook him.

"Woman, leave him be! Ye'll kill him and there'll be no good o' it," said Jock. He turned to Mad Jamie. "Jamie, lad, ye ken me, and ye ken I'll no' harm ye. Did ye see the man? Did ye see the bonesetter?"

Jamie nodded his head.

"And was he lying down, Jamie, lad?" Jamie

nodded. "Was he drunk, Jamie?" Jamie paused before nodding again.

There was a crash as Thomas smashed his cup down on the table. "Useless vermin!" he shouted.

"No' ye, Jamie," said Jock in explanation, as Mad Jamie began to whimper in fear at Thomas's anger.

"We must send for another man," urged Thomas now. "A doctor, anyone who can help Tam."

"Aye," said Jock. "That we should. I was thinking o'—"

At that moment, Tam cried out from where he lay by the fire and Jeannie ran back to him. His eyes were rolling in his head and his whole body shook horribly. Of a sudden, he arched his back and went limp. And the strangest thing – it may not seem possible, but I swear I saw it with my own eyes – was that his lips were blue, which I have never seen on a living person. The grey blue of a dead sea swelling before a storm. Jeannie lifted his head, placed her arm beneath his neck and pulled him towards her. He made not a sound now. And yet his chest still rose and fell, rose and fell. Though lightly, so lightly. I have heard tell of a person slipping away in just such a manner after fearful injury. I know not what it is called, but animals too can pass away through pain and fear, their wide eyes empty.

Iona stopped turning her ladle in the pot and looked to her younger brother, fear in her swollen eyes. There was a stirring among the men, as of leaves rushing together while the equinoctial winds of autumn gather strength.

I felt my arms pinned to my sides. Bess was grabbed by Red, his cheeks suffused with heat, the wiry strands of his beard against her face. Bess and I looked at each other. Her eyes showed little. I remembered times when the light in Bess's eyes would stir my soul and burn my fears away. It would not do so now.

The old woman sat in her chair, rocking a little. She seemed not to know or care what was happening in the room. Her arms were round her body as though she hugged herself and had no need of any other.

Now Jock did not look at us. He turned to where Tam, his grandson, lay near death, and his face was troubled as much as I have ever seen in any man. He looked then towards the others, and to everyone else in that grim dwelling, and finally to us. "Take 'em down to the lower cave. 'Tis low tide – tie them to the wall and when the tide rises, they'll drown, whether 'tis afore midnight or no'. And if God wants to spare them on the Sabbath, he can do such a thing. God rules the tides and…"

Suddenly, with a cry, the old woman rose to her feet.

"Aye, when the tide did rise, they did drown." Her voice, cracked and shrill, pierced everything. And now she stood, small but strong. With her tiny, bird-like eyes staring at each of us in turn, she slowly pointed a bony finger towards us.

There was venom in her voice and it struck fear into my heart.

Chapter Ten

"**B**e these the men? Be these the devil's men?" Before anyone could answer her, the old woman spat her words at us, her eyes burning with fury now.

"I curse their heid an' all the hairs upon their heid; I curse their face, their eyes, their nose, their tongue, their teeth, their neck, their shoulders, their heart, their stomach, their arms, their legs, an' every part o' their body, from the top o' their heid tae the soles o' their feet, afore an' behind, within an' withoot.

"I condemn them tae the deep pit o' Hell, tae remain wi' Lucifer an' all his fellows, an' their bodies to the gallows, first tae be hangit, then takken down an' left tae rot wi' dogs, an' swine, an' other foul beasts, abominable tae all the world. An' may their light go from oor sight, as their souls go from the eyes o' God, an' only in three thousand year will they rise from this terrible cursing, an' mak satisfaction an' penance. An' so I curse their souls."

I could not speak, could not breathe after her words. Already my skin seemed to crawl with a creeping chill as though the words of her curse already had such power.

We were innocent! We had no hand in the old man's death, nor Tam's terrible injury. Yet how could these people be made to know the truth? Or, with such a curse on our shoulders, was it too late?

Into the silence came a rough laugh. It was Red, his head thrown back in mirth. "Look at ye! Afeard o' an old woman's words! Ye had better fear our intentions and the stomach o' the sea, no' an old wifie's words. She talks o' things long past. They are the words o' a mad woman and no' for ye." And he made a movement of his finger across his throat, grinning again.

The woman sat on her haunches again, her eyes glazed and unseeing now.

I knew not what to believe. The words of the curse were powerful. There was hatred in them, which seemed for us, even if Red said she meant it not for us. And perchance her words would have power even so. Mayhap a woman like that has such power, once her mind is detached from the ordinary world and lives with madness. I had heard of such things, the powers of lunatics. It is said that

71

such persons hear the voice of God. Could the old woman have such power?

There was little time for these thoughts. The men who still held us dug their fingers painfully into my arms and we were pushed towards the side of the room opposite the door, where Mouldy and another man were moving a large wooden chest. This other man was the one whose religious strength meant that we would not be killed until the Sabbath was past – and I feared that this time could not be far off now. I suppose by the time the tide rose over our heads, the Sabbath would be past and his conscience clear.

Where the chest had been, they scraped dirt from the floor and revealed a wooden door set into the ground. With a tapering piece of metal, Mouldy prised open the door and lifted it up. A gust of chill air rushed through the room, bringing with it the odours of the sea, dead fish, seaweed and rotten wood. In the fireplace, the flames drew themselves tall, swaying backwards, the smoke gusting outside the hanging chimney hood and swirling instead around the head of the old woman. And still she sat, her lips moving, her eyes closed.

Bess looked at me. A little fear showed in her now, I thought. And how might it not? To think of drowning…

"Wait!" we both said together, my voice little more than a croak, hers light and high, a woman's voice. Did anyone notice? Perhaps it would help us if they did? I still did not know, could not decide. The two men pushed us again towards the open hatchway.

She spoke again. Her words came fast. "My friend has some knowledge. Of bones and such injuries. He can cure your child, can return him to life, I swear." She should not make such claims! The boy was past earthly help, I was sure. And yet...

Before I could add my voice to hers, there came a sharp, barked word from behind me. "Wait!" It was Red. He stood up, a little unsteady on his feet, and walked slowly towards us. Towards Bess.

He knew.

Thomas made a movement as though to stop him, but Red silenced him with a dismissive gesture. Thomas looked to his father, Jock, who merely shook his head, and looked intently at Bess, too, his eyes narrowing.

I knew now that Red, and perhaps Jock, too, had guessed that Bess was a girl. If I had wondered before if perhaps it might save us, when I understood the look in Red's eyes I saw that it would not. How could I have been so foolish as to think that they might treat us more lightly if they thought Bess

73

were female? In my old life, perhaps, where gentlemen treated ladies as though they were fragile, petal-soft – but here? Where only the laws of the wilderness held sway?

Now Red had reached Bess. Everyone was silent, even Mad Jamie, who had stopped chewing on a stick which he kept dipping in a pot of something and who now looked wide-eyed as Red removed the kerchief slowly from Bess's throat. She looked at me then and I knew what she was thinking. She needed me now.

It was I who had brought her to this place. I had been wrong.

"Yes," I said, loudly, desperately, "I have a way with sick creatures. I can do all that your bonesetter might do. I can mend your child's arm and I know I can save him." Heat rushed to my face as I considered what I was saying, the promise I was making – if I failed to keep it, what would they do to me then?

But I could only buy some time.

And all the while I watched Red, his finger under Bess's chin, tilting it up, leering at her. She did not turn away. I worried what she might do. Once before, I had seen her held in a man's sway like this and on that occasion she had spat in her captor's face. No good had it done her or us, though I had not blamed her and I would not blame her now.

Though again it would do no good.

But what difference would it make? Little enough.

"I have need o' a wife," said Red. "But I have no need o' the wife's lad." He did not glance at me as he said this, only walked round Bess, looking at every part of her as she stood there, the muscles in her face tight and still.

Thomas laughed. "Ye are o'er old for a wife."

"Mebbe, but I would look after her better than ye did your own wife!" retorted Red. Thomas leapt towards him, but was held back by Jock. Mouldy pushed me and Bess once more towards the trap-door. Another man was there – who I think was Billy, the gentle-seeming giant of a man with a worried soft face. "Poor Billy," Jock had called him. I think he was somewhat simple, with little under-standing behind those odd-shaped eyes. But he was strong, that much was obvious. He looked from one man to another, awaiting instructions.

Now I could hear the rhythmic crashing of waves in the far distance, the hollow moaning of the wind as it whirled through whatever tunnels must twist their way between this place and the ocean. I shiv-ered, clamping my teeth together so that no one would see my fear.

Now Jeannie spoke. "Are ye all eejits? Are ye no'

thinking? Jock? Are ye having one o' your sore heads again? We could use these two, and the Lord kens – if the lad can save our Tam, then why should we throw him to the tides?"

Jock scowled. "Woman, I'm no' needing your words o' advice. When there's thinking to be done, leave it to me." He passed his hand across his brow. "Aye, my head's sore, but no' so sore that I canna think for myself." He paused, as though coming to his own decisions. "Aye, the lad can try his hand wi' Tam – for there's no' any other hope. The lass, well, she is wee and thin and could be o' use. Think on it, Thomas – if Tam canna go down to the cave then we'll need one that can." I did not know what he talked of, but it seemed as though there was hope for us yet.

If I could save the boy. If not…

Red took hold of Bess's arm, but Jock stopped him. "Red, ye'll no' have the lass. She's o'er young for ye."

Thomas laughed, loudly, in agreement with his father. With a whisky-sodden roar, Red drew back his arm as if to hit him, and would have done so had his father not held his arm up to block the blow. Jock stood with some difficulty, swaying somewhat and screwing up his eyes against the pain in his head, but staring at his son angrily.

There was conflict here. A father who seemed to suffer from some ailment, who seemed to be losing his strength, and two sons who fought each other. Another son, the quieter one with the obedience to God – I did not know his spirit as yet. But I knew that Red was a dangerous man. He reminded me in no small way of my brother. A fiery temper and volatile eyes, a bitter bile, and hating most of all to be held in check.

The look in Red's eyes was dangerous. Whisky inflamed any reason he might have had and it was only his father's next words that stopped him from going further. "Red! Think on Tam! He is in danger o' his life and ye can only think on your pride! I am your father and I will be obeyed!"

At that moment, without warning, Red rushed towards the door and ran from the dwelling.

Jock looked after his son, anger on his face, before turning back to me. "And now, what can ye do for my grandson?" He did not smile, and still there was a threat in his eyes, but he was doing the only thing he could. He was using reason. As was I.

My senses were dizzy, from hunger and fear, and from the confusing change of events. Only a few moments before, we had faced a journey to an unknown cave where we were to be drowned. Now, suddenly, the men who had been hungry for our deaths looked to us with a kind of hope. Jeannie, holding Tam's head in her hands and pinching his cheeks to waken him, pleaded with her eyes.

I had no choice. I must act. And pray. And do whatever could be done.

"I need some whisky," I said.

Chapter Eleven

"Iona, liquor for the lad!" said Thomas.

The girl looked at me hesitantly from beneath her river of red hair and handed me a cup, near full of whisky. I knelt by Tam, and, first looking at Jeannie so that she would see I meant no harm, I tipped the cup slowly against his lips. She saw my meaning, and lifted his head, using one finger to open his mouth. The fumes waked him somewhat and he looked into my eyes with an empty gaze, seeming nearer death than I wished him to be. The liquid slipped down his throat and he choked and spluttered. Jeannie held his head fast with one strong arm, his mouth open with the other. With much spilling, we slowly poured the whole cup down Tam's throat, though much was lost along the way.

It took two cups of whisky before his eyes closed and his body went soft, a smile on his thin face. Already his breathing was easier, though I knew this would not last for long. The whisky was for one purpose only – to make what was to come easier. For the boy, and for us as we listened. For I would not have the child scream as I set his bones.

As well as its use in relief of pain, it is well known that whisky or any such spirit is fair powerful for bringing a person out of collapse. And I think a boy could not have been nearer collapse than Tam.

Now I told Jeannie what I needed. "You must hold the child's arm above the elbow. You will need to be strong, as I must pull the bones away further than they were meant to go, before I can set them by the feel of them. Are you able to do this?"

How I was able to command this older woman in such a way, I know not, but from somewhere came the strength. From necessity, I suppose. And because they looked to me to do what they could not.

Jeannie nodded, glad perhaps to be told what to do, to be acting instead of listening to the arguing of the men. She tucked a strand of dusty orange hair beneath her cap, and wiped some sweat from her brow. Her eyes looked tired and dull, the skin beneath them dark and sagging, a deep line etched between nose and mouth. I could not tell her age but I suppose she must have been around forty-five or more.

I turned now to Bess. "Be ready to tie the arm as

we did before. Will you do that?" She nodded, and looked at me without smiling, though without anger either.

Everything was in my hands.

Jeannie settled herself on the other side of Tam, kneeling, placing a folded cloth beneath his head for comfort, and held him by the arm above the elbow. Bess and I began to untie the bindings. Men shuffled positions behind me, muttering. I looked not at them and I tried to put them from my mind. A dog scratched itself near by and the fire hissed and crackled.

Kneeling on the hard floor, I laid my hands on Tam's deadened wrist. Its coldness was shocking, its greyness ugly. No lifeblood flowed in it at all. This was a limb which would rot and die for certain, if I could not straighten it properly. I knew little enough how to do it, but I could visualize those displaced bones and surely it must be a matter of common sense how to pull them straight. Common sense and a deal of resolve.

I must save the arm and thereby the boy's life. There lay our only hope. Without that, we would find ourselves drowned at high tide.

Dizzy specks swarmed across my vision. Unable to quell my panic, I took my hands from Tam's wrist. "More whisky," I said. Moments later, a cup was placed in front of me. Taking a deep breath, I took several large mouthfuls, gasping with the shock of it. And, in the spinning amber haze that followed, I took Tam's wrist again.

Quickly, firmly, I pulled the hand towards me.

The boy moaned, and a line of drool came from the corner of his mouth. The reek of whisky was everywhere, its heat still in my head, somehow separating my mind from what my hands were doing.

It was as though I watched myself from above. I saw myself cup the broken arm beneath my hand, watched my fingers feel for the edges of the bones beneath the swollen flesh, felt them slide apart as I pulled his wrist again. I felt a space between the edges, was aware of Tam writhing beneath me, though oddly I heard no sound, only the rushing in my head and my own words, "Be still! Stay quiet! I have nearly finished." I think Bess turned her head from what I did with my fingers; I know her eyes were narrow as slits, her mouth clamped shut as though she would keep a scream inside.

With a crunch which I felt but did not seem to hear, the bones slid onto each other beneath my fingers, fitting like a jagged stick, safely, straight. "Now," I said to Bess and, while I held his arm steady with both my hands, she tied the piece of wood to him again, her fingers fumbling at first but soon finding their way. And now, though I know not why I did this except either by some instinct or because of some dim-remembered saying from one of my father's kennelmen, I placed my hands on the boy's upper arm and shoulder, massaging the life back into it. And I would swear I saw some colour return slowly to the pallid flesh.

For some long moments, we watched, all of us. I stood up and felt the blood rushing to my own feet after I had knelt for so long.

I know not what the reason is for any of this – whether some miracle of God, or that the boy would have recovered even without me, or whether perhaps I have some hidden skill in medical matters – but the boy lay quiet and peaceful now and, though fast asleep, yet with a rosier complexion and smooth breathing. I think perhaps he needed only to sleep and the whisky gave that to him. Perhaps sleep took away his mortal fear, quietening his heart and soothing him. I believe it was not anything else I did.

Whether in truth it was my action that saved that boy's life mattered little, for his family thought it was. And I was happy for them to think so.

Tears were in Jeannie's eyes, as she looked gratefully at me before lifting Tam and lying him down more comfortably in the box-bed. She covered him with warm blankets as he muttered in his drunken sleep.

Now the strength went from my legs and I found myself on the floor, my head spinning.

"Give the lad some food!" called Thomas, picking me up and slapping me heartily on the back. And very soon I was being led to the table, where a wooden plate with a steaming meaty substance was placed before me and another for Bess. I had not eaten since the day before and it was difficult not to gulp the whole plateful without pause.

I know not what that food was, but it was tasty indeed. I think it had oatmeal and some finely chopped meat, lamb perhaps, with a thick dark gravy to bind it together. Heavily salted it was, and with a fiery taste. This was what the girl had been stirring when we arrived. I tried to look my thanks at her but she would not glance my way. Well, I have indicated before that I did not like her and I did not.

A piece of doughy cake was placed beside me and gestures made that we were to wipe our plates with it. I did so, and took much pleasure from the crumbly, savoury stuff, rich with the taste of toasted corn or somesuch. It was warm and comforting, and at the end of it I felt a great deal better.

Still my head ached from my earlier injury; still it spun with the effect of that and the whisky; but I felt now no fear and my stomach was full. I had reason to be content, after so much danger.

I could not tell what was to come, but it could not be worse than what we had faced. Bess's black eyes seemed once more to smile at me. She looked tired, though, very tired, with shadows above her cheeks, her face pale as opal, her hair straggly and limp. And her lips, usually so red, were now bloodless.

"On your head be the consequences," she had said. But I had saved our lives on this occasion. I had been right to come here, and if it had been a close thing, then close things are what make life worth the living.

Now, perhaps, we could begin to live our lives?

I thought perchance we could stay here a few days and then move on. I thought that we could rest, eat, give the horses time to recover from the journey, and then leave, proceeding to whatever life might have in store for us.

But it was not to be.

Chapter Twelve

I marvelled at the behaviour of the men that evening. They had been so ready to kill us, but now seemed to have forgotten our presence, as they huddled on stools at the far end of the room, away from the fire. It was as if they did not take our lives seriously – it had mattered so little to them whether we lived or died that our escape from drowning did not stir their emotions.

I suppose now they talked of the old man's death and what they might do about it – but I could hear only parts of what they said. The argument between Thomas and Red seemed forgotten. Red had returned from outside, with a rolling gait, seeming forgetful of what had happened, though at no point did he come to thank me as the others had. The other men took me by the hand or slapped me on the back, until my face was tired from smiling back at them.

Though they might seem suddenly to be our

friends, I did not trust them as yet.

The boy of my age – Calum, I had now learnt his name to be – was not there. He had been sent outside for some reason I did not know. Mad Jamie, too, had gone, back to wherever he came from, I presumed.

Iona sat by the fire. She was deftly weaving willow to make a basket, when Jeannie handed her a slate and instructed her to copy out some lines from a huge black Bible. At first, she grumbled, but Jeannie had said something about Sunday being a good day to write words from the Bible and she had gracelessly taken the slate and begun to write. I wondered at this – that in such poverty, a girl would learn to read and write.

The old shepherd's corpse still lay on the trestle table at the far end of the dwelling, near where the men sat now. I had heard mention of waiting for the minister – their word for churchman, I guessed – to come, but I knew not when that would be.

There was much I did not know or understand.

Whereas before we had been held as captives, now suddenly we were treated as guests. This seemed strange to me, though I was too tired to wonder at it. Perhaps they wanted me to tend to Tam when he should wake. And what had Jock said about Bess being small enough to go down to the cave? What did they plan for us?

What if we wished to leave? Would they be so agreeable then?

I had barely strength to remain awake. On the floor I sat, resting my head against the ragged wall, soothed by its cool stones. Bess sat near by on a stool. I could see her looking towards the old woman every now and then.

The old woman for her part sat on the floor by the fire now, her legs crossed like a young child at play, staring into its flames and muttering every now and then to herself. "I curse their heid an' all the hairs…" she would say. If she meant not us, it was not clear whom she meant. I only know I did not like her words, or her voice, or anything about her.

Jeannie lay on the bed beside her grandson, leaning on one elbow, and stroked his hair as he muttered in his drunken sleep.

She looked over at me once, and at Bess. "I thank ye again. The both o' ye. I ken no' how ye came to be here, but I thank God that ye were, for Tam's sake. 'Tis a sad day, but Old John was ready for the next world. And there's nothing that weeping can heal." She threw a look towards the old woman. "See Old Maggie, she doesna even grieve for her man. She understands nothing. She lives only in the past, and nothing from today makes a difference to her. Blessed she is."

"What of her cursing, her anger at us?" I asked.

"She speaks not o' ye. She curses the men who killt her father and mother for their faith, and who deformed her face as ye see it. Seven years old Maggie was when the King's men tied her mother to a stake and drowned her in the rising tide, along wi' another woman. They shot her father as he prayed. And then they took a burning sword and burnt her face. A wee child – would ye believe it! No' even English they were, nor even Catholic – just soldiers who would do all their masters tellt them."

"Why? What had they done?"

"They would no' sign an oath o' duty to the King. Their duty was to God above all others but the King would no' have that. Our forefathers had a Covenant wi' God and they called themselves Covenanters. Brave they were, though much good it did them. Now, we have other ways o' fighting agin a King's government." She nodded towards where the men sat. "Ye'll see soon enough. And if ye take my advice, ye'll do what they tell ye. Ye are either wi' us or ye are agin us. And they will put ye in the cave if they think they canna trust ye."

Bess had been silent during this time and I knew not if she listened. But now she spoke. I saw her hand go to her throat, where she touched the locket beneath her shirt.

"Seven years old? And she has carried her anger so long?"

"Aye, and more than eighty years old she is. But 'tis a kind o' madness has taken her mind. She can no' say what she had to eat this morning, but she can tell ye what her mother wore as the tide drowned her."

"All in white, an' never weeping," said Old Maggie now, staring somewhere into the rafters, her thin lips quivering. "An' the soldiers shouting, 'Repent!' but she wouldna. No' my mother. Brave she was, braver than any. Curst we are now. Curst that we were no' pure enough."

"No, Maggie, we're no' curst." Jeannie spoke with a weary patience, as though she had heard this many times.

"No' ye!" the old woman snapped. "No' ye. Ye are no' o' my blood!" And she began to rock again, muttering, "Curst we are."

Bess moved to sit nearer to the old woman. She stretched her fingers to touch her hand. The woman started, looking suddenly at Bess, seeming a little frightened.

But Jeannie was speaking now. "Dinna fret yourself, Maggie. Ye're no' curst. And ye ken I dinna like ye to speak like that in front o' Iona and wee Tam."

Now Old Maggie blazed, her eyes bright and her body leaning forward, her bony finger pointing at Iona. "Curst she is too, like all the women o' my line." Suddenly, she stopped and her face became like a child's, the back of her hands rubbing her eyes. "I am going tae sleep."

Iona stood up and left the dwelling quickly.

Jeannie called to the men, "Billy, help me get your grandmother ready for bed. She will sleep here wi' us tonight, no' alone in her own cottage. She needs her sleep, do ye no', my love?" And Old Maggie nodded. As Jeannie carefully climbed off the bed, avoiding the sleeping Tam, Billy came from the group huddled at the other end of the room and walked towards us, his huge frame rolling, and yet with perfect balance and ease. Gently, he took his grandmother beneath one arm, while Jeannie took the other, and they led her slowly from the dwelling.

Jeannie was a woman who would do what needed to be done, I could tell. Such women, I see now, hold the world together, while men rip it to pieces with their wars and their false justice, always claiming God as their guide.

Why could my mother not have been as strong as these women? But the women of my mother's sort, high-born and soft, were worse than any man, for they did nothing, only took their easy lives and thought of no more than scent and silk and servants. This I had come to understand.

Tam, meanwhile, began to stir, groaning. I went to him, not knowing if this was the whisky or a worsening of his condition. He opened his eyes and groaned again and gagged. I turned him gently so that he lay on his side, his good arm, and I reached for a tankard and held it by his mouth. He gagged again, but at first nothing came from him save thin, bubbling spittle. And then, indeed, he did vomit a little, as I held the tankard by his mouth.

It was the whisky. He would suffer a sore head in the morning but he would not die. Now I dared hope further that we would be safe. As I stayed by him, reassuring him and adjusting the cloths where they bound his arm too tightly, Bess turned to Iona, who had returned from outside with a large jug of water. Calum was still away and the men sat and talked quietly at the other end.

"Iona, what did Maggie mean about the women being cursed?"

Iona did not look at Bess but her answer was clear enough. "She is mad, aye she is. She says I'm cursed. Well, I am no'! She does no' even care that her husband died today!" She did not cry, but her eyes were bright and I thought tears were not far away.

"Iona!" Jeannie was back, leading Old Maggie,

with Billy helping. They had, I suppose, been out to the latrine and were now going to put the old woman to bed. "Where's your heart, Iona? She doesna understand, ye ken that well." Iona's face clouded.

"Aye, I understand," said Old Maggie. "He drowned at the stake, for he would no' repent."

Iona looked away with a slight shake of her head. For a moment I thought less badly of her. What did she have to look forward to in this place? She was surrounded by madness and filth and men who drank whisky in quantities and the best she could hope for was to marry into another family who might be no better.

"Iona, take our guests to the well and the latrine. And then find them some blankets. We should sleep soon." Wordlessly, Iona took a long metal stick, pierced it through a clod of peat from a pile, lit it in the fire, and walked out with no more than a glance at us. We followed. I carried the tankard of Tam's whisky-reeking vomit. I, too, would do what must be done.

It was by now nearly dark but it seemed early to be going to bed. However, I would not argue, tired as I was. Still my head thumped slightly behind my eyes.

I breathed deeply in the fresh twilight air as we walked across the yard, our way lit by the blazing peat torch. Curlews called above us and the smell of the sea came salty and dry.

"Tell us about Old Maggie. Why does she say you are all cursed? You don't believe in such things, do you?" I asked.

Iona spoke freely now, outside, away from the undercurrents of anger inside. Still she did not look at us and there was an edge of bitterness to her voice. "When I was wee, I used to. I used to dream o' terrible things happening to me, every night, as soon as it was dark and the shadows came. But now, I dinna know whether to believe or no'. By day, I dinna, but by night…" This I understood all too well.

"And why does she say you are cursed?" asked Bess. I sensed a dislike in her voice, as though she had little sympathy for Iona.

"She said one o' the soldiers cursed her, when he was taunting her mother and telling her to sign the oath. Then, many years later, the gipsies took her only daughter for a wife. And her youngest grandson, Hamish, my uncle – the one who would no' have ye killed on a Sabbath – had a daughter who died only four days old and another is blind. My two other uncles, Red and Billy, have no children, nor wives neither, and nor does Mouldy. So she thinks the women o' our line are none o' us pure enough in God's eyes, because the soldier made her impure by

touching her as he did, and so we deserve our curse. And my father has one daughter." At this, she pointed to herself. "So Old Maggie is waiting for something bad to happen to me. And if it does, she'll no' be weeping – she'll be pleased to see her words come true."

Silently, I rinsed out the tankard in well water. It was a story with power and yet it had begun merely with the cruel and ignorant words of a soldier. And belief in those words had grown it into a story with the strength to hold for generations.

"The soldier merely used the words of a curse to frighten her mother so that she would give way," I argued. "It has no power." Bess said nothing and I could not tell her thoughts from her face in those shadows.

"Aye, but the women in her line have all come to a bad end," said Iona simply. "It must have power. I try to tell myself that it means nothing, but I canna help but fear it."

The peat torch sent its smoke swirling around her head, lending her a ghostly appearance, sending black shadows across her face, and I shivered. It seemed to me that Old Maggie had lost her heart and held only onto her hatred. And her hatred was keeping the curse strong.

A curse may be a powerful thing. I knew that

much. It holds even the wisest man in its grip and in the darkness and the wavering shadows anything is possible.

That is its power.

Chapter Thirteen

I did not sleep easily that night. My head throbbed dully. Never had I slept with so many bodies in one room, and I do not think Bess had either. Tam, Jeannie and Old Maggie slept in the box-bed near the fire. Thomas and Jock slept at the other end of the dwelling, Jock on a pallet which they pulled from under a smaller box-bed, and Thomas on this box-bed, with Iona. I know not where they normally slept. I think perhaps Jeannie and Jock would have had the main box-bed. With Tam? Or Iona? I did not know about the others. I only knew that in my own home we had each had a separate bed and that in the homes of the poor there was much need to share.

The corpse still lay at the other end of the dwelling, the trestle table pushed to one side.

Billy sat hunched by the window, with the shutter a little way open – he watched, for what I knew not. Calum still had not returned from wherever he was.

Mouldy and Red also were not with us – perhaps they had one of the other two cottages around the yard. And Hamish was at his own abode over the hill, I had learnt. Bess and I lay near the fire, the floor hard and lumpy beneath us, but we were warm enough under the thick, hairy blankets that Jeannie found for us.

Iona had become silent again as we went inside. She would not look at Old Maggie. She had kissed her father, Thomas, good night, and Jeannie had ruffled her hair and wrapped her round in her big arms, but Iona seemed not to like this. She shrank away and looked cross, as though too old for such things.

Jeannie bade us sleep while we could because we would be woken early. No one told us why, until Iona had said we would be "running a cargo", which I did not fully understand but took to be a seaman's term. I would not show my ignorance in front of the girl, although she was softening towards us slightly and I to her. There was a silent anger about her, which I was coming to understand. She was trapped in a hopeless world. She must have felt weighed down by the curse that she believed hung over her.

Lying awake on a cold night, alone with her thoughts, she must have feared what might happen to her. As I had, when the man had cursed me. "The devil take the sheriff's son!" he had said, with all the poison and hatred he could muster. And still I feared those words sometimes, though I was far away now and I considered myself no longer the sheriff's son. I had paid for my father's sins, had I not? Had I not done enough to shake off the power of any curse, especially one that was wrongly made?

But could I be entirely sure?

One thing I didn't worry about as I tried to sleep that night – the horses. We had seen to them before we slept and they were dry and comfortable, with some dusty oats and fresh water. These people might be harsh in their treatment of fellow men but of their beasts they would take good care. We had been given back our saddlebags too, and though they contained little of value it meant something to me that we were now trusted by these men. Not that I wished to stay long, of course, but I felt that we were safe at least for a while.

Our pistols and swords were not returned to us, not yet.

The fire hissed and crackled, sometimes spitting a violent spark onto the hearth. Snoring there was aplenty, and the muttering of men sleeping uneasily. Every now and then, Tam moaned in his sleep and I peered at him through the darkness, hoping that he was not slipping into fever. And from outside came the faraway crashing of waves and the nearby whishing of a night wind ruffling the heather-lined thatch above us. Every now and then, a draught from the window moved the spinning-wheel a little, and then it settled with a click.

The scrawny dogs licked themselves regularly with a wet slapping sound. Eventually, someone sent them outside, where I suppose they found shelter where they could.

But more than these noises, it was my thoughts that kept me awake.

I had changed in the last few weeks since running from home. My reasons for leaving seemed like a story from another life. Did it matter now that my father and my brother had despised me so? They had been wrong, and I had punished them in full.

At first Bess had shown me how to survive, but now I needed no one to show me. That thought was strong and good. Yet the future seemed full of confusion. I did not know where I was going, what choices I might have, what chances. I could see the silhouette of the spinning-wheel in the darkness and the image came to my mind of the three Fates, spinning our lives for us, the thread twisting and strengthening, then weakening, then snapping on a whim.

At last, I must have slept, because it seemed a very small time before I was woken by the confusion of voices and other commotion. Someone was shaking my shoulder. It took many moments before I remembered where I was. My mouth felt horribly dry, hunger making my tongue taste foul.

In guttering candlelight and the glow from a quiet fire, Thomas and Jock were pulling on their jackets and boots. Mouldy, Red and Billy were there too, taking up items such as rope, and sacks, and fastening them about their bodies.

Few words were spoken. Jeannie bustled around, giving the men hunks of bread and some cheese, which they ate, ripping at the food with their teeth. She gave the same to Bess and to me. "Do as ye are tellt, and no harm will come," she said quietly. She touched Bess's shoulder, as a woman to a girl, and stroked a finger on her cheek. Bess smiled back at her.

Two men removed the chest from its place alongside the wall and brushed aside the dirt, revealing once more the trapdoor. I shivered as the dank smell of the sea rose through the opening.

Tam still slept, as did Old Maggie. Iona stared up from where she lay, saying nothing.

Calum returned, rushing through the door. Wild-eyed he looked, with exhaustion and excitement together. He carried an unusually large lantern. "Well done, laddie," said Jock.

"Ye're sure, now?" asked Thomas. "'Tis the right one?"

"Aye, I'm sure," said Calum with some irritation, pushing his hair from his eyes. "The signal was good and strong and they saw mine too." He glanced at the lantern as he said this. He looked towards his father but Thomas had turned away.

Now Jock spoke to Bess and to me. "Now we'll see if ye can be o' help or no'. And if no', then ye'll ken too much and ye may guess what'll befall ye." We nodded. Although his voice seemed full of vigour now, I could see traces of exhaustion, and perhaps pain, in his eyes. Was he merely ageing or was it more? "Then follow close. If ye lose a step, the waves are waiting. This is no' for the faint-hearted. This is our business, our way o' life. And if ye're no' wi' us, then the devil or the exciseman can take ye."

At the mention of the exciseman, I began to know what we were about. My heart started to race. Smuggling! Buying goods before the taxes were paid to the King, and then selling them to those who would happily buy illegal goods.

Breaking the law. Was I not accustomed to that now? I had already joined Bess's life as a highway robber, robbing the rich to help the poor, and if we were sometimes the poor, then it seemed fair and reasonable. I knew not what the rights or wrongs of

102

a smuggler's life were, but I had learned enough to hold my tongue and wait to know more. Besides, did I have a choice?

Jock, Red, and Calum went before us. Billy, Mouldy and Thomas went behind. Hamish was not with us.

When it was my turn, taking a deep breath, I swung my legs down through the trapdoor. Cold air rushed up from below and the darkness seemed to swell, hanging over the lip of the hole, drawing me down into it.

Chapter Fourteen

I found metal rungs set into the wall for hands and feet. Bess came after me and I could hear her breathing as she climbed down, her feet just above my head. Darkness was below, only a dim light above, and I must rely on my other senses and try to remain alert.

After perhaps twenty or thirty steps downwards, I reached level ground. Someone called to me. Very dimly, I could make out the shapes of the men pressed against the wall of a narrow passageway. I stepped off the bottom rung and went over to them. Soon Bess stood beside me.

Thomas, the last man to climb down, brought a burning peat brand with him. With it, he lit another lump of peat on the end of a stick, this one held by Jock, and now I could see properly. Steam rose like spectral breath from the damp walls of the narrow passage and smoke stung my eyes. The faces were ghostly and hollow, but I took comfort from their presence, though I knew them little enough, and not yet enough to trust them fully.

We made our way down a steeply sloping passage. "Mind your heads," said Red. And indeed, sometimes the passage was not high enough for me to walk upright. Strangely shaped rocks protruded, and thin stone shards hung down, sharp enough to slice the skin of an unwitting passer-by.

Few words were spoken. The only sounds were the soft crunching of loose stones underfoot, the occasional curse as someone slipped on the steep slope, and the distant noise of water: waves, roaring and crashing against rock. Hollow and echoing. Coming closer.

These were the waves that would have caused our end. How terrible it would be to drown in a quickly rising tide. At first an occasional wave would splash against a victim's mouth. He would stretch his neck upwards, pushing his face as high from the water as possible, yet knowing that this would only delay death by a few terrifying moments. He would arch his neck, turn his face to the sky, closing his mouth as each wave came, faster and faster now. He would take deep breaths, hold his mouth tight shut, refuse to take a new breath in while the water covered his face, gasp as the wave receded, snatch ever smaller, ever more frantic breaths. As the water rose, wave by wave, rhythmically, like the heartbeat of the ocean, the salty brine would lap into the open nose and mouth, choking, bitter in the back of the throat, bubbling in the lungs. He would be overcome with helpless coughing, until there was no room for air to pass, and soon he would be still. Then, at last, the waves would wash over his eyes and the top of his head. I did not know how long it might take, how long one might struggle, at what point one would give up. Or would one ever give up? Would one struggle until death took choice away or would one choose the final breath and then slip into Heaven with a smile? I did not know.

We moved quickly downwards, the slope steepening all the while. The noise of the waves came closer still. The air was thick with salty spray, too fine to see, yet dampening the face and hair, stinging the eyes. The torches fizzed and spat.

"Hold!" The man in front of me raised his hand. It was Jock. He turned to look at us. "We are near the most dangerous part. 'Tis just past high tide and the water rises in the tunnel to this place. Ye've to jump o'er the water. One slip and ye'll drown. Watch Billy and do as he does."

We walked a few yards, following Billy and Jock. Suddenly, without warning, a plume of water shot up in front of them, with a hissing roar. It fell back down again. Moments later came another, and then another. We gathered round what appeared to be a hole in the rock below us, with the sea forced upwards at every wave.

The noise here was immense, the all-powerful crashing of a furious, greedy ocean.

"Watch!" shouted Jock, pointing at Billy. Billy was standing at the edge of the hole, waiting. Another plume shot into the air and, as it began to fall, Billy leapt, landing on the other side with a grunt of effort. He turned and grinned.

With a tightening in my chest, a shiver of horror, I understood that we would need to do the same. Could I do it? Bess and I looked at each other.

Now Jock waited for the next wave to pass. But he did not jump – instead he threw the burning brand and Billy caught it easily. Now I could see properly where he stood, on a wide ledge, flat and safe, though over a gap larger than I would wish to leap, especially in the wet and slippery conditions.

With a roar, an immense wave shot into the air and I leapt back.

After the next wave, Jock leapt over the gap and was caught by Billy. My surprise was great: Jock was an elderly man, and yet he leapt that terrifying space – not easily, I may say, yet without fear.

Now it was our turn. I looked at Bess. "I'll go first," she said. Her eyes shone. She had no fear of this. Strangely, suddenly, I felt no fear either. This was an adventure and we were working together. We need make no decisions, only act. It seemed somewhat unreal, like a dream, in this wet underground world of noise and shadows and burning peat brands and cold, dripping walls.

She stood poised on the edge, waiting for the next wave. With a frothing crash it came. "Now!" shouted the men, and Bess leapt. Billy and Jock grasped her arms and pulled her towards them, though they had no need to do so.

Another pause, another crash, another shout, "Now!" and I was over, before I had time even to think, to consider the raging waves beneath me. I caught a glimpse of the cold sea's hungry maw, its tongues swirling. With a grin of relief, I joined the others, pressed against the wall. And within a few more moments, we were all over.

What now? There seemed nowhere to go, only a few steps hewn into the rock face, but no passageway, no opening, just bare dripping rock. I watched Billy. He climbed strongly up the few steps, then turned and pointed. Jock went after him. More cautiously, I followed and saw where Billy meant.

Back over the swirling passageway, across the

hole again, though higher up and onto another ledge.

This time the gap was wider. Surely he could not jump so far with safety?

Billy handed the torch to Jock, took a deep breath and launched himself over the abyss.

Chapter Fifteen

Billy landed on the other side, throwing his body forward with astonishing agility for one of his large frame, and grasping onto something. When Jock threw the peat brand and Billy caught it, I saw that it was a rope, looped over a projecting rock. This he swung a few times and then threw the free end for Jock to catch.

I tried to ignore a dizzy fear that came over me when I looked down at the raging waves below. They were like a caged wild beast that snaps and snatches at the people passing, a beast too strong for the flimsy bars.

This was something these men must have done many times. And Tam must have done it with them, for I remembered that Bess was here to replace him, being smaller and thinner than the rest of us.

I must trust myself to these men.

Jock was preparing to leap. He held the rope,

winding it round one wrist, and rocked back and forth a few times before launching himself across the gap. And then I saw the need for the rope – he had not the speed and strength of Billy and without the rope he would surely have fallen backwards into the waves. Indeed, for a terrible moment, I thought he would not reach the other side – his legs seemed to falter and weaken as he leapt. But he was able to use the rope to pull himself forward, and, with an effort which I think he tried to hide, he was over.

Bess and I must now do the same.

I took the rope, winding it round my wrist as I had seen Jock do. I looked over the edge. The waters were black, with spume like white teeth, snapping fiercely against the sides of the tunnel, sending their fountains of water high every few moments. My mouth was dry, my skin cold. A weakness spread through my legs.

"Dinna look down!" shouted Red.

"Jump!" shouted Billy.

I jumped. But I did not jump with enough strength. I did not swing back and forth before my jump as Jock had done, and my foot slipped a little as I leapt. Only a little, but it was enough.

My feet crashed against the other side of the tunnel, too low, inches lower than the ledge I was aiming for. Frantically, I scraped at the rocks with my boots, dislodging pieces of stone. Only the rope round my wrist held me, and the screaming muscles in my shoulder. I was flung sideways, my hip and arm crashing into the rock face, and I hung, desperately trying to find footholds.

Panic rushed through me and I think I cried out. A wave sent its icy water over my back. I hung there, dangling uselessly against the rock face, the rope pressing so painfully into my wrist that I could barely keep my fingers closed.

With an even sharper pain in my shoulder, I felt myself being hauled upwards, until my other hand could reach the ledge. Then that hand too was grasped and I found myself being dragged onto the shelf by Billy and Jock, my thighs scraping against the sharp stones.

They said nothing to me. Only unwound the rope from my wrist and called for Bess to jump. They had no need to say anything.

Moments later, Bess landed beside me, her face white and wide-eyed. I rubbed my wrist. I could feel bruises on my side. "I'll jump further the next time," I said, smiling, as though I had not noticed how close death had come.

"Watching you made me jump the further – I should thank you for that!" and she smiled at me too.

Within only a little more time, everyone was safely

over and we now followed a rough passageway. Often we had to climb over huge boulders or squeeze between rocks the size of a man, through a space smaller than my shoulder width. Several times, I saw tiny caves in the rock wall. Some were big enough for a man to hide in. All were pitch black. Once or twice I heard something scuttle away. I knew not what creatures could inhabit these caves and passages, with their wet and slimy walls: a lightless, dank world without heart.

After some time spent stumbling, my body was beginning to cry out with pain, my legs quivering. I did my best to keep a good pace, wishing not to show any further weakness. Bess, too, was breathing heavily. We were used to riding horses for many miles, but this was different. I tried to ignore my exhaustion and laboured breathing, and simply keep my mind on placing each foot safely for the next step.

The sounds of the crashing waves could no longer be heard. The salty smell of the sea was fainter now, or else I was accustomed to it. Our torches grew dimmer as the peat burned down. What would we do when they burnt out entirely? We would be in complete blackness.

But I need not wonder for long because without warning we had come to the end of the passageway. With one more clambering step, I was out of the tunnel and in an open space. Pausing to recover my breath, I looked around in amazement. We were in an enormous cave, the size of a small church, though not quite as high, its ceiling vaulted by the natural arches carved by centuries of wind and water.

Here the air was surprisingly fresh, and the floor almost entirely dry. My fear about the peat torches was answered, for Billy took them both and with them lit three more clods from a pile in a corner. He then placed each of them in braziers around the space, all made ready for such a need.

I wished to look around some more but there was no time. We were being led to the left towards one end of the cave, where the floor sloped suddenly downwards. Some roughly cut steps descended steeply into a space which became narrower. Now I could hear the waves again, and a whining wind weaving its way through the slits and fissures in the stones. We came to the bottom of the steps, and the space opened up around us somewhat. There was room for us all to stand quite easily.

But where would we go? In front of us was nothing more than a small hole near the ground.

And it was too small for us to pass through.

Was it not?

Jock looked at Bess. "Now ye must earn your keep."

Chapter Sixteen

Thomas pointed at the hole. They meant for Bess to squeeze through the tiny passage. She looked at me. Then, biting her lip and taking a deep breath, she nodded.

"What shall I find?"

Jock spoke. "Crawl a few feet until your hands meet empty space. Then ye've to climb down no more than an arm's length and ye'll find yourself in another cave. And if Calum read the signals aright, and if we've no' been duped, ye'll find boxes. If there's no' any moonlight, call and we'll send a torch on the end o' a rope. Then, open the boxes and call to us."

With one more look at the tiny opening, Bess crouched and then lay face down on the ground. Wriggling, she pushed her way into the hole, arms in front of her. I could hear her grunting as her legs slowly disappeared. Strangely, I felt my own chest become tight and yet the air where I stood was plentiful.

Now she was gone, and the only sound of her was the scuffling of the stones behind her.

"Let me go too!" I said. And I began to crouch down.

A hand grabbed my shoulder and Red's snarling voice came to me. "Ye'll go nowhere! Ye'll stay here. Ye think we'd trust the two o' ye?"

Their faces were grim and ghoulish in the torch-light. He was right. I could not blame them. For my part, I didn't fully trust them either.

Now Bess's words came faintly through the tunnel. There was excitement in her voice. "I see the boxes. And there's a little moonlight."

Jock crouched down at the opening and called to her. "What's in the boxes?"

There was no answer for some long moments and then her faint reply. "Bottles. And small sacks, bags of something wrapped many times over."

"Whisky and salt," said Thomas, with pleasure in his voice. The men became excited, grinning. Billy jumped up and down like a huge child, punching the air with his fists. "Whisky and saut!" he kept repeating. "Whisky and saut!"

"Hush!" said Jock, and Billy obeyed. Jock called to Bess again. "Wait!" Now Red and Mouldy passed some ropes to Jock, each with a bag tied to the end, and a small stone in the bag, and he deftly threw them

116

along the passage towards Bess. "Put the goods in the bags – no' o'er much in each – and shout when ye're ready."

Some moments later – during which time I heard very little, save the heavy breathing and occasional sniffing of the men and the distant crashing of the sea – Bess shouted once more. "The bags are full!" And, very slowly and carefully, the men began to pull the ropes towards us. Soon, the goods were with us and the men quickly removed the contents, throwing the bags back for Bess to fill once more. The ground around our feet became covered with bottles and packages, until there was barely room to stand.

"Give us a hand wi' these," said Mouldy and I followed his lead, taking as much as I could manage and carrying it to the main part of the cave, where we stacked everything. Several more loads were brought in this way, until at last Bess called that there were no more. Some moments later, her hands appeared at the opening and two of the men pulled her towards us, slapping her on the back as though they had forgotten she was a girl.

Red no longer treated her as he had before – there were no lascivious looks now. Perhaps he had accepted Jock's decision – but I think it more likely that all of them now had thoughts only for their smuggled cargo and the money they would get for it.

And Bess had been part of that.

There was now a great deal of good humour and laughter among the men. Bess turned to me and spoke quietly. "Another cave lies through that hole, not as big as this, and opens onto the sea. There's no beach, just an opening in the cliff face and the water right against the rock. I suppose a boat had landed the goods there at high tide. It is clever, very clever!" Her eyes were shining.

I did not know what sort of life we were falling into, or what would happen now, but I was glad that both of us had proved our worth. It would be some weeks before Tam's arm had recovered sufficiently to do such arduous work. We were of value to these men and I hoped our value would serve us well. If not...

Jock, I saw, was sitting down, seeming suddenly tired, rubbing his temples. He gestured for the rest of us to put the goods into the large sacks, which Mouldy, Red and Billy had brought from the cottage. Red exchanged a glance with Thomas, as if to see if he had noticed their father's weakness. Thomas stared back at Red.

But soon we were being hurried again, climbing back up the steps into the main cave, Jock bringing up the rear. Every man carried a sack or two swinging over his shoulder, loaded with several bottles and packages of salt. Bess and I did the same, imitating every action of the men. And now we must return along the passageway. I tried not to think of the gap over which we must jump.

Tiredness and hunger began to overwhelm me now. I trudged along the steep passage, doing my best to carry my load carefully – for I had no wish to incur their anger if I damaged it.

I think perhaps my head had not fully recovered from its injury, for I know no other reason to explain the strange visions and voices that crowded into my mind as I walked. My head, my thoughts, seemed to float above my body, and the crevices and deep splits in the rocks around me tangled my vision, so that a kind of madness danced before my eyes. Into my dizziness came the faces and voices of my parents, my sisters and my brother. They were laughing at me, as they had so often done before. Their laughter still hurt me and I could not shake it off.

I had left my home because of hatred and anger. Later, when I had discovered my father's corruption, I had taken revenge and at the time it had felt good. But had it changed anything? Still I hated my father and what he had done. Were revenge and punishment ever the end? Would evil not then go on and on, a twisting line of pain, until the memory of what had begun it had faded into dust?

I had thought that what I had done was just and proper. But now – now, I was carrying smuggled goods for some whisky-soaked men mired in a brutal poverty on the wrong side of the law. Was that just and proper?

I wished to do right, even to change some evil in the world. But I was powerless, driven by the actions of others.

For the moment, there was no other course but to be led. To wait.

But I would not be satisfied with only this for ever. There must be a better way to live. There must be something of worth I could do.

With these confusing thoughts, I stumbled with Bess and the other smugglers, along the passageway and back to the places where we must leap across the jaws of the sea once more.

Chapter Seventeen

The leaps back over the spouting waves were a little downhill, and easier. Besides, the tide had fallen further and the sea no longer threatened us. The men had a routine for passing the bags across the abyss on ropes and before long we had safely crossed the openings and were soon making our way up the steeply sloping passage until we came to the rungs set into the wall. We left the goods at the bottom and began to climb.

The trapdoor was open and Jeannie and Iona waited for us. We were greeted with food and mugs of a thin ale. The mood was warm and festive and I allowed myself to drift into its comfort.

Jeannie seemed concerned for Jock, who went straight to bed, pain etched in his face.

I tried to put my earlier confused thoughts away from me. For the moment, I could do nothing. For the moment, for a few days at least, I must stay here.

There was one thing useful that I could do, and that was to ensure that Tam was comfortable. His face had a warmer colour now, not the pallor of approaching death. He was awake, though lying still in the bed. When he saw me, he even smiled and I confess I was glad to see this.

"Thank ye!" he whispered suddenly. Were these the first words he had spoken since his injury? Jeannie was beside me now. She touched my shoulder and smiled.

"Aye, he has found his speech again and he has tellt me all. He said the men who killt his grandfather were nothing like ye and your friend. And if ye had no' brought him here, he would be dead for sure. I kent ye were no murderers, but the others, they were no' sure. And now ye must stay. Ye can have the cottage that Old Maggie and John had together. 'Tis too big for her alone and she needs the company, the way she is, and there is plenty o' space. 'Tis just o'er the yard and…"

I knew not what to say and I let her chatter on while I tended to Tam, adjusting his bindings. I had no wish to stay. Nor did I think that Bess would relish the thought of a grim life with these people.

Soon, we all slept, for there was still some while till morning light. To my surprise, I slept deeply and peacefully, without dreaming, through sheer exhaustion, I suppose.

When I woke, Jeannie was sweeping the floor of the dwelling. Early sunshine streamed through the open shutters.

Bess was sleeping beside me and I stared at her resting face for some moments. As if aware, she opened her eyes then and smiled at me, raising herself up. We both found water to wash our faces in and quite soon we were dressed. None of the men was there, as far as I could see.

Old Maggie sat, smiling happily to herself at something. It was as if she suffered no memories of the fact that she had learnt of her husband's murder only a day before. Perhaps Old Maggie was happier than anyone, understanding nothing. And yet, what life was that?

As we returned to the fire, Old Maggie turned to look at Bess, seeming to see her for the first time.

"Who are ye?"

"My name is Bess."

"Bess. Bess." The old woman seemed to roll the name round in her toothless mouth and in her mind. "'Tis a strange name for a lad."

"I am no lad," Bess replied. "I dress sometimes as a boy because … it is easier."

"Aye, well." And she touched her scarred face, though her eyes told of no emotion.

123

"Will you tell me your story?" asked Bess now. Jeannie heard her and looked little pleased.

"No, she will no'," she said firmly.

Maggie's mouth twisted into the raw anger of a small child. I had seen my youngest sister do this, before her governess had taught her that she must not show her feelings so. And now my sister, all my sisters, sat straight-backed and kept their lips closed hard like oysters, merely tilting their little chins and controlling the colour in their faces so that nothing more than a tight rosebud of anger prickled under their cheeks.

"I will so!" said Old Maggie now. I wished not to listen. The old woman disturbed me, with her ancient anger and how she kept the fire of it stoked till the flames blazed as high as ever. I feared the chasm of her mind, empty of all the things she should know – her husband's death, her children's births, her grandchildren's lives. The here and now. The present and the future meant nothing to her as much as the ancient cause of her anger.

And it seemed to me wrong, and ugly. I found her ugly, too, her wrinkled face like the skin on a bird's leg, the terrible stretched scar gouged from her other cheek, her twisted eye, even her hair like a ghostly halo. I did not like that she was so old and yet so like a child. She made me uncomfortable.

124

So I wished not to listen. But her voice drew me in, weaving a web around me until the sound of it was held close around my head, weaving its way inside my ears.

Its power was hard to resist.

Chapter Eighteen

Old Maggie told of the day they came for her parents, and she only seven years old and trying to hide in her young mother's long skirts. She told of the feel of the thick woollen material against her face and the smell of her mother, the smell of all mothers. She told of the marsh gentian they had been picking for medicine when the men came and how her mother had dropped the purple flowers, scattering them as she ran back to the house with her daughter, as the soldiers clattered in the yard and as they shot her husband while he knelt and prayed.

Maggie had heard the shot and seen her father twist and fall, surprise on his face. They had taken her mother and thrown her on a cart with Maggie clinging to her. Other women had been on that cart but, when they reached the beach and saw the thick salt marsh with the tide coming in, all but two had sworn the oath to the King. Her mother and one much older woman had not.

Maggie told of how she had been torn from her mother, and how she had stood in water as the tide swept higher, dumb with fear and confusion and disbelief – still thinking of the scattered flowers and the waste of it – her bare feet sinking into the silt on a soft summer day, a tiny breeze ruffling the water, the wavelets lapping as they stroked her skin.

Her mother's eyes had been wide with fear but she would not swear their oath. Silently, her mother had stood waist-deep in the sea, chained to a wooden stake. Her skirts and bodice had been ripped from her and she stood only in her undergarments, white and drifty. The other woman was similarly tied a few feet away. This woman, the older one, shouted abuse at the soldiers. Her shift was torn and her bony shoulders and thin arms were exposed. As Maggie spoke, I could picture them, like the twigs on a winter tree.

For an hour Maggie's mother stayed silent. Then the soldiers had brought Maggie to her, wriggling and screaming above the thickening water, and had threatened to burn the child's face if her mother would not swear the oath to the King. But her mother had not done so, because God was watching her and God would keep her safe or take her to a place of peace.

And perhaps she did not believe that the men could be so cruel.

Many people then had shouted to Maggie's mother, telling her that she should save her daughter and that God would forgive her, but her mother had not listened. Because she knew that it is by God's grace that we go to Heaven and not because of the things we do or wish for. She had stayed strong.

Maggie understood none of this but felt her mother's love and knew that God did indeed watch over her because if her mother said so then that must be right. Then Maggie had seen a light settle above her mother's head, a soft glow, warm, fluttering, flickering like a candle in an evening breeze.

The soldiers put Maggie back on the beach and she was carried away from the water by some other women. They had planned to take her where she could not see what was happening, though Maggie twisted round in their arms and saw the waves lapping at her mother's throat now. The strengthening breeze began to whisk the surface of the water and she could see her choke and splutter as a wave washed over her mouth.

Now some of the soldiers, who had been throwing insults at the two women, came for Maggie. They tore her from the arms of the women who carried her. When a woman tried to fight back, a soldier slashed her across the face with the back of his hand and the woman was thrown off her feet, landing hard on the ground. Blood dribbled down her chin.

Maggie did not like the way they touched her, these men, with their hard fingers on her bare skin. It was as they touched her that one of the soldiers shouted the curse and Maggie did not know if it was meant for her or her mother.

I watched old Maggie's face as she told this story, her words making sense, her thoughts in order, as they usually seemed not to be. Her eyes were alive now, her voice strong. It was as though she was no longer a very old woman. It was as though she was still there, all those years ago, living through every moment, every detail. Keeping it alive.

Her story had not finished. As she told the rest, I became unaware of everything around me, of the people and the smells and the spitting fire. All of it receded into nothing as I listened to the end of her story. And as she spoke, I pictured everything as though I had been there.

The soldiers had quickly built a fire. Maggie understood nothing of what they did. She thought perhaps they were wishing to warm her, for she was indeed cold. She shivered through her thin dress, her bare feet painful in the cold. Still she could see her mother, distant now in the water, the waves at her chin, sometimes lapping over her mouth as she desperately stretched her face skywards. Maggie did not cry. She could not.

A soldier's sword lay in the flames of their fire. She wondered dimly at this. Why did he put his sword in the flames? She struggled to make sense of everything around her. Why was she with the soldiers? Why were they smiling at her? Why were the other women standing some distance away, huddled in a group, with other soldiers watching them?

And then two of the soldiers had gripped her at the elbows and their hands felt huge. She thought that if they were not careful they might snap her arms. Another soldier had held her head and another had picked up the sword from the fire. She gasped. It had turned bright orange! She had never seen such a thing!

The soldier came to the side of her head, where she could not see him properly. Still the other soldier held her head tightly. One of her ears was trapped painfully, pinched between his fingers. She wanted to tell him, to tell him not to hold her so tightly. That he was hurting her.

Then a fizzing sizzle, followed by her shriek of pain. Her scream took everything else away, all the pain and all her breath. She fell into a swoon.

But soon, she knew not when, she awoke and

when she looked out to sea her mother was not there. Only the rough waves, licking and spitting. And the sun not shining any more.

Chapter Nineteen

Old Maggie's fingers played in agitation on the twisted skin round her scar. I turned away.

Jeannie remained tight-lipped, a dark look on her face. She had been sweeping the floor around us while Old Maggie had told her story. Now, with a deft and sharp flick, she sent the pile of dirt into the fire, then put her broom aside and said, firmly, "Now ye tellt your story and let that be an end o' it. I'll get your spinning-wheel and ye can do something wi' that and take your mind off the memories. We could all do wi' some new stockings and there's still some o' last year's wool to be spun." She nodded at Iona, who went to the other end of the cottage and, with a long stick, began to unhook a sack that was hanging from a rafter.

Jeannie shifted the spinning-wheel a little and guided the old woman to the stool beside it, unfastening something from the side of the wheel so that it could move freely. Iona now came back, carrying the sack, from which Jeannie took a mass of grey sheep's wool, which she set at Old Maggie's feet. The old woman smiled, as she took some of the wool in her fingers and expertly began to twist it, turning the wheel in her other hand. A rhythmic clicking filled the cottage as thin, strong strands began to appear.

"All in white," she muttered as she spun, her ancient fingers flying fast, her liquid eyes fixed into the distance. She had no need to watch her fingers, so expert was she at this craft.

I stood up. Jeannie looked towards me and spoke. "Aye, 'tis time ye looked at the other cottage, the one I tellt ye about. Iona, come wi' us. Bess?"

Bess was sitting next to Old Maggie, passing wool to her. She looked up. "May I stay with Old Maggie?"

"No, ye'll come wi' us."

Bess opened her mouth as though to argue, but she rose and came with us, though her thoughts seemed elsewhere.

What did Bess think of? I knew she felt some fascination for the old woman. If I am to be honest, I found her fascination distasteful. Yes, I pitied the old woman, of course – how could anyone not pity such suffering? But it was long ago. She should forget it now. She should let it pass and God would judge. What good would it do to keep it burning fiercely for

133

ever? And what did it have to do with Bess?

Even more now, I wished that we could move on and leave these people. As soon as possible.

I wanted adventure, to ride my horse, to have the companionship of Bess, to survive on our wits and feel the open sky above me. I wanted to feel that there were choices I could make. These were things I had come to know since running from my home. No, they were not enough, but they were a start, and they were better than staying with this group of people and becoming part of their ways. I had now seen many lives of trapped poverty, and could measure them against my early life of cushioned softness and silks, and I could not believe that there was no other way than those two.

As I followed Jeannie outside into the spring sunshine, I felt weighed down by small but growing doubts. How would we leave? How would I tell Jeannie that we wished to go? And what if Bess did not choose to come with me?

The cottage, single-roomed like the other, though smaller, was cold and dank. The fire was dead. It had the smell of something rotten. Many things rotten, I decided as I looked around.

Jeannie, Bess and Iona set to clearing the mess. They flung clothes and items into a pile, then folded them and put them in a chest. Iona began to lay the fire, sweeping up the ashes and placing straw and sticks in an expert heap. I must admit that she worked well, though she spoke little and I did not know what to make of her. Bess took a broom from a corner and began to sweep the floor.

I stood there. I could not see what to do or why. I did not want to be here.

"Will, take these pots," ordered Iona. She held towards me a pile of items: a pan with a handle, a wooden platter crusted with something, a bowl smeared with something else, spoons, two thick pottery cups.

"What will I do with them?"

"Wash them?" she said, with a slight smile. Her hair was now bound in a thick plait hanging all the way down her back. She was pretty when she smiled. Her being pretty made no difference to my mood. Still I did not wish to sleep in this cottage which Old Maggie and her dead husband had shared.

And so, in the yard, with sunshine around me, in the icy water that came from the well, I washed the pots. I heard the whinny of the horses, and at the same time their warm, grassy smell came to me and my spirits lifted a little.

I paused in my work and allowed myself to look up, and to gaze past the cottages and out of the yard. In the farthest distance lay the shiny strip of sea and suddenly all the openness, the emptiness, the vast sky, seemed indeed part of my world, a world where I could breathe freely. Perhaps what I did not like was only the grim interior of the dwelling where we had spent the night enclosed with strangers whom we little trusted, their whisky-reeking belches, their fizzing aggression, the undercurrents of what made them so dark and fierce and not of my ilk.

Indeed, the yard seemed well kept enough, though I could see little evidence of farming. I knew there was a cow, maybe more, in a byre which served as milking parlour and stable. Some chickens pecked over by some bushes. But there seemed little else. There were three small cottages, and the stable or byre, a shed which I think was for the chickens, and two other outhouses – one of which seemed to have been damaged by fire and had now a newly made roof. And there was also a latrine behind the main cottage.

Outside the yard, I saw no crops, only rough land, strewn with boulders and thick clumps of tall, reedy grass. A small field, enclosed by a wall, held the ponies. Yesterday, I remembered, I had glimpsed some fields a little way off, newly ploughed, with dykes separating them from grazing land, but I knew not whether these were fields belonging to Jock and his family.

I thought not. I think they had not the wealth for such land. Or the means to farm them.

Then I remembered the sheep. They had lost their sheep when the old shepherd was murdered. What would they do about this? Surely they would report the loss, and the murder, to the authorities? Surely the authorities would act for them?

There was much I did not understand or know. How much of it did I care about?

I used a stick to scrub the pots and dishes until they were as clean as I could make them.

Now, I wished to see my horse, Blackfoot. So I left the pots on the ground, where they could dry in the sun, and went towards the stable. Blackfoot and Bess's horse, Merlin, snickered as they saw me. I rubbed their noses. The hay in the manger was damp and unpleasant. This was the time of year when fodder from the previous autumn would be at its worst, beginning to moulder. They should be outside, eating what new grass they might find. I found some dusty meal in a bin and gave them some from my hands. The soft flutter of their lips against my palms was warm and familiar to me.

"We will ride you later," I said to them. I was about to leave the stable, when I heard a noise in the yard – a clattering, and voices. I hurried out.

A man drove a cart. It was Hamish. Next to him

sat a man dressed all in black. A churchman. The minister. On the back of the cart, a dark cloth covered something large.

Hamish helped the man out of his cart and led him across the yard towards the main cottage, holding onto his arm at the elbow. The minister was blind, that much was obvious. He looked like a crow, hunched and black, walking with a birdlike gait, picking his feet up high and placing them down cautiously. He held a stick before him.

After watching them go, I gathered up the pots and went to tell Jeannie that the minister had arrived. I thought he must have come to deal with the body of Old John.

I was correct only in part.

Chapter Twenty

I did not wish to watch what the minister might do with the body. Nor did I wish to intrude on the grief that the family must show. "Bess and I should ride the horses," I said to Jeannie, as I saw her go towards the main cottage. "They need exercise," I explained.

"Calum will go wi' ye." He had come from behind one of the cottages.

"There is no need."

"Aye, there is need. There are scoundrels and gipsies and villains o' all sorts. 'Tis no' safe for strangers."

Nor was it safe for natives, I thought to myself, thinking of that old man's slit throat. Perhaps, too, she did not yet trust us. Perhaps she was right not to.

"I'll go too," said Iona. It was not my wish that either of them should come.

"Ye'll no'," said Jeannie firmly. By chance, I

looked at her as she said this. I thought I saw her shiver.

"Ye'll help the men," said Jeannie. Iona turned swiftly, anger on her face, and flounced her way into the cottage, skirts swinging below her tiny waist.

And so Calum came alone with me and Bess. I did not wish for his company or like it. I do not think he had favoured us with more than two words and a blank look since we had arrived there the day before. It was not possible to tell what he thought of us, or of anything.

My doubts and my dark mood lifted as we rode out of the yard into the sunshine. We followed Calum on his long-haired, thickset pony, and rode towards the hills. When Thomas heard that we were riding out, he said we should go to Old John's hut and retrieve his few possessions.

With the sun and the sea behind us we travelled north. A dark forest covered part of one hillside, somewhat to our left, its edges clear and stark. On another hillside, yellow gorse stubbled the landscape, newly blooming. Soon we left the road, and to the sides of our path I saw patches of flowers, yellows and pinks and whites. The chill of the North was in the air, though on our backs there was some warmth in the sun.

Blackfoot felt powerful under my thighs, dancing

to the music of spring. At a stream, we stopped, and dismounted to let them drink and eat new grass.

Bess was trying to talk to Calum, I noticed. She asked the name of his pony and complimented him on his riding – as she had complimented me on mine when first she met me, I remembered. I did not think him as good a rider as I.

She asked him about his uncles. His short answers told me nothing I did not already know. That Red was always arguing with Thomas, his brother; that Hamish lived over the hill and was married and had children; that Billy was weak in the head, but was strong and a good fighter.

"Why did Hamish not come to the cave with us?" I asked, more so that I could be part of the conversation than because I wanted to know. Since I had no plan to stay here long enough to need to know, it was of no interest to me.

"His wife does no' like him to. She has some idea o' him as a merchant." Calum smiled. It was the first time I had seen him do so and I saw now how wide his mouth was. "And that he is! He plays no part in the smuggling, as far as his wife knows, but he deals in the goods afterwards. Along wi' his friend, the minister."

The blind minister! Turning a blind eye, in truth!

"And you?" I asked now.

"Me?"

"Is this what you wish to do? For ever?"

The boy looked blankly back at me. A hostile look flashed in his eyes and he tossed his hair back. "How no'?"

And now Bess spoke. "Why should he not, Will? Is it not a way of taking from the wealthy what is not theirs by right? Just as we do?"

"Aye!" said Calum. Did I imagine it or did he really seem to move a step closer to her? "The taxes! What right have they to take a part o' what's ours? Why should we no' buy salt and whisky and malt without that they take a part o' it?"

I said nothing. Ideas such as this were not new to me any more. There had been a man I'd met once, shortly after meeting Bess, and his wife must wash their clothes in cow dung because the tax on soap had made it too expensive. I knew that this was not right. But....

But I did not like the alternative. I found no pleasure in anything about the lives of these people. A highwayman's life with Bess had been one thing, a life of adventure, just the two of us. And we could manage on our own, could we not? But this, this complicated group of people, with their whisky and their fighting, this did not feel like something I could be part of. And the old woman, and her fury, her

142

ancient, futile bitterness – she especially I did not like.

Bess and Calum moved towards the horses and mounted. I followed. We rode on, the two of them riding slightly ahead, so that I could not quite hear all they said. Once Bess turned round in the saddle, smiling at me. "Isn't this a beautiful place, Will?" she said.

I did not want to disagree with her, so I nodded. And indeed, it was. No one could deny the beauty in the rolling hills, some gentle, some rugged, the range of colours, the light and dark splashed across the slopes, the shining sea behind us, the scents and sounds and shades of spring.

It was not enough.

Chapter Twenty-One

We came to Old John's hut at around midday. A patch of dirty clouds now covered the sun as they swept in from the west, but I could see its steely glow above us. We were silent as we approached, and I could not help but look around cautiously, expecting armed men to leap from behind any bush or boulder. Did the old man's spirit linger here?

It seemed much longer than two nights since we had fallen asleep in the hut and woken to find the shepherd murdered and lying in his own blood by the stream. I remembered Bess's mood too, one of gloom, even despair. She had not wished to take Tam with us: I wondered where we would be now if we had followed her advice. But now she seemed light of heart again, and to burn with something like her usual spirit.

I was glad to see her this way once more, though I did not know what had changed her. Perhaps her earlier sadness had come merely from exhaustion, and the memories of losing her cottage to the red-coats' wilful destruction? And now perchance she had put such thoughts to the back of her mind and was living for the moment once more?

I did not know, not then.

I had noticed that she wore her locket, containing her father's ring, outside her clothing, but I thought perhaps this was because there was now no danger of it being stolen.

We dismounted from the horses. Bess reached out to touch Calum's arm and pointed down towards the place by the stream where we had found Old John's body. Calum said nothing, but his face looked grim and he nodded. She touched his arm again, as though to comfort him.

"Bess, come this way," I called. I thought she should leave Calum to his own thoughts. It was his great-grandfather who had died here.

But Calum turned to us now. "I would kill them myself," he snarled.

We looked at him.

"Our enemies," he said. "The men who killed my great-grandfather."

"Reivers?"

"No' reivers. Douglas Murdoch and his men."

"Tell us more of Douglas Murdoch," said Bess.

Calum frowned, his mouth tightening. "An evil man. A Highlander by birth, a Jacobite. No friend o' the English and no friend o' ours. His father has land up north and he threw his son out when he could no' control him. There was talk o' him cheating in a duel and killing a man. Douglas Murdoch owns much land here. He builds walls on common pasture so we can no' graze our sheep. And he grows richer. He takes what he wants and he has his own men who fight for him. All good men round here hate him. But we are afeard o' him."

"How are you sure he killed your great-grandfather? Might it not be reivers?"

"No. This has the mark o' Douglas Murdoch. And he has taken our sheep afore. Because we would no' give him what he wanted."

"What did he want?"

"At first, he wanted money. Everyone in these parts pays him, else his men cause damage, fearsome damage. We paid him for many years, but then Red said we must no'. We stopped paying Douglas Murdoch, so his men stole our sheep in revenge. That was many months ago. And then..." Calum paused.

"And then?"

"Then they burnt our winter fodder and we had nothing for our ponies. And he said if we gave them our ponies, and started paying again, they would leave us alone. But we couldna lose the ponies. Then he saw something they wanted even more. My sister. They tried to take her one day, two months back, but he had sent only three men and we fought them off. One o' them was hurt – he'll no' fight again, I think. Douglas Murdoch said we'd be sorry. This is how he thought to make us sorry. And it'll no' stop here." He looked afraid, and I did not blame him.

But Iona. They would take Iona?

"They would steal her? Like a chattel?" asked Bess.

"For a wife?" I demanded, in disbelief.

"Mebbe. If Murdoch liked her. Or he'd sell her. Some other laird's son would pay a good price. Or the gipsies would. Douglas Murdoch wouldna mind, if he took what is ours. 'Tis his way," he continued, seeing our unbelieving faces. "He takes all he wants. We have paid more money than we can afford since then and he has taken it, but if he wants Iona he'll have her too. He has not tried since the other time – perhaps he is content wi' what we pay now, but he might change his mind. And now Iona must no' go out alone, for her safety. 'Tis his way, to make us live in fear, no' knowing what he might do next."

"If everyone hates him so, why do you not all join together, and stand against him?" Bess asked.

"No one dares join us. Bad fortune follows us and

the world knows it. And now that they have done such a thing as murder, 'tis worse."

Perhaps they were tainted by bad fortune. But they were also mired in their own struggle. If they fought fire with fire, would they not be burnt? Was there not a better way to stop the fighting? A better way to live?

Surely the law would help them? I asked this now.

Calum laughed. "The law is no' for the likes o' us! The law is for the lairds who want to take our land from us for their crops and their cows, so we canna graze our sheep on the common land. The law is for the King, who wants to take our money in taxes. We make our laws and follow God – that's what my father and my grandfather say. If a lawman came to our dwelling, my uncle Red would as soon fight wi' him as ask for his help."

We were silent.

How could something like this end?

Chapter Twenty-Two

Once we had taken the few possessions from the hut, we made our way back in near silence.

On our way, a strange incident occurred. We were trotting gently along the track towards the road. A curlew flew up with a cry from some reeds in the wet ground some yards away, followed by its mate. I was riding a little ahead of the others and it was a few moments before I realized that Calum had ridden his pony off the track and was galloping towards the reeds. I watched him search for something on the ground, his pony's feet sinking into the thick, sticky marsh. He seemed to find what he was looking for, and with a cry of pleasure, he made his pony move on the same spot, kicking and hauling on the reins at the same time, so that the pony did not know which way to go and only stamped and jibbed. After a few moments of this, he rode back to us, satisfaction on his face.

Bess and I looked to him in puzzlement. "A curlew's nest. I destroyed it."

"Why?"

"Because curlews are no' loved by God."

"But why?" I repeated.

"They betrayed the hiding-places o' the Covenanters. When they tried to worship God in their Conventicles. Their secret places o' worship. In my great-grandmother's time. My own ancestors," he said, with some aggression.

"But they are birds! They know nothing!"

He looked flustered "We have always done it." His voice was lame. He turned away.

We rode on, in silence again. I remembered how one of the men had shot the curlew when we had been riding to the farm on that very first occasion. It had seemed like a sport at the time. Did their anger go so deep?

As we reached the yard, Calum held out a hand to help Bess dismount. She did not need such help, and yet she took it.

Hamish's pony and cart still stood by the water trough. Mouldy sat on a stool at the door, tying metal hooks onto fishing-lines, a net in a heap by his side, and a lobster pot or somesuch. He nodded to us as we approached. Inside, the minister sat in the best chair, by the fire, shoulders stooped and all in black.

His eyes, I now saw, were lacy-white and wide. And yet, they did not seem empty. They seemed to see, and yet I knew they could not.

A long wooden box, a coffin, sat on the ground. The body of the old man lay inside it, wrapped round with a clean cloth which showed the contours of his bony face. But the coffin was nearly full with something else, too: the bottles of whisky and bags of salt that we had brought from the cave the night before were stacked around the corpse, pushed into every crevice, distorting its shape. Red was standing inside the entrance to the underground passage, halfway up the ladder, only his head and massive shoulders visible. He was passing packages up to Hamish, who was stacking them inside the coffin. Another man was below Red, handing them to him.

Old Maggie was asleep on the box-bed, her face soft and peaceful now, her damaged cheek hidden from view. Tam was lying beside her, and his eyes lit up when he saw me and Bess. I smiled briefly at him, because I felt sorry for him, but I did not go to him. I did not wish him to form an affection for me.

That coffin was heavy. I know because I helped carry it to Hamish's cart, where we secured it and covered it with a black cloth. Hamish helped the blind minister onto the cart. Not a word did the man say, simply sat, hunched, his fingers clutching the sides of his cloak round him, his white eyes wandering. Did he know what was stuffed in the coffin with the corpse? Perhaps he did not. Perhaps he did.

They rode out of the yard. Those left behind looked at each other.

"We'll keep careful watch tonight," said Jock. "Murdoch's men will be angry again."

"Why?" asked Calum.

Jock paused. "We will no' pay the cut."

Calum's shock was clear. "But we agreed! We decided! To stop them taking Iona and to make peace!"

"Peace!" said Red, with a snort. "Ye ken nothing, lad. We'll no' make peace by doing what they want. They'll take more and more until we've nothing left at all!"

Jock spoke now. "Red is right: if we always pay, they will ask for more. We'll no' pay taxes to the King so why should we pay Douglas Murdoch and his men?"

"But they will take Iona!" cried Calum.

Thomas shot his son a furious look. "Dinna argue wi' us. 'Tis for grown men to judge." Calum looked at the ground and Thomas turned away now, as though he cared nothing what his son might think. Calum said nothing more.

"Aye, they may try to take Iona," said Red, "but

they dinna ken that there are two more o' us now, and good horses, and pistols. Now is the time to strike. We can surprise them when they come, teach them a lesson they'll no' forget. They took our sheep; they murdered our kin. They will pay. We are agreed." Jock, Thomas and Red, all had faces set firm.

Calum nodded now, as though he had been swayed entirely by their words and would do everything they said. He had nothing more to say, only, "Aye. They should pay."

I did not like this. I did not like it at all. This was not our battle. I could not say where it would end but it seemed to me no good could come of it.

But I did not say so. Another thought came to me. "But they do not know you have a cargo from last night. So they will not know you have not paid."

Thomas shook his head. "They'll ken. And they will come for their share. Perhaps no' today. Or tomorrow. But news will reach them that a cargo was run at our cave – these things are no secret. Even the excisemen sometimes ken – and we give 'em their share to keep them quiet. When Douglas Murdoch finds the truth, then will he come. And we will be ready."

I tried now to sound the voice of reason. "But when will it ever stop? If you hurt them, will they not come back in greater numbers, for revenge? Will it not simply continue. For ever? Or until you are all dead?"

"Or until they are all dead!" retorted Red.

Jock passed a hand across his forehead. He seemed to stumble a little. Red took his arm. "Ye should sit," he said, casting a glance at Thomas, who turned away. Jock shook his son off.

"Dinna fuss o'er me!" he said. But he went slowly into the dwelling nevertheless, followed by the rest of us. And he did sit down. His face was the ashen hue of a weak sky. His body seemed a little slumped, his back no longer straight and strong.

He reminded me of my father's hounds: when the pack leader weakened and aged, it would try to keep the appearance of strength. It would snarl more, pace about in front of his followers, its hackles rising more often. A pack leader must seem strong, or the successors will move in.

Now the conversation seemed to be over. Jeannie called me and Bess to see the dwelling she had made ready for us to share with the old woman. Iona was there, her cheeks pink with effort. They had washed the blankets, for which I was much relieved, and now they flapped wildly on a rope strung outside. A fire crackled in the hearth and a large pan hung from the crook handle, steam rolling from it. The table was scrubbed clean, and on a platter was bread. Stools were ranged around.

On the fire sizzled several fish, hissing and spitting, sending a delicious smell around the room. "Mouldy caught them for ye," explained Jeannie. "He likes nothing better than to spend his days watching fish bite."

Something else lay on the table: our pistols. The bags of shot and powder were beside them. Our swords I saw leaning against the wall.

It seemed that we were expected to stay. I looked to Bess, and saw the pleasure on her face.

Iona was speaking. Her cheeks were pinked and her eyes shone as she took the pan off the heat and poured the steaming water into a large bowl. "I thought ye might like to wash. In warm water," she added proudly.

She was right. But I wished to do so without her there, watching me. Now Jeannie added her voice, looking at me first. "We have found some clothes – Calum's will fit ye." Now she turned to Bess. "Ye are taller than Iona so I have set Old Maggie to make a skirt from one o' mine, but she's no' quite finished. For a bodice, I think Iona's will fit."

"Thank you. You are very kind." And Bess took the garments which Iona now held out to her.

They all looked at me. Of course, I was to leave.

At one end of the room, a strip of coarse material hung from a beam, all the way to the ground. I could have gone behind this, but I did not wish to listen to their women's chatter.

Somewhat irritated, I left. I wanted to talk to Bess, to see what she thought. Surely she did not wish to stay? I knew her to be unpredictable, sometimes impulsive, and that she was different from me, but what was there to keep her here?

As I walked from the door and across the yard to the stable, I could hear their feminine laughter.

Where did I belong? Not here, I was sure, not among these people. And yet, not among my own either. Frustration grew in me, a feeling of being caught in a small and airless place.

Chapter Twenty-Three

I t seemed I would not have a chance to speak properly to Bess that evening either. We all ate together: steaming crab, the sweet, chewy flesh ripped from inside the claws with our teeth; some salty cabbage, which I thought not so pleasant; along with a dark bread, which was nourishing and malty, and oozed with soft butter.

After we had eaten, Bess began to talk once more to Old Maggie, who gave answers which sometimes seemed to make sense and at other times not. Every now and then, Bess touched her arm, and once she smoothed the hair on the old woman's forehead.

I moved away.

Thomas called me to sit with the men, and this I did. But I had to fend off their questions. They wanted to know more than I had told them the night before. I had told them that Bess and I lived as robbers of the highway, but not how we had met. Nor did I tell them this now – I did not wish them to know that Bess had almost killed me and that all I had learned about survival had come from her. Nor did I wish to tell them about my wealthy family, though from their questions I think it must have been obvious. I suppose my accent gave me away. I told them that I would not go home, could not, and that my home was far away. It was all they needed to know.

They did ask me a little about my church. I knew not what the right answers were and so I said simply that I knew my Bible and always put my trust in God. They appeared very satisfied with this. I had already seen Iona copying lines from the huge black Bible – kept on the chest which covered the underground passageway – and I had seen Jock sometimes touch it as he passed, as if for reassurance.

And so they seemed to overlook my educated voice, and my Englishness. I suppose that that did not offend them over much, since they were of Hanoverian persuasion, and hated the Jacobite Highlanders more than they did the English. I think they neither liked nor hated me for my roots. I was not, at least, what they hated most: soldier, Catholic, or reiver.

Besides, I believe they so strongly wished that Bess and I should lend our strength and numbers to them that they minded little where I was from. They knew we were on the wrong side of the law, and the right side of God, and that was enough for them. They knew now that we had rescued Tam, and that I had saved his arm. That, too, made us their friends.

Jock appeared to have recovered from whatever had made him ill earlier, though he ate little and breathed somewhat heavily.

They drank no whisky at that time. Just some ale which, from its watery taste, I think had little potency. Red stood leaning against the wall, carrying in one hand a stout wooden club with pieces of metal sticking out from one end. He repeatedly hit the palm of his other hand with its stem. I think he looked forward to any fighting that might occur. Mouldy and Billy took turns to stay outside and watch the track for anyone coming.

Then Thomas took something from where it hung high on a wall. I had not noticed it before. It was a violin. As he took it in his left hand, his rough fingers curling easily round the strings, I thought of Bess and how she had used to play the cittern. Until it had been burnt along with everything in her cottage.

When he began quietly to pluck the strings and to turn the tuning pegs, I saw Bess twist quickly to see. Her eyes lit up, and the more so as Thomas took the bow and began to play a tune, one which was mournful and yet, at the same time, quick and full of life.

"May I try?" she asked, when he had finished. Jeannie and the men looked at her. Only Iona and the old woman did not. Iona was stitching something and she did not stop now. Old Maggie did not notice, I think. She was away in her own mind.

"My father taught me to play the fiddle," Bess said, taking the instrument and letting it settle comfortably under her chin. "I have not played for many a year. I know not if..." She fingered the strings a little, getting the measure of them. She took the bow in her other hand, her fingers curling round, finding their place, and then she hesitantly drew it across the strings, moving the fingers of her other hand as she did so. And a passable tune came from the fiddle, a tune which grew in confidence as she found its voice.

After a few lines of the tune, while everyone in the room looked at her, she lowered the fiddle, and passed it back to Thomas, who smiled and then, imperfectly at first and then with more confidence, began to play her tune as though he already knew it, which I think he did not. Now, a little shyly in this company, Bess began to sing some words. Very soon, I saw that these were her own words, new words. She must have worked them in her head since hearing Old Maggie's story, because that was the story her song told.

When she was not robbing rich travellers on the

160

highroads, Bess was a ballad seller. She created songs, telling the tales of events and lives. She had written a ballad about Henry Parish's death and we had made copies of it and passed them to everyone we met in Henry's town. We had taken no money for this ballad, wanting only that the world should know of the horror and injustice of his passing.

My Grammar school education and my tutors had taught me that the ballad seller's craft is inferior to the great poems of the classics. But as soon as I had heard one of Bess's ballads for the first time, I had felt the great power of its music and poetry. She could turn a man's life or death into words that touched the heart and mind and a listener would not be the same after hearing them. And this she did now, while I watched her, and watched the faces of those around us as she told of the death of Old Maggie's mother.

I remember only snatches of her verses. She sang of the white dress, the child's tears, the cold spume of the sea relentlessly rising. But I remember well the refrain, a refrain that settled in my head and came to me again over the coming days.

The cruel men laughed as the cold tide rose,
While fire burned bright in the martyrs' eyes,
Nor tender years nor yet old age

Could halt the heartless soldiers' rage.
Now when the curlew cries, my friend,
We summon that fury once again,
And ne'er before the end of years
Shall we forget a martyr's tears.

Old Maggie sat with her arms folded round her, hugging herself, shaking her head softly as a tear fell along the cracks in her face. And when Bess had finished, and everyone clapped and slapped their thighs in admiration, Old Maggie beckoned her over and took her hands in hers.

In a quavery voice, but clear, she said, "I am glad ye have come, child. Ye bring new blood tae us. We need new blood. Tae start again. Ye will produce guid sons, strong sons. No lassies. The lassies are curst."

Iona turned her shoulders away but I saw her lips tighten and twist. I could not blame her.

Bess laughed. She tossed her black hair back. It was clean now, and shining from much time spent combing it earlier that day. It fell in spirals about her neck. The locket glinted in the hollow below her throat. Her bodice – Iona's – was a little tight, nipping her waist; the skirt was the new one that Old Maggie had stitched that very afternoon, coarse and heavy, of cheap material. I could see Calum watching her, without speaking, just watching her. His face was slightly pink, but this was perhaps the firelight and the warmth.

"I have no plans for babies, Maggie!" said Bess, squeezing the old woman's hands. "Will and I are not…"

"No," said Old Maggie. "No, foolish lass. I talk o' Calum. Calum should be married soon and ye are a pretty thing. And Calum's fair o' face hisself, is he no'?"

A snort of derision came from Red, still leaning against the wall. He muttered something, but I know not what. Thomas rose to his feet, pushing his stool back with a clatter. "Well, ye'll no' have her and that's for sure!" and he stood before Red, pushing his chest out. They were of the same height, and as broad. Their faces were inches from each other, their eyes blazing, their lips apart.

"And who's to stop me?"

"I am." It was Bess – standing tall herself, fury on her face. She dared put her hands out and pull the two men apart, before Jock, too, intervened and settled his sons down. "I am not yours for the choosing," she said, coolly.

Red smiled, his large frame relaxing against the wall again. "Dinna be afeard, lass! I'd no' dare! Ye're o'er strong for me!" At which she, too, smiled.

At first, I was pleased that she said she was not

theirs for the choosing. I thought she was choosing neither Red nor Calum. But then I understood: she was looking only at Red. She did not address her remarks to Calum. I looked at him more closely now. And although I did not think him to be fair of face, with his sullen expression, his hair over his eyebrows and his mouth overlarge, yet what did I know of a girl's preferences? Had she not seemed to be easy in his presence? Could it happen that Calum would turn her heart?

If he did, surely she would not choose to stay here with him? But why not? And would I mind? I had no feelings of that sort for Bess, had I? And yet we were together, she and I. We had faced death together. Calum could not say that.

I knew Bess's story and she mine. She knew of the corruption of my father and I had heard of the tragic death of hers. She had let me watch her as she threw crocuses into a waterfall to remember her parents' murders at the hands of the redcoats. I had seen her sadness. And her fury. She had witnessed my shame when my father had hanged an innocent man. Together we had watched Henry Parish shot dead and we had picked crocuses for him too.

Calum could never mean anything to her. I would not believe it.

Chapter Twenty-Four

Of a sudden, I had a need to go outside, to breathe fresh air. Telling them that I would take my turn watching, I left the dwelling. Mouldy stood there, puffing on a pipe, and I bade him to go inside.

A half-moon dropped its milky light across the landscape. The vast sky, dizzying above me, was flecked by stars on this clear night. Not a breath of wind ruffled the air and the sweet smell of tobacco lingered, hanging there.

I went to check the horses, to make sure they had food and water. As always, my heart lightened with their warm, musty breathing, their tangy smell, their trust.

As I walked back again some moments later, Bess was coming out of the dwelling. She said she would join me, so we both went towards our own cottage and I waited outside while she fetched her cloak. Then we walked together, watching for any men or horses approaching along the track. But the night was empty and quiet.

"I have wanted to talk to you," I began.

"I too," said Bess, turning to me. "I wanted to say thank you, for bringing us here. You were right, to help Tam, and to take the risk. These are decent people, with honour and loyalty. They suffer, like all the poor, yet they have made us welcome…"

"How can you say that?" I demanded. Anger flared in me, from so many hours of wishing to say what I felt, of hiding my frustration at this place, these people. "How can you say that these are decent people? These are smugglers, good for nothing. Fighting each other and their enemies. They almost killed us!"

"They do what they can, what they must. Who will help them if they do not help themselves?"

"But what kind of life is it? You would not wish to stay with them, surely? They live from day to day in fear. What are we doing even now? Watching for marauders who wish to steal a young girl! What kind of a life is that?"

"It is not what you are used to, of course," retorted Bess. "But it is a life! It is not without honour and reason. I would gladly stay, at least for a while. Besides, they need me – to go through that passage-way. They need us both, to protect Iona. You would wish to do that, would you not?"

Would I? Of course, I did not wish Iona to be taken or to suffer. But would I lay down my life for her?

Bess continued. "We could make a good living, Will. Think on it! They will give us our share and, who knows, we could still ride out of a night and rob the rich carriages as they pass. We need not stay for ever, not if we do not wish to. But we have a place to stay now and we are welcome. For now, I wish to stay."

"And Calum?" I asked, trying to keep a bitter edge from my voice.

"What of Calum?" I was not looking at her so I did not see her expression but in her voice I thought there was amusement. A slight hesitation before the name, perhaps even a rolling of it on her tongue.

But I could not ask her further. I did not know how to say it. Or perhaps I knew how to say it but did not wish to hear the answer.

A scuttling in the grasses by the corner of the chicken shed made us look in that direction. We walked towards it, each with a pistol before us. But we saw the shadow of a small creature darting off – a rat perhaps, nothing worse.

No wind ruffled the grasses. No owls called. No persons were passing by, no carts at this time of night. Only in the distance the soft shushing of waves on shingle and the occasional faraway curlew crying.

I needed to say something to break the silence. I wanted to say we should not stay, to persuade her to come away with me, but I was afraid that she would not.

"You seem to like Old Maggie," I said instead, my voice level.

"She is so filled with anger. Such ancient anger."

Bess was shaking her head as she said this and I thought I understood her meaning. And so I replied, "Yes, and she should forget her anger. It has poisoned her, made her mad, I think."

"She should not forget her anger! How should she forget? You know what the soldiers did to her and her mother. To forget would be to betray them."

"But she has carried her hatred for near eighty years! What good has it done her? Sent her mad and brought her only bitterness."

"Jeannie said Old Maggie cannot remember what she had to eat yesterday but she can remember every breath of that awful day. Such is the power of her anger! That such evil deeds should never be forgotten. It is only seven years since the redcoats murdered my parents and I wish never to forget. Because that would betray them. And that I will never do."

And now, at last, I realized what had brought back Bess's spark, her old passion for life – it was hatred and anger. That was what she breathed. And it was Old Maggie who had rekindled it. Old Maggie, whose ugly venom seemed to me distasteful, repellent, and yet to Bess like something else entirely, something she might call honour, justice.

I knew not what to say. I had thought I understood her hatred, respected it even. After all, I was no stranger to anger of my own.

But now I had begun to think that revenge is not the way. Holding onto anger is like keeping a thorn inside oneself – it will turn to poison.

Perhaps I was fortunate because I had settled the score with my father and brother. But Bess, too, had surely settled her score? She had killed a redcoat in cold blood. She had finished Henry Parish's work for him, by taking money to his bereaved mother and by ensuring that his death was remembered in song. But then the redcoats had burnt down her cottage, destroyed all her possessions. Did she now need revenge for that? And what then? When would it end?

That too was a reason not to hold onto anger. Did not Shakespeare say, "blood will have blood"? It would never end, it seemed to me – the circle of revenge and anger and hatred would spin for ever.

Almost beyond living memory, Old Maggie's mother had been killed for her religion. And still Old Maggie and her family hated Catholics because they answered to the Pope, and Episcopalians because they answered to bishops, and even any Protestants who believed God spoke through an earthly king. But did we not all have the same God? What would He say about such anger?

I did not understand, only that I had no will to be part of it.

"Be careful your anger does not turn you mad. Like that wizened old woman, muttering about curses." There was spite in my voice.

Now her anger blazed out. "Do not tell me how I should live! You've not had to suffer as I have, rich boy that you are! And how dare you speak of Old Maggie like that? She is strong. Her anger and her hatred make her strong. I should not be ashamed to be like her!"

She turned away from me now. To quarrel with her was not what I wanted. I did not wish to lose her friendship.

And so I told her I was sorry. I *was* sorry – for many things, for the obstacles fortune had placed in her path. But I do not think I was wrong.

She looked at me, her face milk-white in the moonlight. "Do not condemn Old Maggie," she said more softly now. "I wish to be her friend. I understand her."

Oh, I could understand Old Maggie. But that did not mean I thought her right.

Later, as Bess and I prepared to go to bed, I think there was some slight chill between us, though we tried to hide it with conversation. Old Maggie was already asleep in her box-bed, and Jeannie had closed the curtain round her for warmth. I was glad not to be able to see her, though I could hear her rough breathing.

As I lay wrapped in a blanket, on a lumpy pallet that was too thin, I stared into the softly hissing embers, and tried to sleep. I did my best to settle my thoughts. I tried to tell myself that I would stay for a while, and that Bess would soon tire of the company of these people. Then she and I could leave together, move west, or north, or anywhere we chose. Even America! Many people did so, I knew. We could start a new life there. But I would not say anything to Bess now, would not try to persuade her. I knew her to be stubborn – she would not wish to feel that she was being pushed.

I would be patient. I would pretend to be content with these people, joining their smuggling activities, doing what was necessary. And when the time was right, Bess and I would leave. Together.

First, however, ill luck played its part. For that night, in the darkest hours, when sleep is deepest and when dreams and demons play with our fears, we were woken to terrible news.

Iona was gone.

Chapter Twenty-Five

I do not recall what sound woke me first. Was it Jeannie's screams? The shouting of men? Was it the crashing against our door? "Open up!" Thomas's voice was raw and full of agitation. Bess and I scrambled to our feet, pulling on such clothes as we could find in the dark.

I felt sick with panic, as I struggled to grasp what it was we should fear. Bess hurried to light two candles from a glowing ember, and handed one to me. As I unbarred the door, it flew open.

"'Tis Iona! They have taken her!" Thomas's face was rigid. This was his daughter. This his worst fear.

"Get your boots on. We are riding after them," he shouted, turning and running towards the stable. Setting my candle on the table, I rushed to pull my boots on, fumbling with my stockings, and then my coat, fastening the buttons as best I could.

A sound came from behind the curtains of the bed

where Old Maggie lay. I parted them slightly, thinking to look in and reassure her, but I saw even by the dim candlelight that she slept peacefully and only murmured in some dream. She was better not knowing. And I was better not hearing her talk of curses. Snuffing out the candle once more, I left her sleeping, closed the curtains behind me and rushed out with Bess, leaving Maggie in darkness.

In the dimly moonlit yard, by the door to the other cottage, was only more confusion as the men argued about what to do. Thomas and Calum wished to ride after them, knowing that they would be heading towards their lair. But how long since Iona had been gone? They could be safe in Douglas Murdoch's tower by now.

Red also wished to ride after them. He struggled to tie his belt round his waist, to hold his trousers up. Billy stood twisting his hands in distress, knowing not what to say, waiting only for instructions. Mouldy, carrying two burning torches, tried to argue for waiting till daylight, but his voice was barely heard.

Jeannie, her eyes wide and hollowed in the light of the torch she also carried, looked to Jock. "What will we do, Jock? Surely ye'll go after them? Ye canna leave wee Iona, no' even for a night. Who kens what could happen to her? If I could get my hands

174

round that man's neck, I would kill him!"

"Hurry, for God's sake!" shouted Calum now, his voice tight with fear for his sister. He was already on his pony. Thomas had one foot in the stirrup and now swung into the saddle. Red was fumbling to saddle his pony.

"No!" said Jock now.

"Aye!" urged Thomas. "We canna wait!"

"'Tis foolish," said Jock. "Think on it carefully. No harm will come to her this night." I was not so sure of this, but I kept my silence. Some things are better not spoken aloud. But Jock was still speaking. "We go in the morning, when 'tis light. We take money and we offer a ransom."

"A ransom?" shouted Thomas now. I had not seen him so angry before. "A ransom? We should kill them all for this!"

"Aye, that we should!" Red was in rare agreement with his brother. "And the moon is clear enough – we need no' wait for morning, when it might be too late." He picked up his club and slapped it hard into the palm of his hand, with a loud thwack, and began to mount.

It was at that moment that I saw a shadow move, out of the corner of my eye. Over by the door of our dwelling. I narrowed my eyes to see more clearly. There was nothing. But did I not also hear a small noise, as of something moving? I thought I did. Yet it was impossible to be sure.

Bess saw me look. I shook my head. "It was nothing," I muttered.

Besides, I had begun to be properly awake. Questions clamoured to be answered. How had intruders come into our midst so silently? Was no one guarding? How could they have entered the dwelling, without waking someone? I suppose they must have waited till Iona went outside, perhaps to go to the latrine. But they must have waited for a long time. How had no one seen or heard?

It did not seem possible.

And so I asked, "How did they enter? How did no one notice?"

"What are ye saying, lad?" Red snarled.

"Only that they must have been very quiet," I said, levelly.

"Are ye saying that I was no' watching? Is that what ye're saying?"

Jock moved between us. To me he said, "Red was guarding. He went behind the cottage once because he thought he heard a noise. And when he finished his turn and came to get Mouldy, he saw Iona was no' here." It seemed reasonable.

"Are ye coming or no'?" shouted Thomas.

And that was when I heard something else. The

sound of a horse's hoofs, galloping. As one, we turned, all hearing it at the same time.

Spread on a hillside not far away, was a small wood. Out of its darkness, a horse was moving. A single horse, with a rider, clear even in the light of the half-moon on this near cloudless night. "Follow me!" cried Thomas, glad now to be able to act. And he and Calum rode apace from the farmyard, followed closely by Red, and the clatter and clash of their hoofs rang around us as they rode away.

"Stay," said Jock to the rest of us. "There's no more to be done till morning. They'll no' catch him." His voice sounded very tired now and he pressed his forehead with his fingers.

I knew he was right, but they had disobeyed him. He walked back to the dwelling as though broken, not thinking even to comfort his own wife. Jeannie, meanwhile, clasped her hands in silent prayer for some moments. Then she put her shoulders back, straightened herself, drew her cloak round her and went after her husband. The rest of us followed, to wait with them until the others should come back, but Jeannie turned and spoke to me and Bess.

"Ye should rest and wait for morning. There's nothing to be gained wi' all o' us waiting up. Go and see that Old Maggie needs nothing."

So Bess and I returned to our cottage, saying little.

177

What could we say? This was a cruel world we had found ourselves in. To think on what might happen to Iona was not easy, and so I tried to put it from my mind.

And I could not say who was right – Jock, or Thomas, Red and Calum.

After finding our way back to our sleeping places in the dark, we lay down. But we did not sleep. We had no chance. For almost as soon as I wrapped the blanket round me once more, a piercing noise tore through the night.

Old Maggie was screaming.

Chapter Twenty-Six

I was on my feet in an instant. Quickly, Bess was beside me, a candle in her hand. Old Maggie was thrashing about behind her curtains but before we could reach her, a figure had climbed out. It was Iona. Standing in her shift, looking frightened.

"What are you doing here?" Bess and I demanded together.

"How long have you been here?" I added.

Iona shook her head. "I canna remember."

"You had everyone fearing for you!" exclaimed Bess. "Your father and brother have gone in search of you. Red, too. They saw a horseman." Iona looked startled – worried, I supposed, for her family riding off into the night.

"Why were you here?" I asked again.

"I… Mebbe I was walking whiles asleep. I canna remember anything." She rubbed her eyes and shivered. I moved to fetch a cloak for her. Bess, meanwhile, went to comfort Old Maggie.

As I put the cloak round the girl's shoulders, I saw her troubled eyes. She shivered with more than cold.

And I knew why. Or I knew a part of why. Though I could not begin to guess the rest. I spoke quietly so that Old Maggie would not hear. But Old Maggie was railing and cursing and pointing wildly at Iona, while Bess tried to calm her. I did my best not to listen to the words. "I curse their heid an'..."

"Tell me the truth, Iona," I said softly, turning her shoulders to look at me. She twisted her face away but I held her firm.

"'Tis the truth. I've walked whiles sleeping afore."

"Our door was bolted," I said.

"A window is open," she said. And it was. I had not noticed, as the shutter was almost closed, but when I went to it now I saw that the catch was off. I cursed our carelessness, though it was impossible to imagine a man climbing through such a small space.

But I had some extra knowledge, which she could not have known I had. "You were not here when we left to search for you. I know. I opened the curtains of Old Maggie's bed to see if she was asleep."

And now her eyes looked the more afraid. Her lips began to move but no sound came out. There was bad trouble in her, and I knew not what it was. She glanced at Bess and the old woman but they

180

took no notice of us. And now Iona turned to me. "Please!" she whispered. "Please, dinna give me away! They would kill me if they knew! Please!"

I thought she exaggerated. Why would they kill her? Had they not ridden out by night to save her, to find her and bring her home safe? Did they not plan to kill Douglas Murdoch and his men rather than hand her over? She was a silly girl to be so afraid.

"Why were you in our cottage? Why did you not return to your own bed?"

"Ye all stood close to the door. Ye would've seen. But this door was open and I slipped in." Still she shivered. But her voice had the air of truth.

Old Maggie now was calm. Bess stroked her forehead as she lay there. Still she muttered and when she saw Iona again she scowled.

"I'll take Iona and show the others she is safe," I said now. "Someone will need to ride after the men."

"But..." said Iona.

"Come with me," I said firmly, and took her arm, guiding her out of the cottage. Some clouds had begun to cover the sky and the moon was not visible now. As we slowly picked our way like blind men across the yard, she urged me again and the tremor in her voice was no pretense.

"Please, dinna tell them I was no' there afore!

Please! Ye dinna understand! They will kill me!"

I did not believe her words, but I believed her fear.

"Then tell me where you were."

"No!"

"Then I cannot help you."

"I was … I was wi' … a lad. We love each other!" she blurted out.

I laughed. It was the way she said it. But she was serious. I saw it in her eyes and the way they sang with the truth of her words.

"And they will kill you for that?" I asked, in jest. Surely they would be happy? It could be new blood for their group. Perhaps it would help Old Maggie think the better of her if she settled down and made a marriage for herself. She was not too young for her family to think of such things.

But a small doubt crept to the edge of my thoughts and just before we came to the door, I repeated my words, though more softly this time. "They will kill you for that?"

"Aye," she said, simply, her voice fragile. Could she be right?

And then, as I rapped my hand against the door to the dwelling and called out that I was there, I understood suddenly why she thought they would kill her.

The boy she loved worshipped God in the wrong way.

But surely, this would not be enough for them to want her dead? I could not believe it.

Chapter Twenty-Seven

I needed to know more, much more, but there was no time now. The door was hauled open and there were Jeannie and Mouldy. Billy stood behind. With a cry, Jeannie spread her arms and took Iona to her. Her words tumbled over each other.

"Oh, thank the Lord ye are safe! Where have ye been? Oh, how afeard I was!" Then she looked at me, her eyes bright with tears above Iona's flame-red hair.

"She was asleep in Old Maggie's bed," I explained. "She must have come there in her sleep."

"Aye! Aye! I mind she has walked while sleeping once afore, but just into the yard and we found her standing there. But the door – was it no' bolted fast?"

"Perhaps she came in when I left for a few moments. I did so more than once. I had some stomach pains." I did not look at Iona's face as I lied for her. But I was angry with her, angry that I found myself in this position, lying for a silly girl who would cause nothing but trouble.

And yet, why should she not love whom she wished? Why should it matter how the boy worshipped God?

But I would rather she did not love him. It would be the cause of endless trouble. And although perhaps she exaggerated when she said they would kill her, yet surely ill would come of it.

Could I persuade her to leave this boy alone? If I could make her fear the results of her love, then perhaps she would change her heart.

Yet why should I mind? I did not care for her overmuch. She was like the froth on waves, without strength or substance. Pretty, of course, with that river of tumbling red hair, and eyes the colour of sea moss, and her cheeks with their sandstorm freckles, but a girl to be looked at and not listened to. A silly girl, not worth the fuss.

But I felt sorry for her, trapped as she was by walls not of her own making. This dangerous love was not of her making either. And by loving someone forbidden by ugly rules, did she not show spirit? Was she not, in her way, fighting against the terrible hatred of Old Maggie and the others?

So, was she not right? And strong and brave?

And as Iona disentangled herself from Jeannie's

185

embrace, and as Jeannie began now to scold her for the trouble she had caused, the girl looked at me. I saw her eyes then, and there was no fear in them at all. With a small, tight smile, she thanked me without words and I knew then that I would continue to help her.

Because I pitied her, yes. But also because I believed she was right to love whom she wished to love.

I did not like these people and their hatred. They were poisoned by it and if Iona was strong enough to fight against such poison, then she deserved my help.

Chapter Twenty-Eight

We slept no more that night. Mouldy had ridden fast to tell Thomas and the others of Iona's return. It surprised me greatly that he managed to catch them, but I learnt that in such times they used a system of signals, using fires on a hilltop, or lanterns, or burning peat brands, and sometimes by imitating the call of curlews – though they might regard these birds as traitors, yet they would use them.

They had not reached Douglas Murdoch's place, for the fleeing horseman had led them in a different direction, and then they had lost him. And so they had returned, and were now full of joy at Iona's safety.

I wondered if they would be as pleased if they knew the whole truth.

Soon a raw morning light spread across the sky and daylight brought much activity. All of us had our allotted tasks: cleaning, repairing, cutting wood, preparing food. I cleaned out the shed where the horses were. This was a task I had no need to undertake at home, having always had servants to do such things for me. Throwing filthy straw onto a pile with a pitchfork, sweeping the floor and washing it down with many buckets of water from the well, was pleasant work indeed. Good, honest work. Having only the horses for company made it all the better and soon my tiredness began to fade.

The ponies were in a large sloping area behind one of the cottages, enclosed by a ramshackle wall. The two cows were outside the wall, untethered, grazing on what they could find, though the grass did not look plentiful yet and the ground was marshy in parts. One cow swung its full udders; the other cow seemed smaller, younger, and followed it as though it was the larger one's calf. I let the horses into the field, and watched in pleasure as I saw them run, kicking their heels in play, twisting and turning as they enjoyed the spring weather. The ponies began to gallop with them. At the bottom of the slope, they turned and galloped back towards me.

Iona came from round a corner, walking towards the place where the cows were. She wore a dark green skirt and bodice, a clean fawn-coloured apron round her waist. She did not see me there and I simply watched her as she took a slim, bendy stick and flicked it at the cows, driving them expertly into the yard and towards the byre. She made clicking noises with her tongue, and they seemed to understand where she wished them to go. I watched her guide them into the byre.

Wishing to talk to her, I hesitated for some moments, then went after her. As I reached the doorway, my shadow fell across her line of vision, and she looked up. For a moment, there was nothing, and then came a small smile, though perhaps a worried one.

"May I watch?" I asked. I did not particularly wish to watch. I wished to speak to her, but I did not know quite how to begin.

She nodded.

The farm cat, a sleek ginger creature, well fed on mice and birds, stirred from its place on a patch of straw warmed by the rays of sun through a window. It got to its feet, stretching, and came to rub itself against Iona's feet.

Reaching for the small stool, she settled it behind her, positioning herself close to the larger cow, spreading her skirts so that her feet were wide apart. The beast towered above her, its bony rump swaying slightly. With expert hands she grasped the udders and began to pull downwards, one hand at a time, and within moments spurting streams of milk fell noisily into the bucket. Rhythmically she did this, leaning forward, her hair like an armful of autumn bracken hanging down her back, loosely bound in a piece of cloth.

"There is little milk left," she said. "Her calf is growing older."

"When will the calf produce milk?"

She laughed. "Never! It's no' female!" My foolishness made me blush. "He will go to market later, for meat. And then we can buy another cow in calf or we can get this one wi' calf again and sell her milk."

She squirted a little milk at the cat. It jumped, but immediately set to licking the creamy liquid from its chest, purring as it did so.

"Last night," I said, to change the subject, and because I had no wish to talk of cows. "I need to know everything. Otherwise I cannot help you."

She looked fearfully over my shoulder. "Shh!" she whispered.

"There is no one here," I assured her. Bess and Jeannie had gone to the nearest town – Wigtown, they said – to buy provisions, with Billy driving the cart. Jock was resting, his head paining him again. I could see the others outside, two mending the roof of the chicken shed, another chopping logs, another making rope. Calum was sharpening knives on a whetstone near the yard entrance. I remained standing in the doorway, where I could see them.

"I must know. If I am to keep your secret. Who is the boy and why can you not tell anyone?"

She hesitated in her milking. The cow turned round to look at her and stopped chewing its cud. She resumed. The cow returned to its chewing. Iona did not speak, though she opened her mouth to do so but perhaps could not find the words. "Where did you meet him?" I asked, thinking to loosen her tongue with a lighter question.

"Some months past, when I was in the town. It was no' difficult and sometimes I would see him at the market. I had more freedom then and it was no' difficult, until the trouble grew worse between the Murdochs and our family. And now, we meet in secret, and not often."

"And would your family have been so angry that you loved a boy?"

She looked up then and something tightened in her face, though she continued with the milking.

At that moment, I knew that I was right. "He is of another religion, is he not? A Catholic, or from the church of bishops – I have forgotten what you call it."

She nodded, biting her lip. "The Episcopalians," she muttered.

So, I had been correct. I wished to say it did not matter. But I knew enough to know that it mattered here. I could only try to persuade her to forget him.

"This will bring only danger and sadness," I began. "Think how angry your family will be. It would be better for you to forget him."

She shook her head. "But I love him," she said, her voice somewhat petulant.

"You can love again." What did I know of this? Of course, I had felt my heart beat faster at the sight of a pretty girl, a stirring in me at the call of red lips or soft eyes, but I had not met a girl who destroyed my reason as love is supposed to do.

But Iona had something else to say.

"There is more. Ye wished to know it all. And when ye hear it, ye'll believe Old Maggie – I am cursed."

I waited.

"His name is Robert Murdoch. He is Douglas Murdoch's son."

Then indeed did I feel the chill of fear. Though I did not understand fully the intricate hatreds of religions, the wrongs dealt through the ages, the pendulum of punishment and anger, yet I knew well the warring between these people and the Murdochs.

Now, too, I feared for myself. For if Jock and Thomas and Red and the others later discovered that I had known, that I had shielded her, what then would happen to me?

Yet, how could I tell them? What might they do to Iona?

There was no choice: I must hold this knowledge to myself.

What if Douglas Murdoch learnt of it? Perhaps he did not hate her religion as much as her family hated his? After all, he had planned to take her, for what purpose I knew not. It might be better for her to be taken by them. Could she then live with them, perhaps marry this lad and be happy?

Sensing a glimmer of hope, I asked her. "If Douglas Murdoch knew of this, what would he do? Perhaps he would not be as angry as your father would."

She stared at me. "Douglas Murdoch would rather his son were dead than wi' me! Ye have seen my father and my uncles when his name is mentioned. 'Tis the same for them. And worse, because he is rich and to him we are nothing more than dirt. He would take me for his servant, no' his son's wife, and it would go ill wi' me. So they must no' hear of this. Ye must tell no one! Promise me!"

"I will tell no one," I promised, quietly. "But they killed your great-grandfather, the old shepherd, did they not? Can you forgive him for that?"

"Robert hates their violence," she retorted. "As do I hate my family's violence. He had nothing to do wi' the killing, and if he had, I wouldna forgive him. I loved my great-grandfather. He loved me, and he always tried to stop Old Maggie railing at me. Now he's gone and no one will take my side." She wiped the back of her hand across her eyes and took a deep breath.

"Now, tell me I am no' cursed!" she said, her eyes bright. She stared at me with defiance. I said something – mere words. Clumsy, muttered nothings. She just tightened her lips and looked away with a shrug.

Was she cursed? Perhaps so. And in truth, she believed herself cursed. Her family, too, seemed to think it.

A thought came to me. These people trusted so strongly in the curse, that they were merely waiting for something terrible to happen to Iona, the only girl left in the family. They did not wonder if it would happen, but just waited for when it would. But is the future set down already? If it is, then why do we concern ourselves with how to act or what is right?

If fate, or God, has already decided what will happen, then can anyone be blamed for anything?

This could not be the way of it. God judges us on what we do – the Bible had taught me so. But if the future is set down, we cannot choose what to do. And if we cannot choose anything that we do, how can God rightly judge us?

And if the future is not laid down, then a curse can have no power. If fate had not decreed that Iona would suffer a terrible fate, then she might *not* suffer a terrible fate.

Perhaps a curse only has power if we believe in it. If we fight against it, we may turn the future to a different outcome.

Perhaps that is what hope is for. I knew the story of Pandora. When disobedient, curious, interfering Pandora let all the evil into the world by mistake, only Hope was left.

And so I could hope. But I could act, too – act to protect Iona from danger. Because it seemed to me that Iona, by falling in love with a boy from a different religion, was the only one not poisoned and trapped by endless hatred.

This was something I could do to fight against all that Old Maggie stood for: hatred, anger and revenge. And in their place put something better.

Chapter Twenty-Nine

The rest of the day passed without further event. There was no chance for me to speak alone with Bess – always she was with Jeannie or Old Maggie, helping with chores. There was not quite a coldness between us. She smiled when she saw me. But she was busy and did not seem to need to speak with me. It was as though she was settled, in a way that I was not.

What did I wish to say? I cannot be sure. Not to tell Iona's secret, though it was indeed a heavy burden to bear. If I am honest, I know not what Bess's response would have been. She cared little for Iona, perhaps because the girl showed no love for Old Maggie. But Old Maggie showed no love for the girl, nothing but crazy words and fearsome curses – how should Iona have acted differently?

And Bess's admiration for the old woman was something I could not share. I pitied her suffering, but that was all.

I wished Bess did not admire her so. I wished more than ever that we could both go away. But that could not be, not now, for I could not leave Iona to her fate – though I knew not how I could help her. And Bess, it was clear, would not come away.

That night, too, was peaceful enough, with no intrusions, no alarms.

That following night, the Wednesday, however, another cargo was expected. By now I had picked up smatterings of conversation and understood something of what would happen. Calum would go to a place on the cliff and watch for a particular light over the water. This was the sign that the cargo had been offloaded from the cutter sailing from the Isle of Man, or Ireland, and onto a smaller boat. This boat would be manned by two seamen from the cutter, who were in Jock's pay, and would be rowed to our cave at high tide. When Calum saw the signal, he would run back to tell us and we would go down the tunnels as before, and collect the goods when the tide started to fall and the cave would be safe from ambush. Next day, the goods would be taken to nearby towns and sold by Hamish. The blind minister was a useful way to avert the attention of the authorities. No exciseman would dare search a coffin for smuggled goods, and he always had a coffin with him. And Hamish did such things as taking the money to the seamen and learning when the next ship might be passing.

During the Wednesday afternoon, I began to have a sense of the work these people must do if they were to eke a living simply from the farm. It was difficult land, in places soggy marsh, in others stony and fit only for gorse. Mouldy told me that the best and most fertile land was enclosed by Douglas Murdoch's walls, that his cows and sheep grazed the richest grass and his fields grew the sweetest clover and flax for linen. Murdoch even had his own linen mill, though he paid his workers little.

We had to drain a piece of marshy ground for planting. After paring the surface with a hand-plough, we had to divide it into runrigs – so that the water could run along the channels and some kind of crop be grown along the ridges. Quickly, my back became stiff and painful, but if I had thought we could rest when this was finished, I was wrong – we must now dig the last remaining winter turnips from the ground – soft, thin things they were, but better than nothing with all the fodder now gone.

So it was with aching limbs that I went to sleep that night, not heeding the noise of Old Maggie snoring, the rustling in the thatch, or the wind snarling at the shutters.

Chapter Thirty

As we had been warned, we were woken in the middle of the night. It was Billy who came banging on our door and led us over to the main cottage, lighting the way with a burning peat torch. Lamplight filled the dwelling and faces glowed. As before, Jeannie gave us food and drink. There was excitement in the air and I felt a sense of why these people did what they did. This was better than farming the waterlogged land around their home. Highway robbery is little different from smuggling, perhaps, and something thrilling rushes through the body when adventure beckons. My doubts slunk to the edges of my mind and I threw myself into the action.

No fear did I feel as we climbed down the rungs and then along the steeply sloping tunnel. It was high tide again and the waves shot fountains into the air as we leapt across the churning passageway. We climbed the few steps and then leapt across again.

This time, I did not slip and I had no need of helping hands to pull me onto the ledge. I felt Mouldy slap me on the back. Even Red split his face into a grin on my behalf.

Jock did not come with us this time. Jeannie and his sons had persuaded him not to. I think his head pained him again. Certainly, he pressed his hand frequently to his forehead and seemed not to wish to stand. There was no colour in his leathered face.

Soon, we were in the cave again, a little out of breath, sweating lightly. I looked at Bess and she grinned at me, her black eyes sparkling, cheeks pinked, lips a little apart. Her thick hair was tied behind her with a red kerchief, and shone in the dancing light of the peat torches.

Now it was time for her to squeeze through the narrow space at the bottom of the steps. No one spoke; there was no need. She dropped to the ground, pushed her hands through the hole and wriggled quickly out of sight. A few moments later, she called that she was through. We sent the ropes after her.

As before, we heard the noise of her opening the first box, the lid splintering. As before, we heard her voice as she called out what she had found: malt and bundles of lace this time. As before, we felt the tug when the first bags were filled, and we pulled the bags towards us.

Then, horribly, echoing through the caverns and crevices, caught up in the roaring and crashing of the waves, came a scream. And then another. Some scuffling, and another smaller scream.

Chapter Thirty-One

At first, I could not move. No words would come. We all stared at each other, eyes wide in the torchlight, the shadows casting our faces into the shapes of ghouls. What had happened? My mind fought to make sense of it.

I crouched on the ground and shouted through the opening. "Bess! What has happened? Bess!"

Then her voice, brittle with panic. "A snake! I've been bitten by a snake!"

"Tell her to take hold o' a rope and we will pull her back through the tunnel," said Thomas.

But Bess's voice came back, weaker now. "I can't see, Will. The torch fell. Help me! I can't see…"

"Bess! Listen! You must tie the rope to your wrist and we will pull you."

"Will! I am … I feel … dizzy. I can't…" And then there was a scuffling sound, a soft thud, and silence. I had not thought a snakebite to be so dangerous, so fast acting. Perhaps she had fallen into a faint from the fear.

I pulled my jacket off and dropped to my hands and knees. Already, my chest felt tight. Already, my breathing was faster. I must somehow squeeze through that narrow space. It could be done. Bess had not found it difficult – but I was somewhat broader. Could I do it?

There was no choice. Stretching my arms in front of me, I plunged into that dark space. At first, I could see nothing. Utter blackness pressed down on me. The rock felt cold against my hands as I pulled myself along, using my toes to push. My face was inches from the tunnel floor and only inches more separated the back of my head from the rock face above me.

Panic rushed through me and I struggled for breath. At that moment, some dust or grit entered my mouth and I coughed. There was no room to draw enough air and, as I choked, I felt the rock close in round me, darker, colder, harder, heavier. I needed to push myself upwards, to give my chest room to move, but I could not do so, for above me was rock.

The thick rope underneath my body lay still and useless, pressing on my ribs. I pulled myself forwards with my hands and pushed with my feet, scraping desperately on the floor of the tunnel. I must move faster. Still there was darkness in front of me, dust in my throat, no room for my shoulders to move.

Now the passage narrowed further, sloping downwards. Surely my shoulders could not go through this space? My feet could get no purchase now on the grit and dust. I felt around frantically with my fingers, looking for something to grasp, in front of me, or to the sides, or above. Yes! A rocky overhang. I gripped it hard and tried to pull. With my arms outstretched and my shoulders squeezed together, I thought now that I could not move, or even scream.

I was stuck. My eyes were wide open, but only speckled blackness spun round me. For some moments I felt that I was spinning too. No longer could I feel the hard walls, the rocks pressing against my body; no longer could I smell the dust, taste the grit between my teeth. My body softened. The black became red, rushing across my eyes. Fear was still there, but it seemed somehow to matter less. I think if this is how we die then death is not so fearsome after all. I felt my mind spin, closed my eyes and let myself slowly drift. No longer did I need any air.

"Will!" From far away, I heard my name called. "Will! Please!" It was Bess, her voice weak. And now terror rushed back and with one last effort, I pulled, squeezing myself past the narrowing until the tunnel opened out – a little, but it was enough. I could breathe again. Now my heart beat fast, as I sensed how close I had come to death, how nearly I had given in to it.

Forgetting that there would be a drop at the end of the tunnel, I fell headfirst for a few feet, my hands landing painfully on the rough rock floor. I gasped the air, fresh air straight from the sea.

The darkness here was not so deep. No moonlight shone directly into the cave but I could make out the mouth of it, see the ebony waves glinting under the waxing moon. A groan to my right told me where Bess was, but before I moved to her I heard Thomas shout to me, "Pull the rope." This I did, and almost immediately a burning torch spiralled towards me along the tunnel. I caught it and looked around.

Bess was crouched against the wall, surrounded by scattered packages. The snake was nowhere to be seen.

"It's in the box," she muttered. Her voice sounded thread-thin, ready to snap, her breathing fast and shallow. I fought to control my fears – the bite from a snake in this country would not usually kill, I thought, but I was not sure.

She looked up at me as I crouched beside her. "It's my hand," she whispered, holding her left wrist in her right. I raised it and held the torch near by. Two tiny puncture marks sat on the fleshy part under her thumb. "I can't see properly, Will," she said. "I'm going blind!"

I pulled her hand to my mouth and clamped my lips over the puncture wounds, sucking as hard as I could, then spitting, spitting, spitting over and over again onto the floor. I knew not what else to do. I could see that her hand was swollen, her wrist too. Then a sudden memory came to me of one of my father's stablemen doing something when a hound was bitten by a snake. I needed a knife.

Peering around with the torch, I found the blade she had been using to break open the box. Holding my breath and clenching my teeth, I quickly slashed her hand, just above the snake bite. She gasped and snatched her hand away. Blood pumped out. Placing the torch against the side of the box, I whipped the kerchief from my neck and tore it into two pieces. One I quickly bound round the highest part of her arm, allowing the blood to flow freely from her hand onto the ground. After a few moments, I made the other one into a pad and pressed it on the wound. "Hold tight to that, Bess," I urged.

A voice came thinly along the tunnel. "What's happening?"

"I'll tie her hands to the end of the rope. When I tell you, pull."

"The snake!" slurred Bess now. The snake. It must be killed, or we would not be able to come here again in safety. I peered into the box. Nothing. I held the torch closer. Something flickered in a corner. A shadow? Was it my imagination? I held the brand closer still.

It was the snake. Coiled in a corner, its tiny eyes staring, its tongue flickering. I had never been so close to such a creature. I knew not what sort it was – its black zigzag markings meant nothing to me. All I know is that it looked evil.

Without thinking on it further, I thrust the torch with lightning speed into the dark corner. Almost as fast, the snake moved, but not fast enough. It seemed to me that it screamed, but I do not think this possible. With a sizzle and a brief horrible writhing, it was dead. I clamped my mouth shut, or I think I would have vomited.

It was as I was about to turn away that I saw a piece of paper in the box. At first, I thought it must have been part of some wrapping, but it was not like any of the material on the goods that lay scattered about.

"Hurry," whispered Bess. "Please."

I picked up the paper and was about to put it in my pocket. For she was right – we must hurry. I didn't know how the snakebite would affect her but

I knew we must leave this place as quickly as possible. But as I took the paper, my eyes caught the words scrawled on it. In the light of the fading torch I read them.

I burned them then, holding the corner of the paper until every word had vanished into charcoal nothing. No one would ever read those words.

Chapter Thirty-Two

Now I forced my mind to other matters. Though my heart raced with a terrible panic, I leant the torch against the wall and turned to Bess, grasping her beneath the arms.

She was too weak to stand. Half carrying her, I dragged her to the opening. I grabbed the rope that dangled there and tied her wrists tightly to it, telling her to continue pressing the pad on her cut. I then hoisted her body up onto the ledge and held her while the men pulled the rope, firmly. I winced for her pain as she was hauled over the stony surface.

As I prepared to return through the tunnel myself, I tried to quell my horror of the narrow space, the pressing rocks. I had done it once so I knew it could be done.

But it was not to be. Not yet. For another shout came, followed instantly by a rope and then another, each with a bag tied to it.

"Load the cargo, lad!" called Thomas.

"But she needs attention! And fast!" I shouted in return.

"Then ye'd better load the cargo fast, had ye no'?"

Angrily, I stuffed the packages into the bags and shouted that they were ready. They disappeared rapidly and I heard the rattling of stones as they tumbled along the passage. For some moments, I was alone. The torch burned more dimly now but a soft moonlight shone from the sea and it was enough. The waves breathed, in and out, in and out, sighing. Every now and then, a larger wave gasped, and then spat against the opening to the cave. The surface of the sea was several feet below the bottom of the cave entrance – no boat could reach it now.

Behind me I heard the ropes being thrown back again, and again I filled the bags with cargo, forcing as much as I could into each.

We must hurry! They did not care enough for Bess. They did not care as I did what happened to her. They needed us, but not so much that they would sacrifice anything to save our lives. Did Bess understand this too? That they were not her kin, no part of her life and story. Their hatreds and their loves were not hers or mine.

I fumed, muttering under my breath. "Hurry! For God's sake, hurry! Why do they not hurry?"

At last, I had loaded the last package into a bag and all the bags had disappeared. Now, I hoisted myself into the opening and, taking a deep breath, I placed my arms in front of me once more and began to squeeze along the tunnel. The rock hung above me. How heavy it must be! What if it fell? What if even a part of it fell? I would be crushed and soon I would be nothing but a skeleton. How quickly would I die? I tried to reason with myself – this tunnel must have been here for longer than man's memory, many hundreds of years. Yet, caves and tunnels sometimes fall. It must have happened before that a person was inside a cave when it collapsed.

My struggle made me breathe faster. But there was no room! My chest was being crushed under the weight of my own body. I wished to pull my arms under me, to push my body up a little, to find space to draw air. But I could not.

I heard their voices urging me on. Not Bess's – no sound did I hear from her. Then, without warning, my fingers touched a rope. I grasped it and felt my arms being tugged forward, my body following. I screwed my face against the pain as I was dragged over the sharp rock face. And now I could feel warm air on my face. I was through!

As I tumbled into their rough hands, I barely heard their words of praise. Such words meant

211

nothing, for I believe they cared more for their cargo than for Bess's safety. Wiping some smears of blood from my hands and brushing grit from where it had sunk into my body, I looked at Bess, where she slumped against a wall, blood staining her clothes. Calum watched her with some fear, I think. But only Red acted: he hoisted her upwards and over his shoulder. I opened my mouth to say that I would carry her, that he should not, but he was stronger than I.

And he was now urging the others to follow. So I believe he did not think ill of her. There was no greedy look in his eyes and it came to me then that he had not looked at her in that unpleasant way since the second evening. I was glad to see him carry her now, as he was strong as a carthorse. Picking up a bag, I followed close behind and we both urged the others on.

Indeed, I was glad of his strength when we came to the place where we must twice cross the roaring waves. There was less to fear now, with the tide much lower, but still I could hear the echoing crashes of the waves further down the tunnel, and every now and then spray spat into the air beside us. There was not even time for me to wonder how he would cross with Bess on his shoulder: he simply ran and leapt over, landing with his legs bent, as if on steel springs. We followed, throwing our burdens across for Billy to catch on the other side.

In this way, we came quickly to the rungs set in the vertical wall and soon we were hauling ourselves into the main cottage once more.

Chapter Thirty-Three

It was Old Maggie's face I saw first, twisted and mad-eyed. She knitted, her twig-like fingers flying fast. And she rocked in her high-backed chair, gazing at us, yet not seeming to see us. She did not stop when she saw Red carry Bess out, and, though Jeannie rushed to our aid, to Old Maggie we might as well not have been there.

Where had her mind gone that she cared nothing for the present? Did she not care for Bess either? I turned from the old woman and told Jeannie, Jock and Iona what had passed.

"Aye, a snake could find its way to the cave," nodded Jock. "There are many crannies through which such a creature could slip."

I kept my silence. I had no wish to fan any flames of anger with my knowledge. Only I knew that the snake had not come to be there by chance. It had not slithered through some cranny.

But I did not wish to say so.

It mattered not, for now Bess spoke out. At first we did not hear her words, weak as her voice was. "Hush," said Jeannie, as she settled her down on the bed. But Bess would not be silenced.

"It came not by chance." She spoke through clenched teeth, her breathing tight and irregular.

All now looked at her. Iona was heating water on the fire but even she turned quickly to look at her.

"How so?" demanded Jock. "Ye must have reason to think so."

"The lass could be right," growled Red. "And we ken who did it, do we no'? They canna get away wi' this." He fingered the knife in his belt as though he would go after Douglas Murdoch now.

"Hold," said Thomas. "We canna say for sure. She could be wrong. Why d'ye say the snake was put there, lass?"

But Bess was overcome by a bout of retching and shivering. "I'm so cold," she said, when it was over. Every part of her shook, her muscles in spasm, her fingers like claws above the blood-soaked cloth.

"Leave the lass be," urged Jeannie. "She must be kept quiet. And I must clean her hand." She looked to me. "D'ye ken how to cure snakebite?" I shook my head and she must have sensed my fear. "Dinna fret, lad: a snake in these parts will no' kill a healthy lass.

215

It will soon pass. But we must clean the cut, or it may turn bad."

But Thomas now spoke to me, as I was turning to go to Bess. "Why would she say this? Where was the serpent? Did ye see it?"

I shook my head, shrugged my shoulders.

Bess's voice came again.

"In the box." The words were clear, horribly so.

"The villains!" snarled Red. "The scabbit bastards!"

"Is this true, lad?"

"I didn't see. Not until afterwards. I think perhaps it hid there after it had bitten."

I saw Bess look at me, but she was racked once more by painful retching and shivering.

"Leave us now!" snapped Jeannie. She called for Iona to bring the hot water and began to untie the kerchief from the wound and from Bess's upper arm. Wishing not to meet Bess's eye, I said I would go and set the fire in our own cottage, to warm the place for her.

It pained me to keep a secret from her. But I must tell no one about the words I had read on that paper. If they suspected that Douglas Murdoch might have had something to do with it, that was one thing. But the words on the paper would fan the heat of their hatred and terrible bloodshed would surely follow.

If I could safely have told Bess, I would have. But I feared that she was too near to Old Maggie's spirit, that she shared too closely her passion for the power of ancient wrongs. Wrongs which should be forgotten now, wiped clean by enough blood to make the seas scarlet.

These were thoughts I must bear on my own. And so I did, raking out the cold ashes from the fire in our cottage, setting a pile of straw and small sticks, as I had seen Iona do, as I had seen Bess do in her own cottage.

As the fire began to catch, lit from a spark from my flint, and the flames to lick the sticks, spitting as they flickered, I opened the door to make a draught pass up the chimney. Dawn was breaking, suffusing the sky with bloody orange, and an owl called eerily from a nearby wood.

Another day had come. I had not felt so alone since the day I had left my own home.

Chapter Thirty-Four

Jeannie's words had stopped me fearing for Bess's life. And in truth there was no need to fear, though she suffered badly for many hours that day. I did not like to see her like this, shivering with agues that twisted her face into a rictus. Her legs shook and she called for blankets. Jeannie and Iona warmed stones on the fire and placed them near her feet. They fed her sips of some herbal potage – I know not what it was. I wished to help, but there was no place for me, no task for me to do, other than fetch firewood.

I needed to ride, to leave the smoke and heat and Bess's suffering, and so later that day I set out on Blackfoot. The weather had turned dull, the sky mottled with cold clouds, and a chill wind blew against my face, but I minded little. I breathed deeply as I rode out of the yard in the late afternoon.

Shortly after, I heard hoofbeats behind me and I turned quickly. My heart sank when I recognized the narrow frame of Calum, his pony cantering towards me. He must have seen me ride out and had followed me. What did he want? I had wished to be alone, to explore the area without a guide.

He pulled his pony to a halt as he reached me, and it stood champing against its tight reins. I think he was a little older than I, but I was taller, and mounted on a well-bred horse. "Calum," I simply said, looking down at him, keeping my face friendly but leaving it to him to speak.

"I was minded to ride wi' ye," he said, tossing his hair from his eyes. Green they were, somewhat like Iona's though not so deep. His wide mouth did not smile. I know not if he meant to be friendly or if he meant to watch me for some other reason. Nothing could be read on his face. "I can show the way to the beach. If ye mean to bide here, ye should know your way around. One dark night, ye might need to know well."

He kicked his pony to a canter and then a gallop and I followed at equal speed, the wind sweeping my hair back and stinging my eyes. But I am always happy to ride at speed, and any doubts I might have had were blown away on the salty wind.

We rode across uneven ground. Yet, where he led, it was firm underfoot and my horse leapt keenly over the bristles of coarse grasses and patches of dead bracken. Tiny rivulets did not slow us and my heart raced as we galloped, faster and faster in the direction of the steely sea.

As we came closer to the cliff, I could see the distant water. We were high above any beach and there must have been a sheer cliff dropping down not far ahead. Yet I did not slow, or even think of it – I galloped alongside Calum, trusting him entirely. I knew not a reason to trust him more than any other man, but something told me that he meant me no harm. He was a good horseman and as such would care for all horses – he would not cause danger to mine or his. And so I let go any fear and simply laughed in the wind.

Suddenly, Calum wheeled sharply to the right, and I followed him, with Blackfoot barely slowing as we veered. Now we rode close along the edge of the cliff and I did not look down. I could sense the drop to my left and did not wish to see it. Soon, the path sloped a little downwards, and now more steeply, and as it did, we slowed somewhat. There was now no turning back – we were cantering down a narrow path set into the side of the cliff. It was wide enough for one mount, but allowed no room for a misplaced hoof, no hope if the horse were to shy and swerve at some unexpected sound. If I were on my own, I would have slowed to a walk, but I followed at Calum's speed.

I did not look far ahead, but kept my eyes on the tail of his pony, my eyes narrow as the stones and grit flew up in my face from its flying hoofs.

Now our path took us through a narrow space, sliced between the cliff face on our right and a tall pinnacle of rock on our left. For a few moments, the world around us seemed dark, the light blocked by the sheer walls. With a squawk, a large bird flew from a ledge and flapped across my face. Blackfoot's head reared back and my leg scraped painfully on the rock to my left. With difficulty, I reassured him, grateful that at this moment we were not riding alongside the drop to the beach.

Now the path opened out again. We were nearly down at the level of the beach. In a few more moments, we were on the sand and we galloped together towards the water. At the foamy edge, we pulled our mounts to a halt and turned to each other, grinning, exhilarated. He was as good a rider as I and I felt some new warmth towards him for that. I knew he had been testing my courage and that I had passed his test.

And now, breathing heavily, we turned and looked back at the orange cliffs and at the beach. The beach was small, no more than a hundred yards wide at its widest point, and perhaps fifty yards from the edge of the water to the rock face. The sand was dark, wet across every part of the beach. I knew it had not been raining, so the wet sand must be from the tide.

This beach would disappear entirely at high tide, I realized. And as far as I could see, as I looked all around the cliff which enclosed the beach like arms, there was only one path, one way off the beach: the path down which we had come.

"D'ye see the cave?" Calum was pointing over to our left, past the beginning of the beach. Here the cliff fell directly to the waves, which lapped softly at the sheer rock face. It was not easy to see at first, for I had to crane my neck awkwardly: but then I saw the opening, more than the height of a man above the level of the water. From a boat, it would have been easier to see. From the beach it was difficult.

"That's the cave where the goods are landed. When we run a cargo." So, that was why a cargo could only be landed at high tide. At low tide, as we were now, a boat could not reach the cave. "When the seamen in our pay have goods from one o' the trading ships, they bring the cargo in a boat to the cave and leave it there at high tide. When we see the signal, we collect it."

I turned to him. "Does anyone else know about this cave?"

"'Tis no secret around here. 'Tis our territory.

Folks respect it. Others use other beaches, other caves."

"What about Douglas Murdoch and his men? Do they know of it?"

"Aye. But our cave leads only to the passage beneath our farm. They would gain nothing from it. They wouldna tell the excisemen, for then our smuggling would end and they would lose their cut."

I was silent. For it came to me that Murdoch's men could enter the cave at high tide, after they saw a cargo being left. They could have done so, and left the snake in the box, disappearing quickly without anyone knowing or seeing. I already knew that our men only fetched the goods from the cave when the tide had fallen a little – so that they could be sure that no one was in the cave. It had seemed a sensible precaution, since Tam would be at great risk otherwise.

Now Calum was pointing to the right, at the other end of the small beach, by the cliff. At first I could not see what he indicated, only the shadows of crevices and protruding rocks. He kicked his pony and, as I trotted after him, I saw another cave, at the level of the ground. The sand was lower here, the lowest point of the beach, and rock pools sat, murky and still, seaweed swaying, sea anemones pulsing. This cave would be quickly covered by a rising tide.

As we approached the opening, Blackfoot jibbed

at the bit, though the cave mouth was easily large enough for us to ride through. He tossed his head, dancing in fear, and tried to turn away. I urged him on. It was only a cave and he should trust me. But, try as I might, I could not settle him. I could have forced him to enter but I did not wish to.

Calum's pony was little keener and we both dismounted, fastening the reins to the saddles and letting the animals go free. They trotted a short distance away along the beach and then stood and watched us.

The cave was small, perhaps ten paces to the back of it. Weeping water ran in rivulets down the jagged walls, collecting in pools on the sand. Lichen and seaweed lay in splashes on the rocks and the whole place was cold and miserable, sunless. I shivered.

Calum was walking towards the back of the cave and I followed him. I saw the passageway before he pointed it out to me. A black hole in the back of the cave, as tall as I and only a little broader.

"Does it lead anywhere?" I asked, thinking that he must have a reason for showing me this cave.

"Ye remember when we leapt o'er the hole in the tunnel floor?"

And then I realized. "At high tide, the waves come through here and push their way to that place?"

He nodded. "The tide rushes through this cave – there's nowhere else for the water to go so it's forced through this tunnel. Even afore high tide, the water fills the tunnel. Ye wouldna wish to be caught in this place wi' the tide rushing in."

Indeed I would not. I had seen the force of the waves, the fierce fountains of water spouting up the passageway.

But my eye had been caught by something else. Quite close by the entrance to the tunnel, set into the stone, was a huge iron ring.

I suppose it was for mooring a boat. Man-made, it looked out of place here and I reached out to touch it. I caught Calum looking at me.

"They would have tied ye to that, ye and Bess. And as the tide rose, ye would have drowned. And when the tide had fallen once again, they would have cut ye free and left ye to the fishes and crabs. And no one else would have known."

"I think you would not have minded much."

"I thought as they did. At first, I thought ye were Douglas Murdoch's men. I thought ye had killed Old John and harmed wee Tam. I would have killed ye myself."

"And then what? Where would it end? Bloodshed never ends."

"I know not." He looked troubled, confused. "I dinna think o' such matters. And my grandfather and my father and my uncles, they decide what we should do."

"And you do everything they say?"

"O' course! How should I no'? I must obey my father."

"They are strong men, that's true," I said, carefully, thinking perhaps to goad him. But he said nothing. Perhaps he had no ambition in him, no frustration, no need to break away. "Do you not wish to have a different life, to leave your home and ... do something different?"

"And what's wrong wi' what we do?" he retorted, turning his face away, biting his lip. "Ye know nothing o' it. 'Tis the way we live, no better and no worse than yours."

I opened my mouth to speak, but I held my tongue. Besides, what did I care what Calum did, what choices he made? One thing I wished to know. Whether he would help Iona if he knew what I knew? If he knew that she was in love with a boy from a different church.

Yet I could not take the risk of asking. Not directly.

We turned and walked from the cave, towards the sea and the horses.

"What think you of the curse?" I asked. "Old Maggie's curse?" It was easier to talk while walking. We need not look at each other.

"I fear for Iona," Calum answered. "She shouldna

226

know her future. 'Tis a heavy burden."

We mounted the horses, and kicked them towards the path once again. I did not look back at the sea – I did not like to think on its hungry power, its greed, its cold depths. Seeing that iron ring had made me think not only of what might have waited for us, but of what had been done to Old Maggie's mother. And I preferred not to think of that.

"So you believe she is cursed?"

"Aye. Why else does everything bad befall the female line?"

"Perchance she will break the curse. Or one day the curse will end."

"Aye, mebbe." He had not seemed to think of that. Or, I think, to believe it.

"And what of Old Maggie? Her hatred of the people who killed her mother is powerful. She curses them and all their descendants. But their descendants are not guilty."

Calum pulled his pony to a halt, roughly. We were some way up the path by now, the cliff dropping away steeply to our right. A stone, dislodged by the pony's feet, rolled over the edge and I was aware of it tumbling, faster and faster to the beach below. A light rain had begun to fall, the wind scattering it to a fine sheeting spray across my face. Blackfoot's mane was whipped sideways. His ears went back.

Calum's face was harsh. "D'ye know what they called those times? The Killing Times. Because they killed so many – men, women, children. For our faith, our true faith, our love o' God. I hate them, their descendants too. They are o' the same blood. Old Maggie is right. Though she seems mad, she is right about that. There is a truth in her, perhaps from God. A holy fool, I once heard my uncle Hamish call her. If one o' their folk crossed my door, I would kill him. And there's many o' our people feel this too. 'Tis right."

I turned away. I could not meet the violence in his eyes. He was no different from the others. The madness of Old Maggie had seeped into him as well.

What good would such hatred bring them?

But worse, what protection would Iona find in her own family if they knew what she was doing? She had no one to protect her, other than me. Yet what good could I do? If Calum was the same as the older men, as steeped in hatred, then how would they ever change?

I wished again that Bess would come away with me and we could leave these people to their warring. It was not for us to be part of it. And yet we *were* part of it now. I was tied to Bess. She seemed drawn to Old Maggie. And Iona had need of me.

In truth, I was trapped.

Chapter Thirty-Five

We came back to the yard in silence, unsaddled quickly, rubbed our mounts dry, fed and watered them. But Calum spoke then, not looking at me. He hung the saddle up on its peg.

"Is Bess...? Are ye...? Is she yours?" He flicked his hair back from his face.

I looked at him, narrowing my eyes. "Bess is no one's."

He turned to face me. "Ye know what I mean." His cheeks had grown red. I knew not what to say, or think. Yes, I did indeed know what he meant. But how to answer?

Bess was mine, but not in the way he meant. She was my friend, my companion, but there was nothing else. And yet, what did I now feel? Was there indeed nothing else? I cared for her more than for anyone. And no one alive cared for her as I did.

If I had thought at all, I had hoped that we could

carry on as before; that one day soon, Bess would tire of this place and we would move on together. But wed her! I could not imagine it. I could not imagine her wed at all. Not to me; not to anyone.

Not to Calum. I could not imagine her staying here for ever, making her home with these people, bearing children, growing old in this place. Calum did not have her need for freedom. He believed too much what he was told. He was not suited to her. But I would not say so. He would find out for himself that Bess would not have him.

"No, she is not mine."

And his smile cast a cloud over me that did not lift for the rest of that day. I watched him walk away with a spring in his step, whistling.

As I went through the door to Old Maggie's cottage, several faces looked up. Jeannie cast me a welcoming look and then turned back to her task of helping Bess take some sort of broth. Old Maggie stared at me with a gaze of utter emptiness. She sat knitting – her fingers flying as her needles clicked together. Iona leapt up from where she sat mending a garment, and went to pour something into a tankard. She passed it to me, her worried green eyes searching my face.

I suppose she wished to know if her secret was still safe, if I was on her side. I smiled at her and her face softened as she held out the tankard.

But it was Bess I wished to see. She looked exhausted, with dark shadows under her eyes. Her hair was tied back, strands plastered across her forehead with sweat. But she was sitting up and seemed not to be in pain. I went to her and took her hands. Cold they were, cold and dry and without strength. A fresh cloth bound her palm where I had cut it, and there was no sign of redness around the bandage.

"I am glad to see you better." I would have said more than that, but only without the others there. What I would have said, I do not know, but there was much to speak of, between the two of us.

She nodded. "I was afraid. Very afraid. I have had nightmares before and none was as bad as this. All the while I was thinking I was in a dream but then the pains would come and I would know it was no dream." Her face twisted suddenly and she stopped, breathing slowly, deeply. "I am sorry – the pain is nearly gone. You saved me, Will." I turned away, wishing not to see her weak like this, the tears in her eyes.

It brought to my mind how, when we first came here, she had seemed weighed down by a burden in her mind. But then she had regained her spirit – though I had to admit that it had seemed to be Old

Maggie who had rekindled it. Now, it was dampened once more.

A movement at my back made me turn round. Old Maggie was standing over me, looking down on Bess. She reached out her hand and touched Bess's hair, stroking her forehead, muttering something that I could not decipher, if it meant anything at all. I liked not her closeness; there was a smell about her, sweet and yet unpleasant.

But Bess seemed comforted. Suddenly Old Maggie spoke, clearly now. "God has watched o'er ye, lassie. Ye're a guid lassie an' God has cared for ye." Bess closed her eyes, peacefully, seeming within moments to drift into a soft sleep. I turned away and looked to where Iona sat. Our eyes met, only briefly, but a world of thoughts crossed between us and we understood much of them.

Outside, I stood at the entrance to the yard. Dusk was falling and in the open doorways of the dwellings moths flapped around the spilling light. The rain had stopped and there was now a smell of wet earth and air. Smoke poured from the chimneys. The dark figure of Mouldy wandered around the perimeter of the yard, a wooden club in his hand and the two dogs running here and there, sniffing. The horses harrumphed softly in their shelter and through the doorway I could see the gently swinging tails of the cows. From the chickens, in their hut closed firmly against night-time foxes, came silence.

And now Iona was walking towards me, her shawl wrapped round her, her bare feet thrust into wooden clogs. It was cold and the recent shower had made the ground sodden and filthy.

Her thick red hair tumbled around her face and shoulders and as she looked up at me I wondered at the danger she was in. It was not right that it should be so. What had she done wrong? She had been foolish, but she had done only what many had before her: loved the wrong person. The wars between religions were not of her making; nor did she care for them. It seemed to me that her one foolish love was worth more than a thousand hatreds.

But if she had known what I knew, would she have been brave enough then? If she too had read the words upon that paper, the paper that I had so hurriedly burned, would she continue in her dangerous love?

Yet, if I told her, might that not indeed help her? Might it not make her think again and choose life over death? Might it not make her give up her love?

Or was there already no choice and was she marked by fate? Cursed, even, as Old Maggie claimed.

But I decided that there was only one thing I could

do. It was better to act, to try, than to stand silent and let a tragedy unfold.

I would tell her what the words on the paper had said. Although it would frighten her, perhaps it might make her take greater care.

As I opened my mouth to speak, that was indeed my intention. But it was not to be.

Chapter Thirty-Six

"I must speak with you," I said, hurriedly now that I had made up my mind.

"Shh!" she said, looking around. Mouldy was walking near us now. Beyond him in the sky two bats swooped fast, diving and swirling in the gathering dusk. He raised his hand in greeting. He thought, I suppose, that we had some assignation. I minded little what he thought. I wished only that he would pass by and I could speak with her.

Soon he was too far away to hear what we might say and I opened my mouth to begin. But Iona spoke first. "I must tell you," she said, her voice spring-tight with excitement. Her next words tumbled, unstoppable. "I plan to run away, wi' Robert. 'Tis our only hope! I will tell him and I know he will come wi' me. When ye find me gone, say nothing, I beg o' ye. Never tell them that ye knew."

Out of my confusion came one clear thought: she

was right. It was the only way. Yet what a terrifying way for her, to leave everything she knew, everything she had ever known.

She would lose her family and all those who loved her. She would lose everything, for love. And she only thirteen years old. Could she give all that up? But I had done so. I had cut myself off from my family, perhaps for ever.

I looked at her eyes. Like a fairy's they were, and deep, full of life and hope. I saw her beauty then, as she sparkled at the thought of her future, the excitement of it.

All I could do was take her by the hands. I know not whether anyone saw, and it would not have mattered if someone had. How small they were, the fingers so thin and yet warm. "I wish you good fortune," I said quietly. "You are brave indeed."

Now I would not tell her about the words on that paper. There would be no gain in that, not for her and not for me. I would keep them to myself. And I would pray for her. I had prayed little in recent days – my childhood of Bible instruction, church on Sundays, religious lessons at school, my parents' dutiful faith, all seemed far away now. But I hoped indeed that God would look kindly on her.

She had great need of His protection. And of mine, if I could help her.

Chapter Thirty-Seven

She did not leave that night. Nor the next. Nor even the next.

During this time, our lives fell into some kind of pattern. The chores were hard and never-ending, simply to survive and put food on the table, to keep the buildings in repair, to fetch sufficient firewood, to find food for the animals. The winter fodder, stored from the previous year, was all but gone, and what there was had turned dank and dusty. New grass was only just beginning to appear. Sometimes a person would come to buy cheese, of which we had plenty – a hard cheese matured over months from last summer's milk. But we had no milk to spare now for passers-by, with the cow producing less each day, as its calf grew older and the maternal milk dried up.

The sheep's wool, which Old Maggie had spun, was sold or used for knitting stockings for the family. Or for darning patches. And with the weather warming now, Jeannie looked through the few clothes they had, deciding which must be mended, which washed, and which Calum, Iona and Tam had outgrown. The womenfolk were expert in unpicking garments and turning them into something else. Every moment of each day was occupied in the business of living.

Sometimes men would come who were strangers to me, and a huddled meeting would take place with Jock and the others. I supposed that these conversations concerned their smuggling activities or the suchlike.

I do know that money was paid to Douglas Murdoch from the last cargo – after much arguing between Thomas and Red. Thomas feared for Iona above all else and wished to pay, at least for now. But Red believed that paying money would not guarantee her safety – he was all for settling it once and for all, with weapons. Jock, clinging to his strength grimly, sided with Thomas, and while Jock was alive, I thought their view would hold sway. And yet, all of them were of a violent mind and would have killed Douglas Murdoch there and then if there had been an easy way. All believed God to be on their side in this, though it seemed to me that Red had less concern for that and more for his love of action.

For the first day after my conversation on the

beach with Calum, and into the next, nothing was heard from Douglas Murdoch. I began to think he was but a figment of imagination. I had never seen this man. Could he be as grim and cruel as they said? Perhaps everything was merely an empty threat. Perhaps, after all, Old John had been killed by reivers. We had no proof of anything more. We had not found the sheep near the tower where the Murdochs lived. None of their enclosures, with their hated stone walls, held our sheep, for Billy had looked. But the men said that meant nothing – that he would have sold them far away. And Tam could tell us nothing – he had not seen the men closely, and it had been dark. Besides, they could have paid gipsies to do their dirty work for them.

Yes, their anger at Old John's murder did not subside, but they simply stored it as one more reason to hate Douglas Murdoch.

There was no talk of running another cargo during this time and of that I was glad. It would be some weeks before Tam could use his arm well enough to return to his duty in the tunnel, and I did not like to think of Bess facing that danger again.

There was little time to talk alone with her. Calum was at her side more than I would have wished. Once I found him showing her how to cut willow for making baskets. And once I saw him sitting close to her outside, as they rested from some chore or other, and found he was teaching her to imitate the sound of a curlew. Her face was alight with laughter at this, as she cupped her hands round her mouth and tried to make the watery sound.

But I kept a pretence that I did not mind. How much did I mind? I know not. If she and I could have ridden out together, with no one else, I believe I could have made her think once more of our life of freedom on the roads and to wish for that again; perhaps I could have persuaded her to leave with me. But there was no chance and I must wait. Besides, I felt a strong duty to protect Iona. Until I knew she was far away and safe, I must stay here.

Jock spent much of one day lying on his bed, sleeping for the most part. When I heard him speak, his words seemed slurred. Many times, I saw Thomas or Red look to him, and I know not what went through their minds. No one spoke of it, or of what might be wrong with him. Once Jeannie came back with physic – from some kind of apothecary, I suppose – but no doctor came. On the next day, he seemed to improve, and wandered slowly around the yard, looking into the distance, seeming troubled.

Bess, on the other hand, had recovered quickly, cared for by Jeannie, and by Iona, who did all that she was told, silently, but without her usual unwilling expression. And Tam helped, too, wielding an axe with surprising strength, chopping wood into tiny pieces and stacking them neatly by our fire. He seemed to need only one arm and to have forgotten the other one still strapped to his body. He could move the fingers of it quite well now, but any pressure or use gave him great pain. It would heal in time, I told him. He smiled at me, like a trusting dog.

Old Maggie could often be found near Bess, sometimes taking her hand in her own shrivelled one, and nodding vaguely. I wished she would leave her alone, but Bess seemed not to mind at all.

Mad Jamie came several times to our farm, sometimes on foot, once on a small, scruffy pony. He was welcomed and given a drink or something to eat, but always he seemed uneasy, frightened, like some small animal that can never trust its own safety. Iona was always kind to him and sometimes I saw her lead him by the hand like a child. Once I saw her give him some freshly baked oat biscuits, wrapped in leaves. He slipped them into his pocket.

Old John was buried on the third day after Bess's injury, a Saturday. I do not know where his body had been resting since it had been removed on Hamish's cart, but everyone set off that grey morning, with a thin slicing April rain behind us. Jeannie, Iona, Old Maggie and Tam sat on the cart, huddled under an oiled cloth, the others following on ponies. Bess and I brought up the rear on our horses.

It was a grim and saddening scene and I will not dwell on it. Bess and I watched from a distance, a little below the hilltop churchyard. Their stooped figures, huddled stiffly together, and yet not quite touching each other, formed thin windswept silhouettes on the crest of the hill.

"Poor Maggie," said Bess softly. We watched them all come slowly down the hill towards us, the ponies' heads hanging low. Together we made our way back to the farm.

The old woman's face showed nothing as we went. Her scarred cheek was turned away from me. But the other side of her face seemed unblemished except by the wrinkling of the years. Her cheekbone was firm and high, her jaw straight. I wondered how she looked when she was younger, on this side of her face at least. I knew what the damaged side had looked like, for almost her whole life. The scar so deep and so raw.

Of course, I felt pity for her. Who would not have? But more than that I hated the way she kept a terrible past alive.

That night, I thought Iona would leave. She had seemed agitated all evening, unable to settle. Even Jeannie noticed, snapping at her more than once when she knocked something over.

Bess seemed irritated by the girl, but then Bess had never formed a bond with her, had seemed to look down on her silliness. And, of course, Bess would have taken Old Maggie's view: that the girl could only turn out bad or would have ill luck in some way. And I suppose she did not think Iona deserved more: a girl who tossed her pretty red hair as she did and had a petulant air about her. Iona had lost her mother – well, so had Bess, and Bess would have little sympathy for a girl who did nothing to make a dead mother proud. I knew enough of Bess to know this much.

And that night, when I was taking my turn at the watch, I did indeed see Iona leave the cottage, her shawl wrapped round her. I shrank into a darkened doorway. Her elfin frame stood in the yard and she looked up at the sky, but simply stayed there for some moments before going back into the cottage. I felt some relief. Though I knew she must go, yet I feared for her.

I continued my watch. A watery moon appeared from behind a cloud and I could see far into the distance now. But nothing stirred, only the soft whishing of rainfall and the distant crashing of the sea.

Soon, Billy came to take my place and I walked into our cottage. Bess stirred and I went to her.

"Shall I bring you water?"

"Mmm, yes, please," she mumbled. I fetched some from the jug that sat by the fire, and watched her hold the cup to her lips. Old Maggie muttered in her sleep and then resumed her snoring, close to Bess in the big box-bed.

"Thank you, Will," said Bess, now, before turning away and falling into sleep once more, one hand resting against the old woman's shoulder.

I went back to my blanket, where I lay, cold and uncomfortable, until eventually sleep came.

Chapter Thirty-Eight

The following day was the Sabbath. Much praying happened that day, more even than I was accustomed to during my childhood. I had thought they would dress differently for church, but their attire seemed little different from usual. I think their hair was neatened and their faces were certainly cleaned. Indeed, I had seen Jeannie scrubbing Tam's face with cold water straight from the well, and had heard Iona squealing as her long hair was tugged by a thick comb until it shone. She then wound it demurely into twists and hid it under a cap. The men, however, looked little different, and still carried their weapons when they rode off to church.

Thomas read from the huge soft-covered Bible before they set off for their church, or kirk, as they called it. They stood as he read, and when he said a prayer, they did not kneel, which I wondered at. I had been about to kneel, but it seemed to me that I had better do what they did. He did not read the prayer from a prayer book, but seemed to speak from his heart.

Calum stood dutifully by his father, his head bowed slightly.

Bess and I did not go with them to the kirk. It had been decided that it was better if we were not seen, so that no word of our existence would get back to Douglas Murdoch – he would not be at the kirk, being of the bishop-loving church that Jock's people so despised, but one of his informers might be. The only person who knew we were here was Mad Jamie, and he would not tell.

Mad Jamie, I was beginning to realize, was trusted beyond what one might expect of someone of such simple nature.

Jock had himself carried to the kirk by cart, driven by Hamish, who appeared scrubbed and glowing quite early that morning. I saw Red and Thomas watching the weakness of their father. But nothing was said. Jeannie bustled round, tucking a blanket around Jock's knees.

Calum was sitting on his pony near me and Bess as he waited for the others to be ready.

"Calum told me that when Old Maggie was a child, they could not worship in a kirk. They met in secret in the hills, and if they were discovered at their worship they would be killed. And soldiers would search the hillsides for them, all day if need be, while they hid. Can you imagine?" said Bess as we watched the others.

I shook my head. I hated the idea as much as she did. But it was long in the past. Now they could worship as they chose, so why did they feel the need still to remember with such rawness?

She turned to Calum. "What was it you called them? The services they held in secret?"

"Conventicles."

"And that was when the curlews betrayed the people?"

He nodded. But he looked at me a little and I fancy he remembered our earlier conversation and my questioning of this tradition. He said nothing. Could it be that Calum might begin to think differently from his father, his uncles, and his grandfather? Could it be that although he followed them blindly – or fearfully – now, he might not do so for ever? I had thought Calum acted towards his father more out of fear than respect, and this was something I could well understand. But I also knew that with strength one can overcome such weakness.

We watched them disappear slowly into the distance. A strange silence settled over the yard. I felt my spirits rise and I breathed deeply in the spring sunshine.

Bess and I must take turns to keep watch. If anyone passed near by, we must not be seen.

In the two or three hours before the churchgoers returned, I saw to the horses, and cleaned out the chicken shed. These were tasks that I enjoyed. My body was thinner than it had been when I left home some weeks ago, but stronger, and toughened by weather and hard work. My hands were no longer a gentleman's hands, the nails engrained now with dirt.

For the rest of the day, when the others had returned, we quietly went about the things that needed to be done. The Sabbath might have been the Lord's day of rest, but there was no rest for these people and many tasks had still to be completed.

My happiest memory of that day is the smell of the shellfish catch that Mouldy brought from the sea, lugging the pots on his pony's back. The crabs and lobsters were still alive, until he skewered them through the head, in a soft place he showed me, and then they died instantly, though their claws twitched for a while. And soon after, we were ripping the steaming pink meat from inside them, and sucking cooked mussels from their shells, tossing them down our throats with a liquor of water and herbs. There is no better smell than the aroma of roasting crab or lobster that an hour before was swimming free. It has the taste of the sea, salty and sweet at the same time, fresh and strong.

My spirits lifted as we ate, so that I almost thought I could stay here for ever.

Almost.

Chapter Thirty-Nine

Morning dawned clear, a soft orange stroking the eastern sky. Over the sea to the south, a milky haze blurred the farthest shore, making it seem further away. The coast of England across the Solway Firth. My country. Suddenly, powerfully, I wished to be there.

The day had a delicate warmth to it, increasing as the sun drifted higher. I do not know what date it was precisely, only that it was sometime in April. The air and the grasses and the branches of all the trees hummed with new life. Seed of rye and wheat grass, stored and dried over winter, must now be sown on the runrigs, and, as I went about this task, with Mouldy occasionally checking on my progress, I savoured the heat on my back and felt my spirits lift. Later, Mouldy was going to show me where to leave lobster pots, and how to tie a wriggling worm onto a hook to catch a young trout or two from the river.

He was a gruff and humourless man, but a good one. There seemed to be nothing he did not know about the land, and little he cared about the arguments between his nephews. Like Jeannie, he simply did what must be done, I believe, and had little time to think on why.

Iona, her hair freshly brushed and tied with a green ribbon, went with Jeannie and Billy to the town, to sell some eggs and buy some items. I know not what. Women's work this was, and Billy's job was to see them home safe.

This, I regret to say, he failed to do. Though, knowing what I did, I could not blame him. Red blamed him, however, and I think he would have killed Billy if Mouldy had not stopped him.

What had happened was this: some two or three hours after Jeannie, Billy and Iona had left, when Thomas was starting to look worried and I was beginning to feel the same, though for a different reason, the cart returned, hurtling dangerously along the track from the road. Alerted by agitated shouts from Mouldy, we all rushed to the yard entrance and peered towards it as it came.

Iona was not on the cart.

Jeannie's eyes were red and exhausted, her forehead creased with fear. She crumpled when she saw her sons and Thomas helped her down from the cart, putting his arm round her shoulders and leading her

251

to the cottage, questioning her quietly as they went. She seemed worn out. She looked as though she had given up.

The rest of us began to follow. Billy could not speak. His lips flapped open and shut but no words came out.

Then Red kicked him, a vicious lashing out from behind, and Billy fell to the ground with a cry, clutching his knee. "Ye useless dolt! Ye were to look after Iona. What have ye done wi' her?"

Mouldy grabbed hold of his nephew, pulling him away from Billy, who cowered beneath him, tears on his doughy cheeks. Mouldy was a smaller man than Red, and much older, but his anger was as great. No longer would you think him gentle and mild. For a moment it seemed as though they would fight, the two of them circling furiously, like hissing cats before they leap on each other.

"No!" shouted Calum. "This will no' help Iona!" At first, the two men seemed not to hear him, but then Red shrugged, spat on the ground, and swaggered towards the main cottage. It surprised me to see Calum stand up to his uncle in this way.

Thomas, too, looked at his older son, though saying nothing.

Billy stood, his great arms hanging loosely by his sides, his eyes wide with remorse and fear, his soft mouth hanging open.

At the cottage door, Jeannie turned round and called, "Billy, ride and fetch Hamish!"

"No," said Thomas. "We want to hear what happened."

"Billy kens nothing," said Jeannie. "It was no' Billy's fault. Let him be." Billy ran to catch one of the ponies in the field next to the yard. On another occasion I would have laughed to watch this great lumbering man chase them with flapping arms as they ran away in disrespect. Billy was in distress and it was this that made the horses run, I knew. I went to help him and soon I had caught one for him. He led it away to fetch a saddle and soon I saw him riding fast out of the yard.

Where was Jock? I asked this now. I had not seen him all morning.

"He's taken ill," Mouldy answered.

Leading Old Maggie by the hand, Bess came from our cottage, her face tired, her hair unkempt, all unwashed. Only a small bandage on her hand now showed that anything had happened. "Iona," I mouthed to her over the old woman's head, by way of explanation. Old Maggie heard nothing: she walked peacefully, with the flat-footed gait of a small child, nodding happily, as though watching butterflies on a summer's day.

In the cottage, Jeannie, her face tight with worry, biting her lower lip, went to Jock and crouched next to him with her hands one on each side of his head. He sat on a stool, a bowl on his knees, retching into it. His eyes were glassy and he did not speak. Pain creased his grey face.

"Jock, my love," she whispered, struggling to keep her voice steady. "Iona is missing." Jock seemed to hear the words as though in a dream. He shook his head, slowly, then retched some more. A thin, green liquid came from his mouth. I know not what ailed him but I did not think it something he would easily fight off.

"We should kill them all!" snarled Red.

"No," said Jeannie. "We dinna ken it was their fault."

"Who else might it be?"

"I think she went herself."

What was this? Need I not hold the secret inside me, after all? I wished to speak, but must keep my silence a while longer. Perhaps bloodshed could be avoided.

Thomas looked to Jeannie. "What d'ye mean?" Even Jock looked up, ill as he was. Everyone watched Jeannie.

"'Twas in the fleshmarket. I was talking to a sausage seller, and when I turned she was gone. Billy was no wi' us – I'd sent him to buy thread and a needle."

"They took her! Snatched her when ye were no' looking!" said Red.

Jeannie shook her head again and then took something from her pocket. It was a green ribbon. I had seen it before. In Iona's hair. Now it was tied in a perfect bow.

"This was in the pocket o' my skirt. I didna put it there. I think she has gone." She clamped her hand over her mouth and shook her head. I was glad that Iona had left this sign for Jeannie – perhaps now their anger would not be directed at Douglas Murdoch. Perhaps there would be no more bloodshed.

A foolish wish.

Now Old Maggie spoke. "Curst she is, I tellt ye all." She wagged her finger at the empty air.

I thought Jeannie would speak against her. I saw her face flash with anger, saw her open her mouth, but nothing came out. Bess took the old woman's hands and settled her to her knitting, reassuring her with a kindly look.

"Then we must search for her," said Thomas. "We'll search till we find her. We'll tell everyone to look for her. Those o' the kirk – they will look for her. Mouldy, go and send word to our friends."

"What if she does not wish to be found?" I asked, with some hesitation.

Red turned on me. "What d'ye ken? She is our

255

blood, no' yours. Ye canna care for her as we do."

For some time they argued. Every now and then they stood and scanned the horizon. Mouldy rode away from the yard. Red wanted to set out too but Thomas stopped him. "She is my daughter – 'tis right that I go."

Nor would Thomas let Calum go. Calum began to argue, but Thomas stopped him, "I need ye here." Then he lowered his voice. "And dinna let your uncles do anything foolish." I think Calum must have been pleased to have such trust from his father.

Thomas galloped away in the opposite direction from Mouldy. Calum paced about, unable to settle. But his father was back in less than an hour, I think, frantic, not knowing where to begin looking.

Soon after this, by which time it was many hours since Iona had disappeared, there was a clattering of a cart and a clashing of hoofs in the yard. Billy had returned with Hamish. We waited for them to come in through the door.

When they did so, they were not alone. The blind minister was with them. And what he had to say put an end to any care that Red might have felt for Iona. It put an end to any hopes of peace.

It promised bloodshed and more hatred.

Chapter Forty

He walked with a rolling step, slowly tapping his way into the dwelling, holding Hamish's arm with one pale hand, and a polished stick with the other. Cloud-white was his hair, hanging like icicles around his neck. He wore a black hat, stiff and tall.

And his eyes were white as bone, rolling beneath thick, steely eyebrows. As he walked, his face flicked now this way, now that, with birdlike movements, as he sought to catch any sound.

Hamish, on the other hand, looked down, at the ground. He met no one's eyes. At first I thought that his grim expression was for Iona's disappearance, but that was only part of the truth.

Into the cottage they came, and, apart from Jock, we all stood up, because a man of the church was among us even though he could not see what we did. Mouldy removed his crumpled hat and the pipe from his mouth, but the others had none to remove. Even

Old Maggie stood, smiling all the while.

"God be wi' ye all," said the minister.

Hamish was guiding him to a seat. He gestured to Billy, who set the chair carefully behind the minister as he sat down. Tension grew within the cottage.

Jock, his face the shade of ash, his eyes narrowed, began to speak between heavy breaths. "Ye are welcome. Welcome." Everyone looked to him to see what he would say further. But his eyes seemed to blur and his mouth to move without sound. He passed his hand across his forehead again, pressing his fingers to one temple. The other men looked away.

But Hamish now spoke. "Our minister has some news. Ye'll no' like it. Ye should sit yourselves down." There was a thump as Jeannie almost fell onto a stool. One hand clasped her mouth, the other gripped Jock's arm.

One by one, everyone sat now, except for Thomas, who moved close to Jeannie and Jock, but remained standing. Old Maggie resumed her knitting. Everyone else looked to the minister. None spoke. Only the fire crackled and a bubbling came from the water in the steaming pot.

One of the dogs scratched itself, the violent thumping of its leg on the ground loud in the room.

And now the minister's voice came again. "I have news o' the lass."

"Oh! What news? Tell me! What news?" Jeannie could not hold back her fear.

"The devil has surely ta'en her for hisself," said the minister, his voice shrill and nasty. There seemed some cruel pleasure in him. He savoured his words as though he wished their flavour to linger on his tongue. He must have known the effect of them; he must have known how everyone wanted to know Iona's fate.

"Is she dead?" demanded Thomas, his voice strident.

"She may as well be," snapped the minister.

"Then she's no'!" cried Jeannie.

The sound of Old Maggie's knitting tapped against the edges of my mind. I tried to ignore it, not to notice the moments when it slowed, or stopped, or gathered speed. If I could have ripped the wool from her hands, I would have. I had never felt such anger at her.

My mouth was dry. When would the minister tell us what he knew?

"A message was brought to me. By a well-wisher. The lass has run off wi' a lad."

"Is that all?" Jeannie laughed, a forced laugh. As though she knew it was not all. There was a shifting among the men. Did they too expect what was coming?

"He is an Episcopalian," said the minister now. Was that a smile, that twisting upwards of his lips? Or a sneer? Did he enjoy the news he brought? More than he should have if he had a heart, I think.

Now I could only watch and hold my breath as the men's angry words tumbled over each other. Only Jock and Jeannie stayed motionless, and wordless. I did not look at Old Maggie but from the corner of my eye I could see her knitting more quickly now, as though her fingers were chased by flames. I was aware that words mumbled from her lips but I wished not to know them and so I did not let myself hear.

We, Bess and I, could only wait. Bess said nothing, though the surprise showed in her face. She looked towards me but I turned away.

What would they do now?

Did the minister know the last piece of the story? That Iona's lover was none other than…?

"There is more," said the minister now. His thin, beaky face was angled and shadowed, as though chiselled from some northern granite. There was no softness anywhere, only sharpness and edge. Silence fell once more, and into it his words. "'Tis Douglas Murdoch's lad. They have run away together."

"I tellt ye!" shrieked Old Maggie now. "Curst, she

is! Curst! I tellt ye she would turn out like this!"

Now Jeannie let fly with her anger. "Hold your tongue, old woman! I'll no' hear ye talk like that ever again, d'ye hear?"

"I was right! Was I no' right?"

But Jeannie leapt at her now and grasped her shoulders. With tears on her cheeks, she shook Old Maggie like a blanket, shouting angry words at her. Thomas and Red grabbed Jeannie, while Bess took Old Maggie and sat her back down, soothing her.

Jeannie wept as she struggled to free herself from the two men. "How can ye let her talk so when wee Iona is in danger? D'ye care nothing for your daughter, Thomas?"

"She has betrayed us!" growled Red. "To go wi' Murdoch's son!"

"Aye, she has shamed us all!" agreed Thomas. "To go wi' an Episcopalian. Does the Bible no' say, 'the tree is known by his fruit'? Am I no' shamed by her act?" The minister nodded, offering no words of comfort.

And then everyone's words poured out. I heard harsh damnation of Episcopalians and those who followed bishops; there was Old Maggie repeating over and over again, "All drest in white they were." Red was for mustering as many arms as we could and going to Douglas Murdoch's place. What good would that do, asked Thomas, if Iona and the lad were not there? But the villain needed to be punished, argued Red. And if we no longer had to fear him stealing her away then what did we have to lose?

"But if she loved the lad!" said Jeannie.

"Did ye ken about this?" demanded Thomas.

"No!" said Jeannie. "But she is the age when such things happen."

"Did we no' teach her our history?" asked Thomas. "Did she no' listen often enough to the story of her great-grandmother? Does she think our people didna suffer enough at the hands of Episcopalians and kings and others who betrayed their own faith? That our persecution was no' enough?"

"She is but a bitty lassie!" cried Jeannie.

"Aye, and she's a lassie who must learn a lesson. When she comes running back, she will find out that God is a harsh judge and we will no' cease in His work," said Thomas.

"'Whoso sheddeth man's blood, by man shall his blood be shed'," the minister's voice rang out. I suppose he meant to justify their need for vengeance against Episcopalians, but Iona had killed no one.

Murmurings of agreement passed around the cottage.

Calum, I saw, sat silent, his face troubled, his eyes going from one to the next. I could not tell what he thought. Did he wish to protect his sister now?

The door flew open and Tam ran into the room. When he saw the minister sitting there, crow-faced, and saw everyone's grim looks, he went quickly to Jeannie, where he buried his face in her skirts and she ruffled his hair absentmindedly, her face rigid as she struggled with her thoughts. Thomas and Red had now let her go and she grabbed Tam's hand and led him to the fire, where she set him to pounding something in a bowl. She would not look at Old Maggie. Tam asked no questions, though he looked fearfully at the minister.

The minister stood and Hamish and Billy led him out.

"All things work to the good for them that love God," he pronounced, as he left the dwelling. I was glad indeed when he had gone. He had brought a chill to the place, a darkness, something not of this world.

Into the shifting muttering of the men when he had gone, came Jock's voice. "We must show mercy," he said. "'Tis no' for us but for God to judge." His eyes looked empty, or as though a thin fog veiled them.

"Ye're a good man indeed," said Jeannie eagerly, nodding and looking around at the others, as though to tell them that he was their leader still.

Thomas and Red looked away at their father's

words. It was clear they did not agree with his mercy. Though Red was more angry that Iona had gone with Douglas Murdoch's son, and Thomas that his daughter had gone with an Episcopalian, both must act in revenge or punishment.

And Old Maggie would not have this talk of mercy. "My ain son! Gone weak! How will God judge us if we dinna help Him in his work?"

"Dinna speak to Jock so!" snapped Jeannie now. "He is a good man. And we do what he says."

"Curst be her heid and all the hairs on it!" said the old woman spitefully. With a noise of pure rage, Jeannie rose to her feet and ran from the cottage, knocking over a stool. Tam fell onto the ground, where he sat crying. She was like a beast gone wild and soon we could hear her sobbing outside. Jock made to get up, but seemed overcome by dizziness, and fell back on his stool.

Thomas and Red looked at each other, knowing not what to do.

Calum stood looking from one man to another, saying nothing. I knew his views on the religion of the Murdochs, remembered what he had said about killing them if they came to his house, and that he did not forgive them for the Killing Times. But I knew too that he feared for his sister and loved her. Which would be stronger? His hatred or his love?

Bess turned her mind to giving Old Maggie a drink, busying herself, while Tam was crouching on the ground, looking from one person to another, wondering what was splintering his world – a world which had Jeannie's strength and love at its centre.

So it was left to me to follow Jeannie outside and as I did I could hear the others continuing to argue, and to rail about bishops and Catholics and the English and the King and Episcopalians. Between them all, Iona had made herself some powerful enemies by her unfortunate choice of boy to love.

I hoped she was very far away by now and that she would not come back, for her own sake and the sake of peace.

Chapter Forty-One

Out in the yard, I found Jeannie staring towards the sea, twisting the sides of her apron. I went to her, with no thought of what to say, only that she had seemed the only one who would not condemn Iona to Hell. She turned when she heard my steps. Her voice now was without power, flat. It was as though a large weight pressed down on her, and she could make only a small sound.

"I should have held my tongue. It's no' Old Maggie's fault. I shouldna hurt her. She is just a poor old woman."

"But it's not Iona's fault either, surely? She cannot choose whom to love."

Jeannie looked at me then, deep into my eyes. After some moments, I had to look away. For one long breath, I almost told her that Iona had confided her secret in me. But it would not have helped. And I did not know how far I could trust Jeannie.

"I think ye care for her," said Jeannie now.

"I am sorry for her," I said. "And I do not like the hatred that is between your families. For something that happened so long ago."

"Aye, but it did happen. And mebbe Old Maggie was right. Mebbe Iona was curst, though I never liked her to hear it. The both o' them grew up without a mother – Iona's died of a fever when Tam was a wee baby. I didna like to see her flinch under Old Maggie's words, but the woman was right after all. The silly lassie has run off wi' our enemy. How could she be so foolish! She doesna deserve my protection any more. I should wash my hands o' her and leave her to her lad." She shook her head, sadly.

Not Jeannie too! Did Iona have no friends at all?

"A silly girl, perhaps," I said. "But does she deserve this?"

"How often in this world do we get what we deserve?" retorted Jeannie now. "Did Old Maggie get what she deserved? Iona should have kept herself from him, if she'd any loyalty, any love for her family."

How much love did they have for her? I could not understand it, any of it. So much hatred, so little hope for better times.

"Jock has need o' me," said Jeannie, straightening her back now. "I have a family to care for. I pity Iona,

but she has brought this on herself. She'd better no'
return, or she will feel the anger o' her uncles and her
father. I wouldna wish that on her and so she should
no' return," she repeated, shaking her head, sadly.
She walked towards the cottage door.

The door closed, leaving only me outside.

I did not follow her. The only person now who
might show any kindness to Iona was Jock, and
Jock was weak and very ill. And it seemed to me
that, without Jeannie's agreement, he would wither
under the anger of everyone else. Besides, I did not
think that mercy was a word much used by these
people. No, his talk of mercy was not something
I could rely on.

Iona had no one other than me. And all I could do,
it seemed, was hope and pray for her to escape.

The sun shone strongly for an April day, with a
warm west wind. I went to the stable and stroked
the horses. Burying my face in Blackfoot's mane, I
breathed in his smell, his grassy, musty, living smell.

Why did I not simply ride away? I could gather
my few possessions from our cottage and slip away
without anyone knowing. My heart sang with the
thought of this, the freedom once more of the open
road.

Could I leave without Bess? Not if there was any
hope that she would come with me. But if I could not

persuade her... Then, I must leave and must find the strength to make my own way, find a new life once more.

Chapter Forty-Two

My first chance to talk to Bess alone came a little later. She had gone to fetch some water from the well, and there I joined her.

"Poor Iona," I said, to see what her response might be. Surely she would not think that these people were right to treat Iona as harshly as they had?

"She was a silly girl," retorted Bess. Her thick hair was greasy and untidy, scraped back from her forehead and tied roughly behind her, the colour of coal dust. Already she seemed to have taken on a little of the harshness of these people. Some of her grace had gone, that mysterious strength and elegance. Her lips now were cracked and her skin lifeless.

"But only a girl," I replied. "Too young to understand."

"Older than Maggie was when she was branded by the soldiers. Old enough to know."

"And I suppose you believe in the old woman's

curse?" I said, with some spite. Why was Bess being so cruel? Did she think that the ancient anger of these people was right?

"Old Maggie is a good woman! She is strong in her faith and no one will sway her. She does not change her heart just because things around her change." Bess now reached up to finger the locket round her neck again, rubbing it softly, perhaps not noticing what she did.

"Perhaps she should! Perhaps she has no heart."

"She has suffered as you never have! One silly girl's error will not change her heart. And nor should it. Iona has proved Old Maggie right."

"Yes!" I said, furious myself now. "And I suppose your mother's error in falling in love with your father would not change her father's heart! I suppose he was right to nurse his hatred and to throw you out when you were a tiny baby! He said your mother and father should never have loved each other and so he caused their deaths. Perchance he said your mother was a silly girl too, until she died. Did he think she was silly then?"

"Be quiet!" she cried. "Do not speak of my mother and father like that! You understand none of it!" She picked up her bucket and ran towards our cottage.

I regretted what I had said, or how I had said it. Yet I knew I was right.

271

It came to me then that Bess would carry her hatred with her to her grave, just as Old Maggie would do.

As she disappeared across the yard, I no longer saw the Bess I had come to know, the brave spirit who would not be imprisoned. And it seemed to me now that perhaps she was suited to these people after all, that she would stay with them and be wrapped round in their own ancient hatreds, passing their anger down the ages until no one could remember why any of it had started.

I did not wish to stay with her if she would not change.

Should I simply leave, without Bess?

If I could not stay, and she would not come, then I must go.

Chapter Forty-Three

I would leave the next morning, I decided. It was now too late in the afternoon and darkness was only a few hours away. In the stable, with a heavy feeling in my heart, I groomed Blackfoot, and ensured that his saddle and bridle were in good condition. Bess's horse, Merlin, pushed his nose into my back, demanding my attention too. Willingly I gave it to him.

I fed Blackfoot well, or as well as I could, and checked his legs for signs of injury, but he was sound, strong and fit, and as ready as I was to make a journey. And the more I considered it, the more ready I felt. A sense of adventure grew in me now as I thought of leaving behind the dark and hopeless lives of these people. In such a beautiful land, why should they hold onto such cruelty? Was it what God wished for them? I could not think so.

But I knew not where I would go. Perhaps to

Edinburgh? I had heard tell of it as a place of learning and erudition. If I could find a way to earn money, I could perhaps afford to go to the university there. Or I could travel to England again. A part of me wished to know how my family fared now, whether they thought of me at all and, if so, in what way. But I did not think I could return and so perhaps I would never know.

This was a difficult thought, I confess. I regretted not one bit that I had left home, but now that I faced the world on my own again, I admit to a small shiver of fear and a sudden wish for the comfort and safety of my home-life again. I wished I did not have to be alone. But there was little point in dwelling on this. I would be alone and I must become accustomed to it.

But I suppose that it was these doubts, these fears, that made me agree to what we did later that evening. Although I knew I would be on my own again soon, I wished to delay that.

When I had finished in the stable, I went to the cottage I shared with Bess and the old woman. No one was there. The fire hissed softly. There was the familiar smell of bodies and boiled kale and damp stone and the smoke-soaked heather in the thatch. The shutters were closed, and these I now swung open, letting the breeze wash through the dwelling. I gathered together my few possessions, items of clothing, my knife, my sword, pistols and their accoutrements, my flint, tallow candles, and the very few coins I had left. I looked at them: they would not last me long if I had to pay for lodging as well as food.

And I suppose it was that thought, too – the need for money – that made me agree to what we planned that evening.

As I gathered everything up in my saddlebags, I was startled by the sudden sound of voices and the door swung open. I looked up. It was Bess and Calum. They stopped talking when they saw me.

We greeted each other, awkwardly. Bess saw what I was doing. She looked at me.

"Yes," I said, in answer to her unspoken question. "I am leaving, in the morning. This is no place for me."

"I wish you would stay," said Bess, after a pause in which I hope she felt some regret, some sadness. I believe she meant her words, but did she mean them with great force? I could not tell. Bess had been happy before I met her and I think she would not mourn my departure now. And Calum stood close to her. It seemed that there was more than a friendship between them.

If I were honest, if I looked deep within myself, I could hardly bear to think of Bess staying here, becoming mired in the choiceless lives of this family.

It seemed to be as wrong as keeping an eagle in a cage. But she had changed in some way over the last days and perhaps now she had lost her desire for freedom. And if she had lost that, then I could do nothing. Because Bess *was* freedom.

Perhaps that was the final reason why I agreed to what we did that evening – that I wanted one more chance for Bess to change her mind and come with me.

Bess looked at Calum now. "I shall tell him." Calum nodded. What did they have to tell me? I said nothing, just waited, though my heart beat a little faster.

"We are to ride out tonight," she said, her eyes bright once more. "You and I. We are after a prize. Douglas Murdoch's men ride with money this night. Mad Jamie has told us. They have been collecting payments from people in the west and they will be returning to Murdoch's tower in a few hours…'

"This is madness!" I retorted. "He is a dangerous man. He will come for revenge and then what will happen to you all?"

"No! Don't you see?" cried Bess, her face shining. "They will not know us. Murdoch's men have never seen us – you or me – and know not that we are here. When they see our horses, they will not think of Jock's people. There is no risk." I said nothing. "He deserves it, Will. And think of the money. If you are leaving, you will need your share. We have little enough left."

"I do not like it. Not at all."

"Then I will do it alone!" Was she angry, or disappointed? I could not tell.

Calum turned to her. "I will come with ye."

"No!" I said now. "It is not safe. You would be recognized," I added when he scowled.

"So you will come?" asked Bess of me.

Where would be the harm in it? There were powerful reasons for doing it, and few against. Once more would I ride out with Bess. And then, then I would leave. "I will come. But I do not like it, nevertheless," I said.

Only a few days ago, I would have jumped at such an idea with enthusiasm, but now this constant battling on the wrong side of the law sickened me. Had I not already condemned my father for corruption? So, how much better was I if I broke the law so easily?

But I did agree, for money, for companionship, for Bess, and for myself.

And, for adventure. Perhaps I went with my heart and not my head. I know not which is the more important.

For the next hour or more, we prepared for our escapade. Calum would come with us a part of the way, to show us a good place to wait secretly for the men to pass, and then he would wait near by for us to carry out the robbery. Bess was fired with excitement.

Seeing her spirit inflamed once more, seeing her eyes shining again, I confess to wishing more than ever that she could come away with me. After tonight, might she choose to? Perhaps she would remember our adventures and the excitement of the open road, and sitting by her fire after dark, telling our stories to each other and planning to fight for what felt right. But when I saw the way Calum hung on her words, and she on his, it seemed to me that the hope was slim indeed.

Bess and I checked our pistols, packing powder into powder horns, counting our lead shot, placing them within easy reach in our belts. Calum had a knife, which he now took pleasure in sharpening against a whetstone. I hoped that he would not need it, but it was better that he should have a weapon than not. My saddlebag was already filled with all my possessions, but Bess, dressed in her male attire once more, and with the locket hidden, also packed what she might need for some hours of waiting, including her flint, tallow candles, and even a small lantern, wrapped in a cloth, in case we should need them.

When we were ready, we walked to the other cottage. Jeannie got to her feet stiffly. She had been tending to Jock, who lay curled on his side on the box-bed. I could not see if he was sleeping but he did not stir. Jeannie's face was grey, her forehead furrowed, her hair unkempt. There was little expression to be read in her eyes. Tam sat near her, throwing small stones into a circle he had marked in the dirt on the stone floor. A dog lay on its side, one eye open, watching the stones land.

Mouldy was stretching rabbit skins on a rack near the fire. Billy sat sharpening sticks to a point – I know not what for. Perhaps for setting a trap. Thomas stared up into the beams under the roof, as though he would find the answer to all his problems there. He glanced at us when we came in. Calum went to sit near him, and Thomas looked at him and I think smiled a little. Calum poured some ale for his father and his father drank it.

Jeannie poured us some bowls of broth and set bread beside them. We ate in a strained silence. I wished to ask what they thought about Iona now, after some time to think on it, perhaps to find some forgiveness. But I could not find the words, and I feared the answer.

How could they appear to have forgotten her so easily? Even Calum, it seemed. How could they think about us going after money when Iona had vanished and they might never see her again?

The silence was broken by Bess, asking Jeannie a question. "How does Jock fare?"

Jeannie shook her head. "I fear mightily for him. He canna walk – one side of his body doesna move right. I have heard of such a thing but…"

At this moment, the door opened and in came Red, with Old Maggie. He led her to the fireside, and set her in the high-backed chair, with surprising gentleness. Bess went and sat with her. I looked away.

Red turned to me, an unusual note of respect in his voice. "So, ye will ride after Douglas Murdoch tonight?" When I nodded, he continued. "We should mebbe try such a thing on the excisemen, one day! 'Tis a good trade, this highway robbery, taking from people what's no' theirs by right."

"We'll use the money to buy more goods when we run a cargo next," said Thomas.

Was this all they could think of? Even Thomas, Iona's own father? Sorrow was grooved in his face, but still he acted as though Iona no longer existed. Was their hatred of the other religion so deep that an only daughter could be lost with so little grief? And no attempt yet to find her and fetch her back?

As we finished our plain meal, wiping up the last thin dregs of salty soup, Old Maggie began to sing some of the words of Bess's ballad. And as Bess joined in, and as I watched her face harden and her eyes light up while she sang those words, I wondered if there was anything that would stop her holding her own poisonous hatred inside her, anything that would soften her heart and allow the bitterness to go.

I understood then that there was not. Bess would grow old and poisoned and damaged like Old Maggie. And I would not stay to see that.

I was sure then that tomorrow, after one more adventure, I would leave without her.

Chapter Forty-Four

With darkness almost fallen, we set out, riding three abreast, with the voices of the men and Jeannie ringing in our ears as they wished us good fortune.

"And if ye meet wi' Douglas Murdoch himself, use your pistols on him and run him through wi' a sword for good measure!" cried Red, with glee.

Thomas had said something to Calum, perhaps to tell him to take care, and his son had nodded. Calum had then swung himself into his saddle with vigour. I suppose he was glad to have something with which to take his thoughts away from his sister, and to prove himself worthy to his father.

The moon was full that night, a perfect circle hanging low in a near-cloudless sky. Silver light drenched the land around us and the inky waters of the sea to our left. To our right, black hills leaned against the sky.

I kicked my horse forward and Calum had to

urge his pony hard to keep up with us.

As we cantered into the night, relief at leaving that place grew into excitement. I looked across at Bess as we rode and she returned my look with a full smile. At that moment, perhaps foolishly, I believed I might persuade her to come with me after this night's work was done. Adventure ran in her blood and now it made my heart beat faster too.

Once we reached the road, we travelled westwards, making for a particular spot which Calum had said would suit our needs. Wordlessly, we cantered along the road. This, I knew now, was the road newly built by the soldiers, taking travellers from the east all the way to the far west coast. It amused me to know that it was the hated redcoats who had made our travel easier.

The chill wind could not pierce my good coat, and the clean kerchief round my throat gave me extra warmth. I was aware of every breath, every sense, every feeling. As we passed a small copse, the bitter scent of fox came to me and an eerie warning bark followed it.

We continued west. We knew not when Douglas Murdoch's men would pass, but we knew from Mad Jamie that it would be well after dark. Red had snarled something about the man being suited to the devil's hours.

Could we trust Mad Jamie? I had asked this earlier and had been told that he would not lie to us – his grandfather had been Old Maggie's cousin. "He's family," Thomas had said. And his information came from one of Douglas Murdoch's men, a friend of Jamie's who, like many of them, had little love for his master.

Family. For a moment I had almost smiled.

Now, I hoped that we could indeed trust Mad Jamie.

We rode on, deep in our own thoughts, straining our eyes and ears in case we might see or hear something to fear. And it was as I tried to discern anything over the sound of our own horses' hoofs on the rocky road that I did indeed hear something else. At first, I thought it might be the echoes of our hoofbeats, but very soon I realized that it was not. I pulled Blackfoot to a halt, urging the others to do the same. They too had heard it.

More hoofbeats. Coming from ahead of us. Hurriedly, we moved off the road and into the shelter of some trees. I leapt from my saddle, flinging the reins to Bess, and, taking the pistols from my belt and half cocking them, moved carefully towards the road. Keeping myself hidden in the shadow of a tree, I peered into the night.

It was a single rider. On a small pony. He came

closer. I strained my eyes. Was it someone we need fear? Who would be riding at such speed, alone, after dark?

The rider's legs and elbows flapped as he kicked his pony wildly. The pony's feet flew and soon I could hear the snorting of its breath.

"It's Mad Jamie!" cried Calum, as the pony flashed past. He was right. And if it was Mad Jamie, he could have information for us.

What made him ride now with such frantic haste?

"Jamie!" called Calum, and we left the trees. I leapt onto Blackfoot and, still fumbling my feet into the stirrups, followed the others in pursuit of Mad Jamie. But he was afraid and kicked his pony to ever greater speed, thinking perhaps that we were villains who meant him harm.

If his pony had not stumbled, I know not how long it would have taken us to catch him. But stumble it did, sending Jamie over its shoulder. He clung briefly to the animal's mane and neck but was unable to stop himself slithering to the ground. His pony, meanwhile, hung its foreleg loosely – it was lame.

When Jamie saw that it was only us, he gibbered with relief and almost cried as he tried to tell us what he knew. He had indeed been riding to meet us, with terrible news. His overlarge mouth spluttered, with too much spittle and too little control over his tongue.

It took some moments more before we could understand exactly what he was trying to tell us. But, in the end, it was all too clear.

Douglas Murdoch had captured Iona and Robert as they tried to take a boat across the Solway. His son had tried to fight with him and in his fury Murdoch had carted him back home and locked him in the tower, thinking that some days without food would bring him to his senses. And as for Iona? Well, as for Iona, she had been taken away to be punished. And Mad Jamie feared for her safety – Murdoch's eyes had gleamed with more than anger, said his informer.

"Where?" demanded Calum now, fearful for his sister, no matter what she had done. "Where have they taken her?"

Mad Jamie shook his head, his eyes staring, snot hanging from his nose. His hands flapped as though he would shake away his terror.

Calum turned to Bess. "We must find her! We can no' leave her!" His love for his sister was clear. He seemed to have forgotten all his anger at her desertion of their religion. This I was glad of. But what would that matter, if Douglas Murdoch had taken her away to do something terrible to her?

How would we ever find her? She could be anywhere.

And then the truth hit me, a kick in the stomach.

I knew where Iona was. I knew it with the clarity of sharpened steel. I knew it with the horror of gunshot. I have had fear like that in a nightmare; but this was not a nightmare. This was real.

I knew where Iona was and why. And it was not simply a guess. There was a reason why I knew, and why only I could have known.

Trying to keep my voice level, I turned to Calum now, and to Mad Jamie. For either of them might be able to answer my question. "Where is the tide now?" Neither of them answered, confused by what I asked. "The tide!" I repeated. "Is it rising or falling?"

After a moment's hesitation, Calum answered. "'Tis rising."

"Then go back to the farm. And hurry! Tell them what has happened and make them open the trapdoor! I'll meet you in the tunnel."

Calum looked at me, his understanding slowly dawning. "God damn them to Hell! No! Ye canna be right!"

"I am right. I know – more than you think. There's no time to lose. Bess, follow me. Hurry!"

"I'll come wi' ye!" Calum was already gathering his reins, turning his pony.

"No! Jamie's pony is lame and you would not wish Bess to go back alone – you must go. Hurry!"

"She is my sister – I should go to her."

287

"You shall – along the tunnel. Meet us, and show us the way. Tell your family what has happened and that they must have blankets ready."

"What? Tell me what's happening!" Bess demanded.

Calum answered her, seeing the sense in my arguments. "Go wi' him, Bess. Will knows where Iona is! And for God's sake, hurry!" And with that, Calum kicked his pony and galloped back along the road with Mad Jamie following on foot, leading his lame pony.

A thought came to me of a sudden. "Jamie!" He stopped and turned, his face eerie in the moonlight. "When you reach the farm, send someone to the cliff path, to fetch our horses. Do you know where I mean?" He nodded and set off again. I could only pray he would remember.

Without further questions, for which I was grateful, Bess followed me as I set off. At first, we travelled in the same direction as Calum had, but very soon we took the turning off the road and onto the track towards the cliff.

And as I rode, desperately trying to recall what the track was like, not certain if I would know when to swing to the right and go down the cliff path, I could not help thinking of that tunnel with the fountains of water smashing against the rock face, that narrow

288

tunnel, that tiny beach, the incoming tide. And that iron ring set into the side of the cliff. I could not help thinking of the way Old Maggie's mother had died, slowly drowned by the rising water.

But most of all I could not help thinking of the words I had read, roughly written on that piece of paper, in the box with the snake; words that I had burnt, intending that no one should ever read them, that no one should ever feel the chill that they sent down my back; that no one should ever know that Douglas Murdoch was truly evil. I had kept them to myself in order to preserve a kind of peace, or at least to stop more bloodshed.

But it had all been to no avail. Now surely there would be certain death: Iona's. And the words were still etched in my memory.

"Curst be the lass, like the wumman drest in white. In such a way shall death tak her by drooning. An' then will there be nae mair. So be oor curse."

It must not be!

Chapter Forty-Five

By moonlight we rode, the path a pale ribbon in front of us. A curlew wheeled and mewed its reedy cry overhead. I had no fear of curlews.

We could be seen, I knew. If anyone chose to watch our progress, the ground here was flat, with little cover of trees, and anyone could be watching. I tried not to think on this. I thought only of keeping to the right path, and of the sound of our horses, Bess's and mine, as they galloped willingly beneath us. We were Iona's only hope and we must not fail her now.

I turned to shout to Bess, the wind whipping my words away. "Take care – the path goes down the side of the cliff. Be ready." She nodded, her lips tight shut, her face rigid with effort.

Just in time, I saw the place where our route must turn. Sharply to the right we swung, and slowed as the path rapidly descended. If I had been full of fear the first time I rode this way, I was the more so now. Though not for myself, but for Iona.

For some moments, the only sounds were of our horses' hoofs dislodging stones, stones which fell with sickening speed and then silence as they tumbled into empty air. Once, Blackfoot stumbled, and I lurched forward, clinging grimly to his mane, but I righted myself and we continued without slowing again until we came at last to the bottom of the path.

The tide was, indeed, rising. In truth, there was scarcely any beach remaining. We must leave the horses there. Once the tide had risen fully, there would be nowhere for them to go.

Bess asked me no questions. She must have understood that there was no time, and trusted that I knew what I was doing – though I confess I knew little enough. We dismounted and sent the horses back up the path, with firm slaps on their rumps. They were unwilling to go, standing looking at us as though to ask why we had brought them there. But we could not pause to consider them.

The strip of beach still uncovered by the tide was perhaps three or four paces from the water's edge to the cliff, in parts more and in parts less. There was no time to lose. "Follow me!" I urged Bess and we ran along this narrow strip. At one point the rock face swelled outwards, and here already the waves lapped hungrily at its base. We splashed through shallow, tugging water.

Now there was no turning back. Within moments that place would be deep with swirling sea. I tried not to think of the horses. They must find their way home. Or Jamie would send someone for them. We would find Iona in time and carry her up the passageway and the horses would be waiting for us at the farm.

How could I hope for so much? How could I not accept that Iona was probably dead, that perhaps we too might drown in those tunnels, that our horses would be lost to us, perhaps captured by Murdoch's men? I know not, merely that I could only hope.

Something rushed through my body, urging me on, forcing me to hope, lending extra speed and strength to my legs. I would not give up!

And now, dodging the nipping teeth of the waves, I could see the overhanging darkness of the cave. Moonlight did not enter here and at first I struggled to discern the back of the cave or the entrance to the tunnel.

Bess was close behind me. I could hear her quick breathing. We both held our bags above our heads, protecting the contents from the water. We would need the wicks of the tallow candles to be dry, for without them we would have no light at all in the tunnel – if we even managed to reach it.

Ahead of us here, the beach sloped downwards, so that the tide had already entered the main part of the cave. Where we stood now, as each wave receded, the water was at ankle depth. As each icy wave rushed in, our legs were soaked past our knees. I gritted my teeth against the clawing coldness. Pressing ourselves close to the rock face, we clung to each other and tried to stay upright as each wave passed. It was impossible not to gasp. Already we were shivering, soaked up to our chests by spray.

But I held onto one hope – that Iona had not drowned. If she was standing upright, she could not have done, I believed. The water was not deep enough. I called her name now, peering into the darkness, still struggling to make any speed through the water.

"Iona! Iona! We're here!"

No reply came. Only the sucking and spitting of the sea, and the whishing of a growing wind.

We forced our legs through the waves, close to the cliff face, with the water getting deeper as the sands sloped further downwards. With a jarring pain, my foot hit an unseen rock and I stumbled. At the same moment, a wave crashed into me and I lost my footing. I managed to stand upright, but another wave hurled itself at my face. Water entered my mouth as

I gasped and my eyes stung with the salt. And I knew, in an instant, that the contents of my bag would be soaked and useless. But Bess's bag was still dry, or its contents would be. I would not think of failure. For failure would spell Iona's death, and perhaps ours.

Strangely, from that moment I felt no cold. A surprising warmth began to suffuse my body, my skin losing its feeling, my mind losing its fear. I thought only to find Iona and the tunnel and safety. Never had the smoky, dirty cottage seemed so desirable. Never had I wished so much to see the swarthy faces of Red and the others.

"Come on!" I shouted to Bess, more for my sake than hers. I firmly placed one foot in front of the other, gripping Bess's arm with one hand and any protruding rock that I could find with the other. By now, my eyes were used to the near-darkness of this cave and so it was then that I thought I saw Iona.

Yes! There she was! I could discern her small shape, slumped forward, against the cliff face at the back of the cave, where the swirling water was at its deepest, tugging at her waist.

My heart leapt. The water had not reached her face. She had not drowned. We pushed forward, further into the cave.

When Iona's family saw the terrible punishment

she had suffered from Douglas Murdoch, then surely they would forgive her? Blood was surely thicker than water, and love stronger than hate.

"Good God!" cried Bess, still holding her bag above the water. "What have they done?"

We reached Iona as the waves snarled and crashed around us. I gripped the iron ring for balance. "Hold tight!" I called to Bess. The sea could beat us yet. She gripped the iron ring above Iona's head and between us we supported the girl's limp body as I took the knife from my belt and began to saw against the ropes that bound her.

I suppose a part of me noticed her coldness, her dead weight as she slumped. I suppose I saw that she made no response, no movement, no sign that she knew we were there. But I could not bear to think what that might mean.

Only when her ropes were cut and she fell forward into my arms, did I try to rouse her. Only then did I fear for the terrible chill of her body. Her face was close to my ear, her head lolling on my shoulder. No breath could I feel, no warmth from her mouth, no beating of her heart against mine. And her skin – how icy it was, how lifeless.

I shook her. Another wave hurled itself at us, stronger, angrier now.

"Hurry!" shouted Bess above the hollow roaring

of the sea and the moaning of the wind in the cave. "The tide is rising fast! Where's the tunnel?"

"Over there!" I shouted, pointing towards the opening, a few paces further round the rock face. I lifted Iona until she was hanging over my shoulder, and pulled myself through the water. Bess grabbed my arm and pulled me too. Between us, we reached the opening.

The tunnel mouth gaped in front of us. It spelt safety. Yet, what terrifying safety! I remembered with what brutal power the waves had spouted through the passageway. I had been told how quickly the sea's strength would force them through the narrow opening. But there was no time to think on that now. The waves rushed in and out, now covering the ground underfoot, then swishing back, spitting shells and shingle and seaweed. The tunnel floor was higher here, the waves slapping only at our ankles and knees, but each wave seemed to shoot into the opening with greater power. There was no time to lose.

Iona was a dead weight over my shoulder as I stumbled as fast as I could into the tunnel entrance. The ground sloped sharply upwards here, for which I was glad. Although my breath rasped in my chest, I had the strength of three men that night. Goaded by the waves behind me and by terrible fear for Iona,

I would not slow down. I could hear Bess behind me.

Climbing steeply up the steps hewn into the rocky floor by man and water, very soon we were above the waves, though I knew they would continue to rise, and quickly. Yet, at that moment, I believed we could climb faster than they.

But I had not counted on the darkness. Within moments, we were in pitch blackness. I stumbled, cutting my hand on the sharp floor and grazing my elbow. I felt Iona's body crash against the side of the wall.

We could not go on. We needed light. I stopped. Bess's voice came through the darkness, reading my thoughts.

"Wait!" she gasped. "I'll light a candle." I gently placed Iona on the ground, lowering her body as carefully as I could. Not knowing what else to do, I slapped her hands together, pinched her cheeks, called her name. She did not stir. I wanted to believe that she was merely in a faint, that she had swooned through cold, or fear.

I feared that this was not the case.

I could hear Bess fumbling with her flint, striking it several times, many times, against the tinder. It must have been damp too, despite her best efforts. God was not on our side and I knew not why.

But suddenly, with a rasp, a spark became a tiny

flame, lighting the wick of the candle that Bess held carefully on the tinder. Quickly she shielded it with a hand and I watched the flame grow. Once the lantern cover was round the candle, it would not go out, not unless a wave covered it.

It was at that moment, in that flickering light, that I saw the worst thing of all. On the side of Iona's head, between the strands of hair, was a small, perfectly round hole, blood encrusted on its edges.

Trepanning. Douglas Murdoch had trepanned her skull.

Chapter Forty-Six

Iona was dead. There could be no doubt. A part of my mind was blank, numb, refusing to accept. And yet, I must accept it. Murdoch had drilled a hole in the side of her head while she was alive. He had tortured her before leaving her to drown.

I could say nothing to Bess. Not now. She needed to believe, to hope. I needed something else to fill my head. I needed to believe that there was a reason why I struggled through that passageway, in the dark, in fear and exhaustion. Because now, indeed, exhaustion began to take hold. As I sat there, uselessly rubbing her hands and trying to stop my tears from flowing, I felt my strength dissolve; I sensed the cold creep over me until I was shivering with an iciness that pierced my bones.

Iona had died a useless, cruel death, just as Henry Parish had done. Bess and I had tried to save them both. And we had failed.

Despair began to take a hold. What was the point in believing in justice? Yes, I would take Iona's body back, because that was right and proper. But what then?

If it were not for Bess, I think perhaps I would have given up at that moment. I am ashamed to say so, because I thought myself stronger. But then Bess did not know what I knew, that Iona was dead and that we had failed.

From the noise of the waves, I knew that the sea rose quickly behind us. I could feel its spray, hear its rhythmic breath, like a huge monster spitting at us.

"Hurry!" urged Bess.

For a moment, I did not reply. But I glimpsed her face in the candlelight. Full of hope it was, her eyes alight, full of determination once more.

Although I had no hope, yet what else could I do but follow her?

"Lead the way," I said. And she squeezed past me as I sat with Iona's body on my lap.

A wave crashing against my back and splashing across Iona's upturned face goaded me to activity. Quickly, I grasped her under both arms and hoisted her over my shoulder, summoning all my strength once more to climb up the unknown passageway.

Sometimes the passage levelled out. Sometimes it twisted round a corner. Sometimes we seemed to climb as if up a flight of stairs, though never have I seen stairs so irregular and treacherous. Always, we moved slowly, painfully slowly. Stones slipped under our feet, rocky overhangs threatened to lacerate our faces, and all the while, over and over again, the waves below us reached up with their grasping fingers or sent their icy spray across our backs.

As we climbed, the force of the waves behind us grew. More than once I found myself hurled forwards, sometimes falling onto my face, Iona's legs beneath me. Although I had no hope of her being alive, I nevertheless tried to protect her body from further harm.

Although I would doubtless have moved faster without her weight, not once did I think of leaving her body to the waves. How could I have borne to see Jeannie's face, or Jock's, and Calum's, if I had not brought her body home? They needed to bury her, I knew that. Even Thomas, though he had condemned her for her betrayal, surely he too would want to mourn over her corpse? When he saw her small frame, her beautiful flame-red hair, surely he would forgive her too?

And so, I carried her, though my heart was as heavy as it had ever been. I followed the small flame that Bess carried before her.

But I did not know how much longer I could keep

going. My head felt dizzy. Pain sliced through my lungs, my chest, each time I took a breath. And my legs grew more and more tired, losing strength, until even lifting them required all my effort.

Yet, every time I thought I must stop, every time I almost called to Bess, another wave would hurl itself against my legs, snatching at my ankles. And when it did, I wanted to scream my anger at the sea.

In my head, strange sounds flitted. The pounding of blood, the roaring of the sea, my own breathing, the crunching of stones beneath my feet, Bess's footsteps in front of me, and voices.

Voices!

Ahead of us! Surely that was Calum's voice! We were almost there – at the place where the passage from the farmhouse met this one, the place where we had had to leap across when the tide was high.

My mind was broken in two parts. In one part, relief at our safety, mine and Bess's. And in the other, dread.

Chapter Forty-Seven

"We are safe, Will!" came Bess's voice from above me. I saw her legs disappear quickly upwards, saw her smiling down, and Calum's face beside hers. The dancing light of two lanterns leapt up the craggy walls. Red was there too, I saw, reaching down with his strong arms towards me.

I said nothing, but prepared to lift Iona high above me so that he could take her. I had only to climb the last few steps with her, before heaving myself over the lip of the hole, and hauling myself over and to safety.

"Hurry!" urged Red, as I gathered my strength. What was the hurry? The waves had not beaten us. We would be safe.

I did not know if I had the strength to lift her above my shoulders. She was heavy, lifeless as she was, and soaked through, her clothes weighty with water. And I was tired. Very tired. This was why I paused so long, summoning all the strength I could find. I almost wished not to let her go, perhaps to hold onto the knowledge that she was dead. I wished no one else to know.

"Hurry!" said Red again. "The highest waves are near. Ye dinna ken their strength."

"I know their strength!" I snapped. "Have I not come this far?"

Now Calum's voice came to me. "The last waves o' the rising tide have a terrible power, Will. Hurry – Red is right!"

And, as he said that, as if the sea had heard, an awful muttering roar came from below me, in the bowels of the cliff. I felt the air sucked from around me, a gathering pressure on my ears, and the hairs on my neck rising. The moment after Red reached down and pulled Iona from me, I grasped the edge of the rock, and an enormous wave hit me from behind, shooting its power high into the air.

For several moments I could neither breathe nor see. I could hear nothing but the roar of water around me, feel nothing but its tugging arms, think of nothing but gripping the rocks for dear life. But when the wave fell back, its vast, dragging power ripped me from the wall of the tunnel and plunged me into its depths.

As the water carried me down at huge speed, I felt no pain, though the rocks tore my clothes and sliced the flesh on my side. In an instant, I was being hurled upwards again. I had no time to think, no power to make any choices at all. I had, I know, resigned myself to a quick death – already my thoughts were drifting into emptiness – when suddenly I found myself hurled to the top of the wave, and grabbed by unseen hands.

Now, the pain was intense as I landed on my side, hauled to safety by Red and Calum, their faces looming over me. I was choking and coughing, vomiting seawater. My clothes were shredded in parts, blood seeping through the cloth above my hip and my thigh. I must have been cut in a dozen places and the air and salt water stung viciously.

Barely able to remain awake, scarcely aware of what was happening, I felt myself lifted into the air in strong arms and I groaned as I was thrown over a broad shoulder. Red was carrying me, I dimly understood. In front of us, I saw Iona, carried in the same way over Calum's shoulder, hanging limp and grey-faced. Bess went first, carrying one of the lanterns, and I saw her look back at me with concern. I did not know whether she understood that Iona was dead, or whether any of them did, though I think they must have known. But I could do nothing now.

And then, at last, I surrendered and let my eyes close on the pain.

Chapter Forty-Eight

I awoke to the sounds of voices. We had reached the trapdoor. Calum had already carried Iona's body up the rungs and the sound I heard above all else was the crying of Jeannie as she tried to take in her granddaughter's death.

"Let me walk," I said now. I would not be carried up like this. But Red ignored me and carried me upwards until I was pulled into the warm fug of the dwelling by other hands.

Blood was all over one side of my body, soaked through my clothing, and the palms of my hands were cut in several places. I must have been a shocking sight, bedraggled and bleeding. For one confused moment, I thought I saw Iona stoking the fire or stirring something in a pot. But it was Bess who brought warm water to bathe my cuts. And it was Bess, drenched through herself, who would not let them question me until she and Red had removed my jacket and trousers. She made me sit by the fire, with only some sheeting to preserve my modesty and a scratchy blanket to keep me warm, while she soaked the scraped flesh of my legs and hip and shoulder with warm water, wincing for me as she did. Someone brought a salve which she pasted onto the cuts – these were not deep, but the ones on my hands bled profusely until she bound them.

I suppose that Calum had already told them much of what had happened when he had returned to the cottage after Mad Jamie's message, though he could not have known the outcome, and much cursing of Douglas Murdoch had doubtless been done as they waited for us to come up the passageway. Of this I was glad: I do not think I could have borne to hear them rant and rail. They seemed shocked into inaction, with no arguments about immediate punishment and revenge.

The horses! "Where are the horses? Did Mad Jamie…?"

"Do not fret," replied Bess. "I have already asked. They are safe. Jamie sent Billy to fetch them. They had stayed where we left them."

Through half-closed eyes, I watched the others. I had not spoken to Jeannie. I did not need to, not yet. With tears still wet on her cheeks, she was stroking Iona's face and smoothing her hair. The girl's body lay on the other side of the fire from me – I thought it should be away from such warmth, but it was not for me to say or to interfere. Jeannie gently removed the wet and torn clothes, shaking her head at the bruising. She wiped away the still oozing blood from wounds which were similar to mine, and wrapped her carefully in some sheeting.

Thomas wept, too, kneeling beside his daughter. His face was white, his eyes glazed. He said not a single word. I know not what he thought, beyond his grief. Did he forgive her now? Calum, I believe, did forgive her, and his grief was indeed real and raw and right.

Old Maggie was not there, for which I was very glad. She would be in her cottage and I hoped she would stay there.

Jock lay where he had lain before. On his side, his face turned away. I suppose he slept. Tam lay beside him, also asleep. Mouldy sat at the table with Billy. Their faces spoke of sorrow and shock and a lack of understanding. They did not know what to do. Red went to Jeannie. He put his arm across her shoulders. It was strange to see him so subdued by events.

A hush now fell across that dwelling.

Bess took hot water from the pot and mixed it with oatmeal. She poured some into a bowl and brought it to me. I thanked her and, although brose was far from my favourite food, I was glad of it then.

"Bess, ye should put dry clothes on," said Jeannie after a while.

I was angry that I had not said so myself. Although the room was warm, Bess was beginning to shiver. At first she refused, but Red insisted, and so did I. Jeannie smiled at her a little as she spoke, "I have need o' ye in good health, Bess. We all have need o' ye more than ever now."

I did not much like to hear this.

Mouldy went with Bess to the other cottage and a short while later they returned, Bess now wearing her woman's clothing. She brought with her some clean clothes of mine, too, though I did not put them on at that time. Then she sat beside the fire with me, on the other side from Iona's body. When she looked at me and met my eyes, I know she thought of Henry Parish, as I did, and of Iona. I could not help but think also of the world's injustice, and I wonder if she did too.

Very soon, the salve which Bess had pasted on my grazes began to soothe the pain and I started to feel drowsy, listening to the hissing of the fire and the whimpering of the dogs, and the soft clink of tankards as men drank the next hour away. And I think some of them began to settle down to an uneasy sleep themselves, to ease away the sadness of that evening, to lose their thoughts in dreams.

But it was not to be. Into my sleepy mind, came a knocking on the door of the dwelling.

Old Maggie. In she wandered when Billy opened the door. All dishevelled from sleep, she was, her matted white hair loose around her shoulders. But her eyes were bright, alert, like an early morning bird's.

Jeannie looked up from where she sat beside Iona's body. Her eyes narrowed, and her shoulders drew together slightly. Her whole body became still, as she waited.

I, too, waited, wishing the old woman had not come here now. Her presence threw a pall over everything. I looked to Bess but could read nothing in her face.

Surely, now, at last, Old Maggie would soften, when she saw Iona's body? Surely she must have some heart left?

Chapter Forty-Nine

Old Maggie walked into the cottage. We looked towards her, those of us who were awake.

She shuffled slowly, clutching a thin shawl round her shoulders. Her feet were bare, the gnarled toes yellowed. Her jaw moved constantly, as though she chatted to some unseen spirit, but no words came, no sound other than of her feet on the floor. Straight to Iona she went. She stood there, looking down on the vivid red hair, the empty face, the peaceful lips, the closed eyes. Jeannie had made her hair cover the tiny mark on her skull.

Old Maggie nodded. Just nodded. And then moved on. Over to the spinning-wheel she shuffled, settled herself down and took the loose thread in one hand. With the other hand, she began to move the wheel and soon its rhythmic click filled the cottage. My eyes narrowed as I looked up into the rafters, where smoke sat heavily, wrapping

311

itself around the twisted beams.

No one had spoken since Old Maggie came in. It was as though they looked to her to make a judgement. Their silence angered me. Her silence angered me. I wanted to know what she thought, whether it was too much for her that Iona had died. I wanted to see how far her hatred would take her.

I would not be silent.

"Are you satisfied?" My raw anger, my rudeness, broke the stillness of that place. There was a shifting of bodies, an intake of breath. I knew that my words, and their harsh tone, were wrong, that I should not speak to an old woman in such a way. She was sick, and frail, and probably mad. Yet she had a power I did not like.

The wheel stopped spinning. She turned to me. Then she looked at Iona.

"I tellt ye. I tellt ye all." It was a simple statement. Yet it said all I needed to hear.

What of the others? Was Iona's death enough to salve their hatred and anger? I felt it my right to ask now, that I had earned such a right.

"Jeannie? Thomas? Will you even now let this hatred grow?" Jeannie looked to her oldest son and Thomas seemed as though he wished to speak, but no words came from him.

It was Red who spoke first. "The lad is right. Iona

has died and we should no' speak ill o' her now. 'Tis an evil man's doing." Calum was nodding at this.

Now Thomas spoke. "Aye, she brought shame on us but she was a bitty lass. She didna deserve this."

"'Twas written," said Old Maggie. For a moment I thought she referred to the words on the scrap of paper, but she could not have done. She only meant that it was written in fate. But I knew that could not be – I knew in my heart that destiny is not written down. If it was, God would have nothing to measure us by when Judgement Day came. "She was curst," muttered Old Maggie. "She was always curst."

"No!" I shouted. "She was not cursed, any more than I am cursed! Think of her – was she cursed with her beautiful hair, her green eyes, her lovely face? Was she cursed to live in this place, with her family? Was she cursed that she found love and happiness? It was men who killed her, not a curse, and they only did so to hurt her family. They only did so to continue the hatred."

Everyone looked at me now, and I saw that Red nodded in agreement. I went on, "I have had an evil man throw a curse on me too, and no bad came of it. And if evil happens to me, it will be through no curse, but through my own actions, or the actions of others, or chance. A curse has no power if you allow it no power."

"All drest in white they were!" said the old woman, her mad eyes blazing still, though with a fragile desperation. "All drest in white, an' the waves rose an' the waves rose an'…"

"'Twas long ago," said Jeannie.

"But 'tis still the truth! Look at me! Do I no' bear the scars o' that day?" And she touched her terrible face.

Thomas spoke now. "If Iona was cursed, she is now at rest. We should mourn for her. We should forgive her."

"Forgive her?" Old Maggie cried now, getting to her feet. "Forgive her! For going wi' an Episcopalian lad? For going wi' the men who killt my mother?"

"Those men will pay," Red assured her. "We will see to that, but Iona is dead and we should forgive her and think well o' her."

"He is right," said Thomas, wearily. "And ye may be sure that Douglas Murdoch will pay for this. Wi' his life."

"Aye! So he will, and all his clan along wi' him," Red exclaimed.

My heart sank. Would it ever end? Had they learned nothing?

And yet, should not a murderer pay? Would that not be justice for the terrible thing he had done?

Calum did not speak.

Old Maggie did not hear their last words because now she pointed her finger at Red and spoke again, spitting her rage. "Forgive? I'll no' forgive her even wi' my dying breath! God is on my side." She pointed now at Bess. "The lass kens. She kens wha' 'tis tae lose a mother and a father. Would she forgive those soldiers?" When Bess said nothing, the old woman was triumphant. "She would no'!"

I looked at Bess. Would she take the old woman's side still? Surely not!

Chapter Fifty

"You have forgotten something," said Bess to her, gently, going over and taking the old woman's hands, crouching down beside her at the spinning-wheel. "Iona did what my mother and father did – she fell in love with someone forbidden by her father. She acted as my parents did, through love and not hate. I am sorry for what happened to you. But hatred is not the way. I know that now." And she looked quickly at me, before leaving Old Maggie and sitting down once more beside me. The locket shone in the fire-light and she put her fingers up to ensure that it lay properly.

And still Old Maggie muttered beneath her breath.

Let her mutter. She was a poor old woman who meant nothing to me now. Not now that Bess was no longer under her spell.

If it had not been for the horrible knowledge that

Iona lay dead in this room, I think I could have felt some kind of peace then.

The night was not yet over. Exhausted as I was, I was the first to hear Billy's shouting in the yard, and then hoofbeats.

Almost at the same time, the others had heard it too. We stood up. As quickly as I could, though in pain, I pulled on the clean clothes that Bess had brought earlier, wincing as the cloth tugged at my raw wounds. We grabbed such weapons as were near by and slipped out of the door, leaving Jeannie and Old Maggie, as well as Jock and Tam, who still slept. Jeannie looked as though she cared little for what might happen now. As I left her, I saw her cover Iona's face with the blanket.

In the yard, with Thomas carrying a lantern, we ran to the gateway. The clear, full moon lit the landscape and we could see in all directions. In the distance, I thought I saw tiny flickering lights, as though of flaming torches. But, much closer, a single rider approached, galloping on a fast horse. No hill pony this, I could tell immediately.

He carried no visible weapon, though perhaps he had pistols in his belt. No sword hung by his side. We were in no danger, outnumbering him as we did.

But who was he?

"Who goes there?" shouted Thomas.

317

The rider hauled his horse to a halt some five or ten paces from us and it stood, its flanks heaving, breathing mist into the night air. The man was cloaked, his head covered. I could tell little of his frame or age, except that he sat tall and straight on his horse and rode well.

"Who are ye?" demanded Red.

The rider paused before answering, with a strong voice. "I am Douglas Murdoch's son."

"Bastard! Murdering bastard!" roared Red, leaping forward, a thick wooden club in his hand. The horse reared in fright and Robert Murdoch pulled it skilfully round, turning a fast circle, keeping out of Red's reach. "Is she safe?" he shouted above the angry noises of the men.

"Iona is dead, drowned by your murdering father!" shouted Thomas. "We have her body safe."

With a cry of horror, the boy leapt from his horse, not heeding the danger he was in, caring nothing for the fury on their faces or the weapons in their hands. He tried to run towards the closed door of the dwelling.

He had no chance. They caught him and brought him to the ground, where he lay face down in the dirt. Red twisted his arms behind his back but he did not cry out.

"String him up!"

"Take 'im down the cave!"

"Drown the murdering bastard!"

"Slit his throat and send him back to his father!"

I could see the boy struggling to turn his face, but a foot pressed his head down. Red and Mouldy between them hoisted him now to his feet. He gasped for breath and then began to try to speak. But Mouldy hit him across the cheek and within moments blood was trickling from the corner of his mouth.

I knew then that this boy had as little chance as Iona had had. Did he hate his father too, for what he had done?

"Let him speak, Red," I urged now. "He had no wish for Iona to die. And remember, his father imprisoned him. Mad Jamie said so."

"He led my daughter to her death!" said Thomas.

"He did not! Douglas Murdoch is the only one to blame for that!"

And in the small pause that followed, Robert spoke, blood oozing from his mouth. "If Iona is dead, I will kill my father myself. But there is something ye know not."

All looked to him. He struggled to control his emotion.

"Even now, other men wish him dead. Mad Jamie has sent word to many people o' what my father has done and they are making their way to our home.

If ye wish to join them, ye should make haste."

"Is this true?" Thomas asked, with a growl.

"Aye, 'tis true. Armed wi' weapons and fire they are." He sounded weary, overwhelmed. Lost.

"One thing," I said. "Mad Jamie said you were imprisoned by your father. How did you escape?" Perhaps his presence here was a trick – who could tell?

"Two o' my father's men helped me. Some o' them are sickened at my father's ways," said Robert. "They say he has gone too far."

By now, the other men had decided to believe Robert. The idea that they might miss such action must have been too much for them to bear. Mouldy and Billy were bringing out the ponies, throwing saddles on them, deftly fitting their bridles. Soon, they were all mounted, Calum too. They rode off into the night, brandishing two blazing torches, heedless as to who followed them.

Bess, Robert and I were left in the yard, the moonlight leaving everything colourless and ghostly. "I wish to see her," said Robert, looking towards the dwelling, as though in truth he feared to go inside. A little light came from beneath the door, and from the slits around the window shutters.

I was about to lead him into the cottage, when Bess held me back. "What about Old Maggie?" she asked.

I knew what she meant: if Old Maggie saw Robert, she would judge him to be the cause of all this. I did not wish to hear one more word of her ranting.

"Take her back to her own bed. We shall stay out of sight." And I led Robert round the side of the dwelling. I had no fear of him, nor he of me. I felt pity for him, and some admiration that he had dared come here. The fact that we both had fathers of whom we were ashamed gave me a kind of kinship with him, too. He licked the blood on his lip.

As we waited, silent at first, a question came to me and I asked it now. "Did you know of the snake? The snake in the box, among the smuggled goods?"

"Aye, but too late. My father's men laughed about it. They boasted o' how clever they were, timing the tide just so. Placing the snake in the box and then disappearing by boat afore ye came."

"Why did he do it? It should have been Tam who found the snake. And instead it was Bess. What harm had either of them done?"

"It would have made no difference if he had known it. He wanted to frighten ye all, to warn o' what he could do. Everyone knows o' the old woman's curse, the story she told to all she met. He laughed at how afeard ye all would be to read those words. He is a cruel man. And I am ashamed to be his son." He clenched his fingers, open and shut. But his face showed little emotion. I think he held it all inside.

"And did your father mean then to carry out his threat? Or was it only to make us afraid?"

"No, I think he did no'. 'Twas no more than threatening talk. But then, he learnt about me and Iona, and he was furious. I couldna tell Iona that he knew it – she would have been too afeard. But she had already told me her idea o' running away – at first, I tried to change her mind, but when I saw that my father knew about us I said we should go without delay. But … 'twas no use."

Robert seemed to wish to tell everything now. I wondered if he had been able to confide in anyone else. I supposed not. "We'd no' gone far when they caught us, and took us back to him. He locked me up and took Iona away. But I was able to send word to Mad Jamie. One o' my father's servants helped me."

I had one more question. It was an idle question; I could not realize that the answer would mean so much. "How did your father learn about you and Iona?"

A noise escaped from Robert's mouth, an explosive burst of disgust before he spoke. "Now there's a man I would see dead!"

"Who? Who told him?"

"John Blakelock!"

"Who is John Blakelock?"

"The minister. A man o' God, no less!"

And then I understood the truth. "The blind minister?"

"Aye. The same."

"But why?"

"Who knows? He came to our home. My father almost barred the door – this was a man who preached agin our religion, who hated us Episcopalians, and who would do anything to see us pay for earlier wrongs. But he said he had information my father would want. And he did. The same servant told me o' it. Another who hated my father."

What treachery! Why would the minister do such a thing?

At that moment, I heard Bess call. We went round the side of the dwelling again and walked towards the doorway, which now stood open, warm light spilling out.

"I told Jeannie you wished to see Iona," said Bess softly. Robert did not move for some moments.

"I am sorry," I said to him, touching his arm. "I wish we could have saved her."

He said nothing. I think he could not.

Bess and I watched him walk into the doorway but we stayed outside, not wishing to see any further.

Chapter Fifty-One

Robert stayed inside for some while. Bess and I said little as we waited, shivering in the night air. We watched the distant hills, where I could see torches dotting one part of the landscape. Were these the men bent on revenge and punishment of Douglas Murdoch? I felt no pity for the man. He deserved whatever might befall him, but I wished not to be part of it and I feared for what would happen next. Would it end? Could it?

How eerie a full moon is. Strange events occur when the moon is whole, they say, when a certain magic holds creatures in its sway. It is as though every night leads towards this perfect circle, when nocturnal powers strengthen, and anything can happen, for good or for ill.

Now that I had time to think, my wounds began to sting more strongly than before. My skin and joints were stiffening in the chill air and my head throbbed with tiredness. And yet I did not think the night's action was over.

Jeannie and Robert came to the doorway. I think that he had been weeping. He pulled the hood of his cloak up again and went towards his horse.

Now, his strength seemed to return and he leapt into the saddle.

"My father will pay for this!" he shouted. And with that, he kicked his horse hard and galloped away, clattering through the yard entrance and along the track towards the road.

Bess and I looked at each other.

"Shall we go with him?" said Bess.

"No. It is not our battle."

"But I fear for him."

"It is not our battle," I repeated.

"Will is right," said Jeannie. "There is nothing can be done. And I need ye here, Bess. Nor do I like to see ye ride out wi' the men. There is better work here."

Jeannie took Bess's arm and I followed them into the cottage.

"There's the fire to be stoked," continued Jeannie. "And I must prepare Iona's body. It must be washed and made ready. And all manner o' things to be doing." She bustled around, busying herself with anything that would take her mind from what had

325

come to pass that night. And what might yet happen.

But nothing could have prepared her for what did indeed happen next.

She screamed. Her hands flew to her mouth, her eyes saucer-wide in the glow of lantern and fire. Bess, too, gasped. I did not at first see what frightened them so.

And then I too saw it.

It was as much as I could do not to scream myself.

Chapter Fifty-Two

Iona's whole body was shivering beneath the sheet. While Jeannie stood too shocked to move, I ran to the fire and pulled the edge of the cloth down. Her eyes were open – she was alive!

I knew not how this could be. Yet she was no ghost. I had heard stories of people being in a deep sleep and waking when all hope was gone but I had never believed such a thing to be possible. Her body had been so cold, so motionless, that we had assumed her dead. Her sleep had been so deep that we had detected no breath, but she must have been breathing very shallowly all the time. And now the warmth of the fire was rousing her from her strange sleep – for sleep was all it had been. Still her skin felt chilled, but there was a softness to it now. There was life in her.

And the hole in her skull? Surely she could not have survived such a thing, though I had heard of people in times gone by being trepanned to release a bad spirit, and I suppose they sometimes did not die.

Jeannie ran to her and gathered her up in her arms, where she lay, still limp, still silent, but with her eyes open, and breathing more strongly. Now, too, Tam was waking, smiling at his sister, never having known that there was anything to fear.

"Hello, Iona!" he said, as though it was morning, any morning, after any night.

Now Jeannie laughed, as she kissed Iona's face and smiled at Tam. Bess and I grinned at each other too, more pleased than I can describe. All that pain, that fear – it had not been for nothing!

Iona's hand went to her head, and Jeannie pushed back her hair to reveal the hole. But when we looked, we saw that the hole had only pierced the flesh covering her skull, and had gone no further. Her skull was unbroken. Murdoch and his men had not trepanned her after all – it was nothing more than a mark from some other injury.

And Old Maggie had indeed been wrong, wrong in every way. Douglas Murdoch still deserved all that might happen to him, but how glad Robert would be that the worst had not happened.

Robert! He was riding towards his father with vengeance in his heart. Although I had no desire to protect Douglas Murdoch, I did not wish Robert to do something he might regret. And if he thought Iona dead, who knew what lengths his grief might lead him to?

Besides, I wished him to know, and to have something to be glad for. There had been enough of the other.

Bess ran to our cottage and changed quickly into man's attire once more, and we saddled our horses again, somewhat against Jeannie's wishes. But Jeannie was so intent on looking after Iona – as well as Jock, who lay now with eyes open but glazed, his lips slack – that she did little to stop us. Tam wished to help her, running about on his bare feet, fetching wood with his one good arm, and stoking the fire expertly.

The moonlight still gave the air a steely gleam, though some clouds were drifting over the sky now, and in the distance we could see the moving pinpoints of torches near Murdoch's tower.

In that direction we rode, fast. My wounds stung but I did not care about that. In some strange way, the pain reminded me that I was alive, and that it was good to be so.

Could this whole ugly feud be stopped now? The power of Old Maggie and her foolish curse was over. Surely, once Thomas knew that his daughter was alive, and once Red and the others saw how nearly they had lost her, and with Douglas Murdoch stripped of his power and his friends, with everyone rising against him – surely now it would be the end of the back and forth battling about who had done what to whom? Surely they could be at peace, and continue with their lives?

This I hoped with all my heart as Bess and I galloped into the night, the rhythm of our horses' hoofs familiar now, my stride perfectly matching Bess's. The fresh wind on my face filled me with new strength. It was with excitement, and hope, that I rode.

Would I leave after all this, as I had planned? Yes, I would, with even more certainty now. Would Bess come with me?

Perhaps foolishly, I dared to hope so.

Chapter Fifty-Three

As we came closer to the valley where Murdoch's tower sat, we could hear distant noises. Shouts of men and the whinnying screams of horses. What was happening? The sky was lightening rapidly, glowing almost orange in the east, in the direction of the valley. Was it so late? Was dawn breaking so soon?

When we rounded the crest of a hill, we pulled the horses to a sudden halt. We sat there, staring.

It was not a rising sun that suffused the night sky with orange. It was fire.

One side of Douglas Murdoch's tower was on fire, the flames leaping skywards, dancing from the wooden roof, whipping the air. Below it, running around it like frantic ants, many men darted about, throwing firebrands through windows or onto piles of sticks against the walls. At the entrance to the tower itself, six or seven men held a tree trunk, which they used as a battering ram, crashing again and again against the door. It remained firm.

Other men tried to breach the thick double door into the low wall that enclosed the outbuildings. But it held firm. One of the buildings inside was on fire too and there was a terrible noise from frightened animals. Then I saw men, Murdoch's men they must have been, running to free the animals from the blazing structure. Horses stamped and whinnied, and cows huddled together at the wall furthest away from the flames.

I could not tell where Robert Murdoch was. It was not possible to be certain where our men were, though I thought I recognized the great hulking frame of Billy, and was that Thomas with him? But there were more men than ours – perhaps twenty or thirty, and who knew how many at the other side of the tower? Douglas Murdoch had made many enemies.

I could see our ponies waiting near by, tied, I think, to trees. They stamped and snorted, fearing the smell of the flames. I hoped they would not take fright and break their reins. Our men would need them.

"Listen!" Bess pointed in the other direction, from the west. At first, I heard only the noises from below. Then I, too, heard it. Hoofbeats. Many hoofbeats. Cantering. Iron shoes on the stony road. Not local ponies then, for they never went shod.

I knew before I saw them what sort of men would ride iron-shod horses, cantering in such great numbers.

Soldiers. Redcoats. Perhaps a quarter of a mile along the road, coming towards us along the ridge of the hill. We saw the moonlight glinting on their bayonets, shining on their white sashes. They had no need to hide from anyone.

We moved off the road and into the shelter of some trees. "Deeper!" I urged Bess, when she stopped. Bess's terrible hatred of redcoats had led her to rash actions in the past. I hated them too, for what they had done to Henry Parish. But this time, I felt, we might be glad of them.

For them to be out at this time of night, there must be good reason. Were they making for Douglas Murdoch's tower? Even if they were not, they must see the fire. They would investigate, would they not?

I watched Bess as the soldiers passed by our hiding-place. She saw me looking, and smiled. "Do not fear! I am not so foolish!"

But now, we must warn Thomas and the others. It would not help Jeannie if some of them were caught and hanged for fire-raising. Or murder, if that was what was happening.

It was then that I heard a curlew. So close by that it startled me. But it was no curlew, I realized quickly, seeing Bess's face. She had her hands curled round her lips, and once more she made the piercing wail, an eerie sound, with nothing human about it at all.

Calum had taught her well. But the men would not hear from here, not above the other noises.

"Take Merlin and stay here with the horses," said Bess. I would have argued, but there was no other way. She dismounted and handed the reins to me.

"Be careful!" I urged her, but she was gone. All I could do was wait and hope.

From my position in the trees, I could not see into the valley, could not see the tower, though the glow in the sky did not diminish. But with the redcoats now far enough from me, I dared to come out from the hiding-place and peer into the valley. I could just make out the shape of Bess, sliding down the slope, dodging from one patch of gorse or boulder to another. I wished that the moon would go behind a cloud but such things are in the hands of God. And God, I think, had left us to chance or our own devices that night, for the moon stayed bright in the sky and the few clouds did not move across it.

My wounds were hurting afresh, my hands sore as I gripped the reins. I tried not to think of the pain.

The redcoats were out of sight, though I knew roughly where they would be by now. Soon, they would be in the valley. I could just see Bess again, crouched beside a patch of gorse. From here, I could faintly hear her curlew sound. At first, the men did not seem to hear her, but then I saw two of them stop, listen, and drop the battering-ram. A few moments later, all the men who had held the huge tree trunk had scattered. Some ran towards ponies, others ran round the side of the tower. Now, the redcoats were upon them, and the noise of shouting, and some shots, filled the air.

"Hurry, Bess!" I muttered, under my breath. I could see her darting up the hillside now and within a minute she was with me once more. She leapt onto Merlin and we galloped back in the direction of the farm.

But when we were safely away from the tower, I called a halt. Of a sudden, I did not wish to return so soon to the farm. I had no desire to witness the moment when they saw that Iona was alive.

It would be better to leave it to them. I cannot clearly explain why, only perhaps that I was tired and I wished not to be part of it any more. It was peaceful out here, with Bess and the horses. It was easier to breathe.

"We are near the stream, Bess," I said, by way of excuse. "I need to drink." We found the water, not very far from where we had found the old shepherd murdered – how long ago that seemed now, though less than two weeks – and I stooped to drink, putting my face to the water.

And then, after the horses had drunk their fill, we made our way slowly back to the farm.

Chapter Fifty-Four

Some time later, while birdsong told of an approaching dawn, I found myself lying wrapped in my blanket, desperate to sleep. The men had all returned safely, though with battle wounds to boast of and stories to tell. Their joy at finding Iona alive was short-lived – very soon, they were arguing about whom to blame. Still they talked of revenge, and their hatred seemed as great as ever, though this time fuelled by strength and the sense of victory.

Iona simply lay on the box-bed near the fire, grey-faced, and silent. She seemed unaware of what had happened or of what anything meant. I feared for her mind then. Her hair, fiery as ever, framed an empty face, her eyes like cold embers. The fairy light had gone from them.

I had not stayed with them longer than I must, preferring my own company. Bess, however, stayed with Calum, to listen to his stories of bravery and action, his face gleaming in the firelight as he sat beside his sister, rubbing her hands uselessly.

And so, in our cottage, I slept at last, with only the sounds of an old woman's snoring and the distant calling of sheep, and the small noises of a countryside awaking without me.

I dreamt of my father again, and of my brother. Again we fought, but this time it was not the same. This time, it was my brother who writhed in the mud, as I stared down on him, my sword-tip poised at his throat. I had won. But I did not know what to do with my victory and strangely there was no pleasure in it. And then, suddenly, the face in the dirt was not my brother's any more, nor even my father's, but a stranger's. I did not know what I had done or why I was there. When I had been the loser, the dream had an end – a frightening one perhaps, but an end all the same. Losing is not difficult. But where was the end for the victor? What was the winner to do?

When I woke from my dream, I felt oddly dissatisfied.

Chapter Fifty-Five

The sun was quite high in the sky. I think it was mid-morning. The shutters were open, fresh air sweeping through the cottage. Bess was shaking my shoulder. And the sound of a cart came from the yard. I pulled on my clothes with stiff and painful fingers. I removed the bandages and found the cuts to be clean and knitting together, so I did not replace them. I ached in more places than I had last night, but the pain was bearable.

It was Hamish's cart. And he brought with him the blind minister.

I was the only person here who knew what this man had done. And I vowed that by the end of the day, I would not be alone.

Bess, who had slept for even less time than I, explained, "It is for Jock. Jeannie fears he is dying. She sent for Hamish to bring the minister." I said nothing as I followed Bess slowly across the yard.

A chill wind blew suddenly and I pulled my coat tight round myself.

I did not enter the dwelling. I did not wish to. If the man was going to pray for Jock, if he was going to be there to help this family through the death, then I did not wish to see his hypocrisy. Nor did I wish to see him pray. Or to look at him, knowing what I knew.

Bess glanced at me as she went inside without me. She didn't know my thoughts, of course. But I would not speak them, not quite yet – this was a man's death, after all, and I had no wish to make it harder for them to bear. Or for Bess, for I sensed that she felt some affection for Jock, some sadness at his passing.

But when the minister had finished, when the time was right, then I would speak to him.

While I waited, I went to the stable to see to our horses. This always brought me peace, as though their easy breathing and their warm eyes contained wisdom beyond words.

It was not long before I heard the voices of Hamish and the others in the yard again. I went outside to meet them, the low sun briefly blinding me. To my side, by the wall, a spray of forget-me-nots, in a single shade of blue, grew in a patch of grass. Three dandelions nodded in a soft breeze. Unseen birds chattered in roofs and trees. Everything was innocent and simple.

My heart beat fast as I walked towards the group, wondering what I would say, and what the minister would say in return. Should I perhaps stay silent? Should I let it pass? This was a man they trusted. Would it help if they lost that trust?

Yet it was because they trusted him that they should know the truth.

Beyond them, I could see the rolling hills of Galloway, rich, fertile. And to the distant right, the crystal sea, herring-silver, gentle-seeming. The smells, of salt and sand, of grass and horse, of dank and marshy ground, were things I had come to know. This land was worth something. It was a place of beauty. And yet it was being sullied.

I stood in front of the minister. "I wish to ask you something."

His face turned in my direction, the hollow white eyes wandering over me. His face was still, though his hand shook on his stick.

No one else spoke, though Hamish frowned. I had never liked Hamish. His face was somehow too clean, too scrubbed, too gleaming. He sweated overmuch. I did not like his wet lips. There was an unnatural silence about him, as though he had things he wished to say but would not say them. I cannot say precisely why I felt this. I can only say that I did not like him.

"What would ye ask o' me?" asked the blind minister now.

"Why did you tell Douglas Murdoch about Iona and Robert?"

"What?" This was Thomas. "What d'ye mean, lad? Show some respect to a man o' the kirk!"

But I would not stop now. "I wish to know."

"Have ye taken leave o' your senses?" demanded Thomas.

"Maybe," I answered. "But what has the minister to say?" We looked at him.

"Then I'll tell ye," said John Blakelock now. "I gave Douglas Murdoch the truth because 'twas right. The lass and her lad were doing wrong in God's eyes and a minister o' God must put an end to that. We look to our place in Heaven, nothing more. 'Be ye therefore perfect, even as your Father which is in Heaven is perfect', the Bible tells us."

A slight smile played across his lips.

And I knew not what to say. Was that all? Simply a minister doing what he thought right in the eyes of God?

"But there is no law that says they might not be together," I said.

"Your King has no' set a law, no. But I obey God's

law, which is higher. And Douglas Murdoch's church follows a bishop's law and a King's law above God's. That is the path to Hell and damnation. I saved the lass from that. 'Twas right."

"She came near death by drowning!"

"There is a worse fate than death. To be damned to Hell is worse, is it no'?"

I knew not what to say. But he was continuing, warming to his theme, his followers around him, hanging on his words.

"The Bible also says, 'Let us do evil, that good may come…' Thus God tells us that the end justifies the means. *Cum finis est licitus, etiam media sunt licita:* when the end is allowed, so too the ways to that end are allowed, as your education will tell ye." The sun glared in my eyes, casting his face into shadow. He continued. "We are faithful people. Good people. God's people. We wish only the freedom to worship as we please. And those who went afore us have died for this, believing that our place is in Heaven, at God's right hand. He will reward us for our faith, our steadfastness, whiles Douglas Murdoch and his like will burn and twist in the flames o' eternal damnation."

"I do not think God would wish a young girl to die because of whom she loved."

"Who knows God's mind? I know His word. 'Tis

written. 'Honour thy father and thy mother.'"

The blind minister turned away from me, without waiting for what I might say, and held out his arm. Hamish took it and led him to the cart. I watched him climb stiffly onto the bench.

He spoke one more time. "'Tis also written, 'Life for life, eye for eye, tooth for tooth, hand for hand, foot for foot, burning for burning, wound for wound, stripe for stripe.'

"'Vengeance is mine,' saith the Lord. And we help Him in His work. Nothing more. We do God's work."

He did not look at me again. Hamish clicked at the pony and drove him away.

Crushed, I watched him disappear. I had not said all I felt – I had not the words for it, did not know where to start. Confusion wrapped itself round my mind. The man carried himself with a haloed air of righteousness. He was so sure, so filled with faith, that I could not argue with him.

I felt lost, adrift on an empty sea.

Almost, for a strange moment, did I believe him. I thought he must be right – he spoke with such power, and he was a man of God, a minister. I must be wrong, I, no more than a boy. It would be so easy to believe him, to trust such a strong voice, a voice that claimed all God's power behind it.

And yet, I knew the minister was wrong. I would not believe him, however strongly he spoke. For I knew, deep down, that he was indeed inspired by hate, even if he hid it behind a minister's robes. I could not change what he thought, but I could believe him to be wrong. In my heart.

For did not the Bible also say, "Blessed are the merciful: for they shall find mercy"?

I had seen what hatred caused and I knew that there was another way – of love, and friendship. Why did it matter how one worshipped God?

But these people would not see it. The men all turned from me and walked into the dwelling. They believed their minister, without doubt or question. It was as if they swaddled themselves in his black cloth, hiding in the dark security of his word, believing it to be God's truth.

I did not go with them. I stayed alone.

Chapter Fifty-Six

Jock died just after noon that day. It was a peaceful passing. Jeannie did what must be done, her shoulders hunched, her eyes red, though her face seemed calm. I spent little time in their cottage, preferring to be outside, or with the horses. I let Tam ride on Blackfoot. He was able now to use his arm somewhat better and seemed in little pain, though there was a crookedness to the bone that made me wince to see it.

When I did go inside, to pay my respects, I saw Iona sitting in silence, twisting the edge of a blanket in her thin fingers. She did not even ask for Robert. It seemed as though her mind had gone. What she had suffered was not something she could forget. And where had she gone, when we thought her dead? Had she seen terrible things in her dreams? Away from this world, had she been in another one? Had she seen death? I know only that she was not as she had been. The spirit had gone from her green eyes and, though Jeannie brushed her hair till it shone, she looked lifeless, like a painting of someone from the distant past.

And I? What of my plans for leaving? I would go the next day, I vowed.

Old Maggie I avoided above all. I will speak no more of her now.

Some news came early that evening, before dusk fell on that long day. There was good news and bad. The good was that Douglas Murdoch had been taken by the soldiers the night before, and would be tried the very next day. It was two redcoats who brought this news. By good fortune, Bess was not there. She had taken Iona and Tam to pick herbs and other wild leaves. It was Bess's idea – she thought that by activity and fresh air, Iona might be brought back to the world and to health. I think perhaps Bess felt some sorrow at what had happened to the girl, and wished to make recompense for her earlier words.

And so, when the redcoats arrived, I had no need to worry that she might cause any trouble. They were, I may say, polite, though they looked askance at the poverty of the dwelling and would not drink with us. They had heard rumours of what Douglas Murdoch had done and wished to take a signed deposition as to our evidence. We told them a part of it.

Of course, we did not tell them of the passageway beneath the farm, only that we had found Iona tied to a ring in the cave, and had rescued her before the tide cut us off. That much was true. We told them, too, about the murder of the old shepherd.

They turned a blind eye to anything else. They had no wish nor need to know of smuggling, nor of feuding. They wanted to know only what they thought they knew already: that Douglas Murdoch was a villain and a murderous man. To find all aspects of the truth was not their purpose. Perhaps they would earn some reward for bringing a guilty man to trial – I knew not the way of the law in these parts. I only knew that they seemed very eager to believe in his guilt, and questioned us only briefly.

I joined in little of this, except to relate how I had rescued Iona. They seemed to respect my voice, my education, and to believe that I must be someone worth listening to, because I spoke like a gentleman. They wished to know who I was. Thomas said I was a schoolteacher in the nearby school and that I lodged with them and taught their children. He added that I was English but was travelling to see more of the world, that I was soon moving onto other parts of Europe. I thought he said too much, but they seemed not suspicious of me in any way.

And that was it. Satisfied, they left and all kept

silence until the hoofbeats disappeared into the quiet evening air.

Then did a cheering and a laughing fill the cottage. As Jock's body lay there at one end, covered by a sheet, the men poured whisky and raised their cups, clashing them together in hearty pleasure.

Did I feel any pleasure? I confess that I did. One might have thought that with my talk of love and forgiveness, I would forgive Douglas Murdoch. But the man deserved punishment for what he had done. It seemed right.

Eye for eye, tooth for tooth? I know not, only that this did feel like justice.

Besides, with Douglas Murdoch out of the way, I hoped that hatred might end and be forgotten. And so, this was good news. And yes, I hoped he would hang. There are men who have hanged for much less.

But there was indeed bad news, too.

Mad Jamie had died. In the turmoil when the men were trying to force Douglas Murdoch from his house, Mad Jamie had tried to help his friend escape – the man who had given him so much information, and who had thus enabled us to save Iona. Both men had died, as Jamie threw a rope to the window of a burning room and the man tried to catch it. So intent were they in their efforts that they failed to see the approaching soldiers. They were the only men who died at the redcoats' hands that night, and perhaps the two who deserved it least.

But none of that did we know until after those two soldiers had left, much later that evening, when some men arrived whom I did not recognize. They were friends of Jock and his family, and they had been at Murdoch's tower. Full of tales they were, once they had paid their respects to Jock's body, tales which grew with each telling. More men arrived during the next few hours, and the noise of their victory rose into the night air, as they celebrated the inglorious downfall of Douglas Murdoch.

Chapter Fifty-Seven

Next morning, I made ready to leave.

It dawned cold, the sky a turmoil of scudding clouds. It had rained in the night. From inside the cottage I had shared with Bess and the old woman, I looked through the doorway into the yard and slung my bag over my shoulder.

Bess and Calum were walking towards me. I had told Bess I would be leaving today. She had tried, a little, to talk me out of it, but she had not said she would come with me. And I had not asked her. I would ask her one time now, one time only.

They came into the cottage, and Bess took the shawl from her head and shook her black hair free. She smiled at me uncertainly. A smudge of soot was on her cheek. She looked, I may say, beautiful. And she was dressed in woman's attire. Suddenly, I wished she was not. Dressed like that, she seemed as though she must stay. With Calum. And not come with me, for adventure and companionship.

I think I knew then that I had lost her. I could not ask her to come with me, much as I wished to. She had made her choice.

"You will not stay?" she asked. Was she asking me to stay?

"No, I cannot," I said. "This is not my home."

"Calum has asked me to stay," she said. "And Jeannie. And Tam. And I think the others will welcome me too. As they would welcome you, if you wished to stay." Still I do not think she was asking me to stay. Besides, I did not wish to, not even if they all asked me. It was not my place. It was not where I could be content.

"I am sure you will be happy," I said. It sounded dull. It felt dull. And I did not believe it but I knew not what else to say. I would have liked to say how I wished we had never come here, how I wished we were still riding the roads at night, doing what we thought was right. I would have liked to say that I would not forget her, ever, nor the things that we had done together.

But I said none of this, and we talked, somewhat awkwardly, about other matters. Bess insisted that I take all the money that we had left – it would last me for a few days. After that, I would need some other source. I would look for work, perhaps. And find a way to university? Anything was possible. We walked, the three of us, to the stable, and Calum gave me some food to take with me for Blackfoot, for which I was grateful.

"Eat and drink wi' us afore ye go," said Calum now. But I did not wish to. "And I thank ye," he said. He looked directly at my eyes, not hanging his head as though he could not look at me.

"I could not have let her drown," I began.

"No, I dinna mean that. O' course, I thank ye for my sister's life, but also I thank ye for coming here. For showing me another way."

I looked surprised.

He continued. "I did no' think o'er much afore. I was no' brave enough, or strong enough. I thought not of why we act as we do. If I thought at all, 'twas to believe that I should do as we always had. But I dinna think so now. I ken no' how I can change my father's mind, or my uncles', but I will. For they are wrong and ye are right. And dinna fret o'er Iona – I will take care o' her. There'll be no more bloodshed. No blood on my hands, I promise. Ye showed me this."

I held out my arm to him then and we each gripped the other's shoulders and smiled. There were no words for what I felt. I had thought I was leaving having achieved little, but I was wrong.

It was as I was leading Blackfoot out into the yard that a rider came at haste along the track towards the farm. He brought news – that Douglas Murdoch had been killed – shot while trying to escape his guards. His corpse had been strung from a tree as a warning to others. And the excitement that this announcement caused allowed me to leave that place almost unnoticed.

Blackfoot and I trotted out of the yard. Bess ran after me. She called me to stop and my heart surged. Would she come with me? But no, she took my hand in both hers and looked up at me. "Be safe, Will. And thank you, for friendship and adventure! My father would have been proud of you." There was a catch in her voice, I think some tears in her eyes. Then she suddenly looked behind me, towards the door to the cottage. A quick smile crossed her face. I looked in that direction. There was Iona, a pale, small figure, leaning against the doorframe. But waving at me, waving and smiling.

In Iona's eyes was life once more, and now, truly, I dared hope that everything would change for her, for all of them. Perhaps not at first, for there were powerful forces at work here, but in time. I believed that indeed Calum could bring about a new way of thinking in his family, helped perhaps by Jeannie, who was, at heart, wise and good. And, I suppose, by

Bess, though it would be a long time before I could resign myself to her decision. But there were the beginnings of change here, and I was proud of the part I had played.

I waved back. And so, I was able to leave that place under the eyes of the two people I cared for. Bess and Iona were the only two who watched me as I rode away. Old Maggie and Jeannie were not there – Old Maggie no doubt in some strange and malign place of her own, and Jeannie, who had bade me farewell already, busy with the grim realities of life inside the dwelling. The men were so busy celebrating their victory that they had not noticed me leave the cottage.

However, I did see Calum standing a little apart from them, watching them. Would he be strong enough? I thought he would. Yes, I felt he would. And my heart lifted.

A biting wind nipped at my ears as I rode away to the east. With mixed feelings I went. A sadness that I was leaving Bess, and that I was alone. But a relief to be away from such a place, with its burdens of poverty and lawlessness. A sense, too, that one day they could be free of such burdens.

Fear, I felt, as well. For myself and the future. But excitement and a longing for freedom. One day, I hoped, I would find a way to live a worthwhile life, if that were possible, if I had that choice. But now, I was young, and many paths lay before me.

Blackfoot cantered willingly, and I kicked him faster. Now the sky seemed lighter in the distance as I rode towards it, the wind in my hair, my sword clanking at my side, all my possessions carried in two bags across my horse's withers. The earlier rain had cleared and the air smelled washed and fresh.

I would ride towards a new life.

Perhaps I would even go home one day. For if I had learned anything in these last few days, it was that hatred and anger are never the answer. That old wrongs can never be made right by more wrongs. And that forgiveness is sometimes the only way, however terrible the sin. However great the hatred and however enormous its cause.

And so, I rode away. Alone. But free. And full of hope.

Chapter Fifty-Eight

In the freshening breeze, my mind cleared, all the ugliness of the last days washing away. For a while, I wished only to ride without stopping, the cold air pressed against my face, my eyes screwed up against the wind, my hair swept back from my forehead. But after a little time, I slowed and then stopped, my chest heaving as I caught my breath.

We were at the top of a ridge, Blackfoot and I. He stamped and shook his head, wishing, perhaps, to continue with me. I twisted some strands of his mane between my fingers and removed some soft willow blossom from his coat.

Taking a long drink from my water bottle, I gazed back to the west. The sky was brightening now, and I marvelled at the rolling colours of the landscape, the heathered slopes, the new patchworks of greens and browns, peppered with ash and rowan, pine, poplar and oak, criss-crossed by stone dykes. A snake of a stream slithered down a hill to my right, and, in the deep distance, further layers of hills stretched as far as I could see, with orange patches where sunlight pierced gaps in the cloud. To my left, the thin strip of seal-grey sea rippled lazily.

It was, indeed, a beautiful land. I would breathe it in one more time, and then I would move on. Blackfoot began to graze at the side of the track. There was no hurry – we would pause here until we were ready to go.

Above us floated an eagle. It hovered over everything, watching, uncaring, before it might choose to pass by. But this one did not pass by. It stayed, hanging in the air, as if watching us, waiting to see us off.

The wind rattled in my ears. With my gaze turned upwards into the dizzying space, I did not at first hear or see the approaching rider. Blackfoot, I think, noticed first. I felt him stirring slightly beneath me, noticed his head come up from his grazing.

A single rider. Approaching from the west, along the road that we had travelled.

Bess! I knew with certainty. I knew from her shape, from the way she and Merlin moved, from the way my heart sang at the sight of her.

She came closer. Her hair flowed behind her as she crouched low along Merlin's neck, moving as one with him. Apart from the loosened hair, she wore her man's clothing once more, I saw, breeches as clean as ever they had been, white lace at her throat, her rapier swinging beside her, as she rode along the twisting road, over the rolling moor.

She came to a clattering halt a few paces from where I sat.

She had ridden hard and fast. Merlin's chest was sodden and foamed with sweat, his eyes wide, his nostrils flaring, his sides heaving as he danced there. It was not like her to use a horse so harshly.

What news had she brought? Good or bad?

Did I wish to know it? I was not part of that world now and if something had happened to any of them – Iona, perhaps – I did not wish to hear. And after hearing it, I would have to say goodbye to Bess once more.

"I wish to come with you," she said now.

This was some game. This could not be. "But you did not wish to before."

"You did not ask," she replied, with a mischievous grin, her eyes dancing.

"I thought you had made up your mind. I thought you would not like to be persuaded."

"I would not. And if you had tried to persuade me, to make me come against my wishes, I would not be here now."

"So, because I did not ask you, you come?"

She just smiled more. Bess, unpredictable as ever. Free as an eagle.

"But Calum, what of him?"

"If I ever thought I could spend my life with Calum, I was not thinking aright. I like him. I like him more than you would understand. But it is not enough. What is enough is that the times when I have felt most alive I have been riding with you, after a prize, or escaping from redcoats, or telling stories into the night. Or trying to save young soldier boys or whatever we thought was right. So," and she paused, smiling at me, her chin jutting a little, "may I come with you? And where are we going?"

We.

But no, it could not be. "There is much for you to do here, Bess. What of Iona, and Old Maggie? And Calum must need you too – and if you like him as you say, you could be happy. And does Jeannie not need your help? Do you not want to stay with them, as they wish you to?"

"No, you were right. It is not our world. And besides, do not fear for them: you did not hear how Calum spoke to Red and Thomas after you had gone. He berated them for how they treated Iona. He said that with Jock gone they must all start afresh. And you should have seen Jeannie's eyes light up! And Iona – you saw her: she will recover. There was a difference in the way they all talked, after Calum spoke like that. And now, I want to come with you. Are you going to make me plead with you?"

I could not look at her. My heart was pounding, my thoughts a whirlwind. And then I did look at her, black-eyed Bess, with her red lips and tumbling hair. And her grandmother's locket, with her father's ring, proudly round her neck, for all to see. Bess was as she was and some things might never change. But I could take that chance.

I knew then that I wanted nothing better than to be with her and that there was no one else on earth whose thoughts met mine as hers did.

I grinned. I could do nothing else, could not say the words.

She smiled. "Where are we going?"

"I know not. Perhaps home. One day. Perhaps nowhere. But first, adventure! And you may come with me – if you can catch me!" And I swung Black-foot's head round and kicked him to a gallop, not looking to see whether she followed. And as we rode, Bess, Merlin, Blackfoot, and I, along the ribboning road, I knew that whatever happened, whomsoever we met, and wherever we found ourselves, we were truly alive. And that feeling alive, and grasping life with excitement and hope and honour, were what mattered.

Love and friendship against hatred. Forgiveness against anger.

There could be no contest at all.

AUTHOR'S NOTE
The Wigtown Martyrs and the Killing Times

All my historical novels are sparked by true events which grab me so strongly that they demand to be told. In *The Highwayman's Curse*, the real events are from one of Scotland's most brutal periods, the Killing Times, when men, women and children were killed for their religion. One of the final and most cruel episodes was the execution of the Wigtown Martyrs, in 1685. But *The Highwayman's Curse* is the sequel to *The Highwayman's Footsteps*, which was set in 1761, seventy-six years too late. How could the Killing Times be relevant?

The problem with hatred, especially religious hatred, is that it goes on and on. It passes through generations, fanned in the hearts of vengeful people. Look at the religious conflict in the Middle East, and other wars, both past and present, between Jews and Arabs, Christians and Muslims, Protestants and Catholics. Even, in the case of the Killing Times, between Protestants and Protestants.

This is the true story of the Wigtown Martyrs: on 11 May 1685, two women were executed by drowning in Wigtown Bay in Galloway, south-west

Scotland. Margaret McLaughlan was sixty-three; Margaret Wilson was eighteen. Their crime? They worshipped the "right" God in the "wrong" way. In Scotland, the Protestant church was divided mainly into two groups: Presbyterians believed that ordinary people should choose their ministers, who would help them understand the word of God; there were no bishops. Episcopalians believed that God chose the king and the bishops, who in turn chose the clergy, and that these powerful people interpreted God's word to the worshippers. There were other differences too, but this was the main disagreement that sparked the Killing Times.

Although *The Highwayman's Curse* is partly about smuggling, it's about much more: it's about hatred carried through generations, especially by an old woman, Old Maggie, a woman teetering between dementia and obsession, traumatized by having seen her mother drowned in the rising tide by soldiers. (Old Maggie's mother was not, by the way, one of the real Wigtown Martyrs – neither the eighteen-year-old nor the sixty-three-year-old would have had a seven-year-old child; Old Maggie's mother is a fictional character, from an imaginary identical execution.)

What exactly was the crime these women committed? They were Covenanters, Presbyterians who